The Return of the Dissolute Son

Or Breaking the Vicious Cycle

Ian Douglas Robertson

ISBN: 978-1-62420-793-8

Credits
Editor: Sherry Derr-Wille

After such knowledge, what forgiveness?
T.S. Eliot.

Chapter One

I spent a disturbed evening, appalled by what I had heard and read, still unable to believe the young man I admired and in time come to love, could commit such heinous crimes. I searched despairingly through the media mire for something that would point to his innocence, some discrepancy, some incongruity that might expose a fabrication, a trumped-up charge. Yet, I had found nothing. Not that anyone had offered any sure-fire proof of his guilt. The evidence was, as they say, circumstantial, hearsay, based on testimonies that were at best tenuous.

They pounced on him soon after he resigned as Artistic Director of the National Theatre, only ten days ago. It wasn't long before he was branded a pariah, a monster. His life was over. The theatre, his great love, was a thing of the past. Even if an astute lawyer were to win his acquittal, he'd be lucky if he were given a job as a delivery boy, let alone a part in a film or play. The media, the social media and the world at large condemned him out of court. He had been publicly executed, lynched by the mob, torn limb from limb. Even a government official, a secretary of state, who should have known better, described him on national television as a 'danger to society.'

It was all politics now, the opposition blaming the government for appointing him to a position in which he could 'prey on the innocent,' the government pleading ignorance of his private life and accusing the opposition of trying to make capital out of a situation that could not have been foreseen. Yet, without a shred of evidence and before any official charge had been filed against him, 'they,' the government, the opposition, the public, the nation had condemned him out of hand.

He would never work again, a brilliant career obliterated in the blink of an eyelid. All his artistic accomplishments, his sparkling performances, his insightful articles on ancient Greek theatre, his delicately crafted productions, his winning interviews, in which he dazzled viewers with his wit and acumen, had been erased from public memory as if they never happened. His past was wiped out and he would survive in the annals of the country only on the strength of his notoriety.

If condemned in court, and it seemed very likely that he would be, he would not survive prison and, if by some miracle he did escape the barbarity of his fellow inmates, he would not be able to endure the isolation, the disgrace, the rejection and, above all, the mental stagnation. Jason, despite all they said about him, was gifted, artistic, sensitive, yes, sensitive, which may seem paradoxical, given the crimes of which he was accused.

They talked glibly of castration, summary execution, bringing back the death penalty. Even if what they said about him was true, I abhorred their self-righteousness, their holier-than-thou hypocrisy. Was his crime worse than that of a terrorist who was convicted of eleven assassinations and was now on hunger strike, drawing crowds of sympathetic demonstrators demanding the state should accede to his demands?

I had seen reputations ruined, sometimes justifiably, often not. In many cases, it had nothing to do with misconduct or incompetence, but politics. The worst crime anyone can commit is to rock the boat, side with the opposition. Seventy years after the Civil War, in which right and left, sometimes members of the same family, clashed in an onslaught of hatred, political fanaticism was still endemic.

If it wasn't dirty politics, it was dirty journalism, which is almost the same thing, as newspapers in my country are, as a rule, flagrantly partisan. Even those that make an effort to be impartial fail to convince a lot of the time. Yes, the civil war is still raging, the younger generation taking over from the old, the children of those who fought in the original bloody internecine war. One wonders whether it will ever end.

So, I clung to the hope that this was yet another attempt to 'assassinate' someone who had declared for the other side. His conservative views on how the theatre should be run were no secret, which was anathema to his left-wing colleagues, who controlled the Actors' Unions and the Actors' Committee of Ethical Practice, whose own practice was what could only be described as 'eclectic' at best.

The evidence, however, seemed irrefutable, the leaked depositions incontrovertible. If their aim had been to charge him, try him and condemn him publicly, they had succeeded. The whole country was in an uproar, as if only now had they become aware of something to which many, including myself, had shamefully turned a blind eye. I knew such things went on but, for lack of facts and tangible evidence, had kept quiet about them. Like so many others, I was not prepared to stick my neck out for fear of being accused of sour grapes or waging a personal vendetta against an 'innocent' personage.

Only a victim could speak out but it needed great courage or great anger, or both. The psychological trauma is bad enough but to undergo the ignominy of public scrutiny, to take on a public giant, an acclaimed member of society is too much for the ordinary person. So, we let it slide, let it carry on, pretending it doesn't matter but all the time knowing that it does, suppressing our guilt, finding excuses not to inform.

Yet, all it takes is one person to speak out for a chorus of 'Me Too' to follow. That person, however, must be extraordinary. It took twenty years for this person to emerge, an Olympic Champion, to reveal her secret, and with it she opened the flood gates that threatened to sweep away professionals from all walks of life; actors, directors, teachers, athletes, coaches, anyone in a position of authority, who used their 'power' to impose their callous will on others.

Jason, no, surely not. I was in shock, still trying to come to terms with what felt like a betrayal. I had been more than just a teacher to him. I had been his mentor. He trusted my judgement and I his. Perhaps I overestimated his talent but certainly not his ambition. He wanted to reach the top and was prepared to work hard to achieve it. As we all know, talent is never enough. Some succeed with very little, while others who have an overabundance of it never do. It is tenacity, determination and diligence which get you places, and he possessed all three in ample supply.

The sound of the doorbell made me shudder. It was past midnight. I was tired and overwrought. I had no desire to face him. For a moment, I considered not answering the door, but I couldn't turn my back on him, after all the years we had been friends, nay, more than that, family even. I could not abandon him now that he needed me more than ever. When he phoned that afternoon, he had sounded desperate, on the point of mental collapse, on the brink of tears, so I gave in. Besides, I had to know for sure, one way or another.

As I went to open the door, I had an outdated image of him in my mind, of an innocent, shy young man, brimming with enthusiasm, with that quaint disarming smile of his. I knew he had lost his youthful good looks. I saw shocking pictures of him on TV. He looked haggard, prematurely aged. I once jestingly referred to him as Dorian Gray, but in his case, it was the portrait that had stayed young not Dorian.

I didn't turn on the porch light or the light in the hall, so as not to attract attention. Yet, he could have been anyone standing there in the semi-darkness, lit only by the streetlamp opposite. He was wearing a cat burglar's outfit, a ski cap pulled down around his ears and an anti-Covid 19 mask, also black, but I wasn't going to take any chances.

Neither of us spoke. He hesitated, possibly wondering whether I might have changed my mind. Had he read something in the strained expression on my face? The onset of repulsion perhaps? I'm not sure.

I beckoned him in. I didn't want him hanging around on the doorstep. I scanned the balconies opposite and the street outside to make sure no one had seen me admit the mysterious stranger, not that they would have connected me with the now infamous celebrity. Our long friendship was no longer public knowledge, as far as I knew.

"Thanks," he said shifting awkwardly in his black trainers, as if still unsure whether I would let him go beyond the threshold.

I had to gently draw him forward to close the door.

"It's good of you to take me in, Patrick. I didn't know who else to turn to."

"Yes," I murmured.

He must have been desperate indeed to seek me out after all these months. As his teacher, we formed a bond of mutual admiration, I of his burgeoning talent, he of my ability to relate to my students and possibly what was left of my fading celebrity status. In hindsight, I think he may simply have felt sorry for me, an old horse turned out to pasture, opting out in my prime. That, however, is another story.

Chapter Two

"It's been a long time," I said, for lack of anything better to say.

I had been useful to him once. Since Alice's death, he seldom contacted me, unless he felt the need to pick my brains on how to interpret a role or stage a scene.

The funny thing is I never considered him a great actor. It was all craft and no soul. His real talent was cultivating relationships, getting people to trust him. He had a quiet, prepossessing manner that conveyed unpretentiousness, not an easy feat for someone who had reached the top. When treated like a god, one invariably ends up acting like one. Yet, he continued, despite his fame, to maintain an air of humility, never too stuck-up to give an autograph, answer a silly question during an interview, or mingle with an adoring audience after a performance. Yet, I think he quite liked the adoration and, by all accounts, he knew how to exploit it to his advantage.

"Too long, Patrick. I haven't had a moment to myself. You know what it's like. You never know how long it's going to last."

I couldn't tell whether he was aware of the irony of his remark. I believe he was still not wholly conscious of how precarious his situation was. "I understand," I said expressionlessly. It was true. I did understand.

He slowly peeled off the layers of his disguise. First, the ski cap. I was shocked to see he was nearly bald. The remaining hair had gone white, overnight, it seemed.

I tried not to look at him. "Sit, Jason. You must be all in."

"I've hardly slept in a week. Only a half-bottle of whisky can give me any respite but it isn't real sleep."

"You should have called me. We could have talked."

He turned his head and looked at me, trying to ascertain whether my concern was genuine. "I didn't want to bother you, Patrick. Besides, I wasn't sure you'd want to."

"You must have plenty of friends?" I said tentatively.

He laughed drily.

So, they had all deserted him. No one wanted to be associated with him now. I was still not sure why I agreed to let him come to my house. Was I clinging to the hope that it was all a fabrication concocted by those who envied the giddy heights he enjoyed? I know first-hand there are plenty lurking in the wings, waiting to stab a colleague in the back. It is the very nature of the profession.

He finally removed the mask from off his mouth. I don't know whether he had forgotten he was wearing it or whether he was still unsure whether he could make himself at home in my house. A look of horror must have manifested itself on my face, but he appeared not to notice it. I would hardly have recognized him, his face was so deeply furrowed, his sallow skin dry and sickly. It was the drooping bags under his eyes that were most alarming. It occurred to me that they were not the result of a week of sleeplessness but of a life of debauchery. I was taken aback by how ugly he had become. That boyish baby face had taken on a wicked aspect I had never seen before, or was it just my imagination, an attempt to adapt Oscar Wilde's story to real life?

He smiled self-consciously, perhaps unnerved by the probing look on my face.

"How did you get here?" I asked, hoping that he wouldn't tell me he had parked his car outside.

"I walked."

"Em," I uttered with some relief. "A bit risky, no?"

"Even paparazzi have to sleep sometimes."

There was little danger of his being recognised. Those washed-out brown eyes peering out from between a ski cap and a mask could have belonged to anyone.

"You'd better sit down. Can I get you something to eat?"

"The truth is I've hardly eaten in days. One, I didn't feel like it, and two, I couldn't leave the house for fear of being mobbed by paparazzi and journalists, or worse. Did you know they've put up 'Wanted' posters all over the city centre? 'Dead or Alive.' Radical groups, left-wing or right-wing, it doesn't matter, have openly threatened to lynch me. 'Innocent until proven guilty' doesn't seem to apply in my case."

"Yeah," I said, repressing my smarting desire to ask him straight out if he was innocent or guilty. "Once the press gets hold of a story like this, true or false, the mob takes over."

"How are the mighty fallen, eh, Patrick?"

"Indeed," I said, in an effort to instil some sympathy into my voice. "Drink?"

"Whisky, neat, if you'd be so kind."

I went to the sideboard and poured him a long one. As I handed it to him, he looked up at me sheepishly. His eyes were as chaste as ever, but I was not going to allow him to entangle me in his web. I had to remain aloof.

"You won't join me, Patrick?"

"It's too late for me. It'll knock me out."

"I wish it would do that to me."

We sat in silence. I didn't know what to say to him. Without knowing whether he was innocent or guilty, I didn't feel like sympathising, and it was definitely not the time to make polite conversation. So, I waited for him to talk, if he wanted to. Perhaps he didn't. Perhaps he just wanted a place of refuge from the vigilantes threatening to take the law into their own hands.

He seemed to relax slightly after he had taken a few swigs from his drink. Even the lines on his face seemed less pronounced.

"I'm in a right bloody mess, aren't I?"

"It does seem like it."

"Do you think I'm a monster, Patrick?"

His question took me off guard. What was I to say? "No, of course not." Yet, I couldn't, without being in possession of all the facts.

"If you do, I'd understand, Patrick. Everybody else does."

I couldn't put off asking the question any longer. "Is it true, Jason, what they're saying about you?"

"You know better than I do the truth depends on how you present it. I could make Macbeth look like an angel from heaven."

I knew he could. In fact, I think he had. "Maybe it's too late to talk. I've made up the bed in my son's room. Shall we leave it till the morning?"

He didn't answer at once, just heaved a sigh and drank feverishly from his glass, all the time regarding me with an intense, penetrating stare, as if trying to fathom whether I was truly interested in hearing his side of the story. "I don't want to keep you up, Patrick. It's already late."

"To be honest with you, Jason, I'm not a great sleeper. It's one of the consequences of getting old."

"As far as I can see, you haven't aged a bit."

I laughed. "Some age internally, others externally. I seem to belong to the former."

He dismissed my remark with a faint, bemused smile. "I would like to talk, Patrick. I need to try and prove to someone I am not a monster. I know you will not pre-judge me."

I wasn't so sure I hadn't already, but I nodded noncommittally. I wanted to believe he wasn't a monster, but I also know there is a brute in all of us, loosely guarded, crouching in a corner, waiting for us to let our guard drop. Most of us manage to keep it in check but there is always a danger that, in a moment of inattention, it will break loose and go on the rampage. "Let me refill your glass."

He looked apologetically at his empty glass but handed it to me anyway. I decided to pour myself one too. I had the feeling I was going to need it before the night was out.

As I went to the drink cabinet, the silence was crushing. I felt as if I was suspended in the eye of a black hole about to implode. The sound of the whiskey sloshing into the glass jarred on my nerves, like a waterfall tumbling over a mountain ledge. I had put myself in an impossible position, agreeing to harbour a man soon to be arrested. I could not help him. I did not know how to comfort him, nor was I sure I wanted to.

I glanced at the wreck of a man slumped on the couch and couldn't help feeling sorry for him. His eyes were half-closed, and he was leaning slightly to one side, like a sack of rotting potatoes about to topple over. Was he on the edge of an elusive sleep? Or was it oblivion he was after?

He opened his eyes with a start when I accidentally touched his foot with mine. He looked up at me, temporarily disorientated. Then, he saw the glass in my hand and took it with frazzled eagerness. It crossed my mind that he might be alcoholic but immediately dismissed the idea when he placed the glass on the coffee table in front of him.

He bowed his head and once again looked up at me. "I suppose you've been watching the news."

I had to admit that I had.

"It's all lies," he muttered dispassionately.

"All of it?"

"It's true I like young men. I like their company, their sparkle, their passion for life, their childish innocence…"

"Their bodies," I wanted to add, but refrained. "They claim they were all underage, fifteen and sixteen-year-olds," I said.

"Underage? What the hell does that mean?" he exclaimed in a sudden outburst of frustration. "You know how many kids have had their first sexual experience before the age of fifteen? Besides, the young men I like to hang out with have lost more than their virginity. They've lost their home, their family and their country. They yearn for love and kindness, someone who cares. I…"

"So, they are vulnerable. Some would say easy pickings."

A flash of anger raised invisible hackles on the back of his neck. "No. It was not like that, believe me. They saw me as the back door into the theatre. I tried to help them; I really did. It's not my fault they didn't have what it takes. Sooner or later, the door would have slammed back in their face."

I could see he had thoroughly convinced himself that he had done nothing reprehensible.

"The thing is, Jason, if it's true what they say, however much you may think you did nothing wrong morally, it was against the law."

"You of all people must be aware that the law is an ass, Patrick. These young men may have been only sixteen or seventeen, but they were far from innocent, I assure you. Circumstances forced them to grow up fast. They were adult in every way, worldly-wise, cunning, aware of how to milk a situation and it seems, quite capable of using the law to gain asylum, even citizenship…because that's what they're after, believe me. They will play the victim, make me out to be an odious predator. The state will take pity on them and compensate them by giving them citizenship - basically to shut them up. It's been done before."

Was he as gullible and innocent as he was trying to make out? Or was he merely trying to justify his actions by self-deception?

"So, you think they have turned on you for personal gain, not to seek justice?"

"Oh, Patrick, for God's sake, of course. It makes me so sad because I loved them, and I thought their love for me was genuine too. I now see it was their intention all along to use me to achieve their ends."

He sighed deeply and let his head collapse into his hands. I waited to hear sobs but only heard deep breathing. It was time to be gentler with him. After all, who was I to set myself up as judge and executioner?

"Maybe it's time to call it a night," I said quietly. I got up and put my hand on his shoulder.

He raised his head so that his hands were now just covering his mouth. "Thanks, Patrick. You have always been kind to me."

He looked up at me, his eyes red and bloodshot. He had been crying. Was it brought on by self-pity or profound sorrow for what he saw as betrayal? I had no doubt he loved those boys, or thought he had.

'The law is an ass.' I considered his statement from his point of view. Sixteen-year-olds had recently been given the right to vote, presumably based on the premise that they were capable of making judicious choices. Yet, the law did not consider them mature enough to decide who to have sex with. An oxymoron, surely? I remember my son at sixteen, completely independent, letting off a fuzzy beard and no doubt having sex with his girlfriend of the time. I remember myself at the age of seventeen when I was solicited by a man passing in a car. It was late and I needed a lift, but I said no. Couldn't they have done the same? Yet, I was sure the law would side with them, assume their innocence, simply because they were 'underage,' as defined by the law.

"I think it's time you got some sleep. I have something that will knock you out for an hour or two."

"Sounds just what I need, Patrick. Maybe I should take the whole bottle."

I didn't smile. His remark was not made in jest. "I can't promise you will come out of this unscathed, but we have to give justice a chance."

"Give justice a chance," he said with a wry laugh. "There will be no justice for me, Patrick, but it is a comfort to know that you will stick by me. Not many would. There's no point in fooling myself. I'm finished. My career is over. I might as well just put an end to it here and now."

I knew they would use him to set an example, *'pour encourager les autres,'* as Voltaire would say. His punishment would be exemplary. For Jason, his life was his career. There was nothing else. He had no family, no permanent partner, no other interest. He lived for the theatre. Without it, there would be no life.

I led him upstairs and ushered him into my son's room. I wondered what Andrew would say if he knew I was offering his room to one of the most loathed men in the country. Andrew was a sensible young man in most things, except when it came to cars, motorbikes and drugs. Yet, he and Jason had been friends. He too had got himself into a mess. Perhaps he would be more understanding.

Jason seemed pleased, no doubt feeling shielded, temporarily at least, from all those who were after his blood. "I have nothing tomorrow morning. So, we'll be able to discuss how to proceed."

"I've already got myself a lawyer," he said casually.

I was surprised. I didn't imagine him to be so well organized. "Excellent. A good one, I hope."

"The best."

He mentioned the name of a well-known lawyer who took on high profile cases, mainly for the publicity, and the money, of course, a man I detested and despised. He was one of those arrogant, know-it-all lawyers, who is not averse to bending or bypassing the law, for the sake of expediency.

"Are you sure he's the right man for the job? It won't help you gain public sympathy. Everybody knows his tactics are not always above board."

"You're right, but the truth is no one else will take me on. They either see me as a hopeless case or don't want to risk blemishing their reputation."

Possibly both, I thought. "Are you prepared to go along with his underhand methods? Even if it means resorting to lies."

"Patrick, do you honestly believe the prosecution is going to treat me with kid gloves? Of course, not. They will use every scrap of false evidence…and any bogus statements they have at their disposal…to bring me down. Why shouldn't I concoct a bit of dubious evidence too, if necessary. I can't spend the next twenty-five years rotting in a prison cell. I'll be nearly eighty by the time I get out."

I had to agree with him but didn't want to encourage him. "It's up to you. I just can't stand the man. He's so reptilian. He even wears suits with a V pattern that makes me think he must be a member of the adder family."

"Do you think I like him, Patrick? He's obnoxious, but what choice do I have? Besides, he hates to lose, so I know he'll put up a good fight."

"Right," I said, still unsure of his choice of lawyer. "Anyway, try and get some sleep. Come down in the morning whenever you wish. Hopefully, you will feel like one of my extremely unhealthy Irish breakfasts."

He smiled but I think food was the last thing on his mind.

"Oh, and keep the curtains closed. We don't want anyone to spot you. The last thing we need is to be inundated by reporters and paparazzi. There's a toothbrush and toothpaste in the bathroom with some clean towels."

"I can't thank you enough. You've put yourself out for me."

"Unlike your younger colleagues, I don't have much to lose, except my friends, who hopefully will not prove fickle. To be honest, I don't care all that much. My own company suits me very well of late. I have become a bit of a recluse since Alice died."

"Yes, Patrick, I'm sorry. I meant to come to the funeral, but I was swamped with work at the National."

A phone call would have sufficed, I wanted to say, but there was no point in adding to his guilt. "Good night then. Just rap on my door if you need anything. As I said, I'm a light sleeper."

Chapter Three

I lay in bed for some time wondering what I had got myself into. I had cavalierly said I was not concerned about my reputation, but I was. I had no desire to alienate myself from those few friends who remained loyal to me. Would they understand I was merely providing succour to an ex-student? Would they be able to comprehend my motives? Or would they assume that we had been lovers in the past? All it needed was some reporter to make the insinuation for it to become a fact. Yet, I saw no way out. I had to go on believing the crimes he was accused of were simply minor aberrations or fabrications. I would not be able to desert him. He reminded me too much of Andrew, or someone who could have been Andrew.

I slept intermittently, with Jason dominating my vivid dreams. I was back at drama school directing a play in which Jason was playing the lead role as usual. We were rehearsing a Shakespeare play, Richard III, I think it was. He was wonderful in the part, the innocuous smile morphing into a scowl of malice. It struck me how complex the human psyche is. How benign we may appear at times, only to become cruel and heartless at others. Who are we really? Is there a truly innocent being in this world? Or is it that some of us are good at hiding our demons?

It was clear what Jason's demon was. Was he capable of acknowledging it and admitting it was destroying him and others? If he could come clean, admit his guilt, plead psychological disorder and agree to undergo treatment, the court might be lenient on him, give him a reduced sentence. With any luck, he might still have a few years to enjoy what would be left of his life when he got out. I made a note in my torpid brain to take it up with him in the morning.

I forewent my early-morning walk, a great sacrifice, as it invariably helps to clear the fuzz in my head, but I wanted to be there when he came down for breakfast.

I also wanted to catch the eight o'clock news to find out what else they had dug up about him. The reporters had not been idle. They managed to get hold of one of the 'victims.' He claimed he had been raped twice by Jason. At first my heart sank until it struck me as highly implausible, as the boy repeatedly visited Jason's apartment before and after the so-called violations. A victim of abuse is surely not going to return to the scene of the crime to expose himself to abuse a second time. Or might he? Drugs and alcohol were involved. Had Jason plied his victims with stimulants to make it easier to bend them to his will?

At about nine, on my third cup of tea, the phone rang. It was an old friend, an actor I worked with in the past. He had been more dedicated to the profession than I and, despite his advanced years, was still pounding the boards. In the good old days, we played together in TV series, films and a few times in one of the popular theatres of the capital.

We had remained friends ever since. I was married. He was not. I discovered in the nick of time that marriage and acting are a combination set for disaster. Acting requires utter devotion and a great deal of pampering. She is a demanding mistress. If you fail to accede to her wishes, she will dump you for someone more adoring, and there are plenty waiting to take your place. So, rather than wait to be ditched, I ditched her first, for a time at least.

Billy went through countless marriages and an equal number of relationships, but acting was always his favoured mistress. Now, though in his late sixties, he didn't seem to mind being alone. He had his ex-colleagues to exchange gossip with, and of course his admirers and his coffee/beer-drinking pals, who basked in the glow that still radiated from his minor celebrity status.

"It's been ages since we had a drink together, Patrick. It's about time you started getting out and about. You can't go on mourning Alice forever. She wouldn't want it. You were a loyal husband. You don't have to be a loyal widower."

"It's not that, Billy. I'm just a bit disillusioned."

"With what?"

"Life."

"You think too much. You need to let your hair down, what's left of it."

"Yes, you're right, I suppose. So, what do you propose?"

"I want you to consider taking a part in a film. It's right up your street. A gentleman of a certain age is forced to choose between supporting an old friend alleged to have committed a number of criminal acts and being a witness for the prosecution. The man is placed in an impossible position, as you can imagine. I can just see you in the part."

I was taken aback. Was the man clairvoyant? Or was it just an extraordinary coincidence? "A nasty situation to be in, right enough."

"An up-and-coming young man, Stephen B, you may have heard of, is directing the film. I was very impressed by his latest film."

"Wasn't he nominated for an award at one of the festivals last year?"

"So, you have heard of him."

"What does he do in the end? My character, I mean."

"Aha, I think I've tickled your curiosity. I'll get the casting director to send you the script. They've all said they'd love to have you on board."

"I'm kind of involved in something at the moment. I'm not sure I'll have time."

"I'm glad to hear you're working but I'm sure you can fit it in. Can you give me a hint as to what it is? Theatre, film, voice? Or is it very hush hush? Have you decided to write your memoirs perhaps?"

"Oh, God no. Nothing so trite, Billy. If there's one thing, I will not inflict on anyone it is my memoirs. It'd bore them to tears."

"Don't always be putting yourself down, man. So, are you going to tell me? Just a hint, so that I know my old friend Patrick is at last emerging from his shell."

"To be honest with you, I have no idea whether it will come to anything."

"All right, keep me in suspense then. If it does come to something, I want to be the first to know. By the way, it seems your star student has well and truly landed himself in the shits. Hard to believe really. I always took him for a quiet, serious type. Who would have believed he was a sex maniac, and quite ruthless with it, by the sound of it? You never can tell with people. Sex. It's a bloody menace. I blame the media and all that porn. It drives a young man crazy."

"It has a lot to answer for, I agree."

"They say he's done a bunk. Or just lying low. I don't blame him. He's not going to get much sympathy from the courts. Sad to see such a talent flushed down the toilet. Has he been in touch with you at all? You were always very vocal in your championing of him."

I hesitated, unwilling to lie, but also reluctant to reveal too much. Billy is a loyal friend, but he also has a loose tongue, especially after a few whiskeys. "We've lost touch. The pupil outstripped the teacher. I'm just sorry he didn't consult me on more personal matters."

"You couldn't have done anything to help him, Patrick. The man is sick, quite obviously. If he does come to you for help, I'd steer well clear. The man's a menace to society and needs to be put away for a very long time."

"I know he's not innocent, but do you think he's as bad as they say?"

"There's no question. Preying on young refugees, it seems. The evidence is overwhelming. What I can't understand is why he wasn't more careful? It's the age-old story, I suppose. Those with clout think they are untouchable. I know you must be upset, but for God's sake, Patrick, don't get involved. It could turn out very badly for you."

Billy made it sound like a threat. It was almost as if he knew Jason had slept under my roof. "Don't worry. I don't think I'm in a position to help him anyway. What he needs is a good lawyer."

"I hear he already has one. That ghastly man, Victor S, who enjoys wallowing in cesspits. Stay clear, Patrick. Stay clear. I only hope he doesn't contact you because I know you - you're too altruistic for your own good."

"I'll bear it in mind."

"Good man. I'll tell the casting director to send you the script. It'll be great to work together again. Like old times."

I turned and saw Jason standing in the doorway.

I hung up before he had a chance to speak. If Billy knew Jason was with me, he'd have been over in a shot to persuade me to get out while the going was good.

Chapter Four

Jason stood self-consciously at the door. "I'm sorry. Did I interrupt a private conversation?"

He must have suspected I was talking about him.

"No. It's best no one knows you're here."

"I've put you in a difficult spot," he said apologetically.

"I offered to take you in, so I only have myself to blame."

"Why are you doing this, Patrick? You owe me nothing."

"To be honest with you, I'm not altogether sure myself. Let's say, you—or anyone for that matter - deserve better than to be thrown to the wolves."

"I'm glad you think I'm worth it."

"Everyone deserves a fair trial. Come and sit down. Do you like porridge?"

"Porridge? I don't think I've ever had it."

"A good way to start the day. Cooked oatmeal with milk or cream. Some like a bit of honey or sugar with it. As a child, we used to add a pinch of salt."

"I'll try anything…once," he said dubiously.

"Did you sleep?"

"You were right. Those pills knocked me out."

I enjoyed watching him eat a hearty breakfast. It was obvious he hadn't had a square meal in days. After he finished his second piece of toast, he said, "I think I'll need to go back to bed after all this…to sleep it off."

"A good idea. You have some catching-up to do. Have you and Victor S talked about a strategy?'

"I'm leaving it up to him."

"Is that wise?"

"He's a very experienced lawyer."

"Yes, but you must remember that it is as important to win over the judges as it is to produce counter evidence. Showing remorse could get your sentence reduced considerably."

"That's assuming I'm sentenced. Victor S is convinced we'll be able to get the case thrown out."

A good night's sleep seemed to have done Jason a world of good. He was far more positive than the previous evening, almost irrationally so. Did he honestly believe his case would not come to trial? "Isn't he being a little over-optimistic? Given the allegations?"

"He assured me he has ways of discrediting the witnesses."

"I just hope he's not going to make your situation worse than it already is. My feeling is, given the public outcry, it would be better to submit to a psychological assessment and undergo the recommended treatment. As I see it, that's the only way the courts will be lenient on you."

"So, you believe I am unhinged, Patrick?"

It was unclear whether it was a question or a statement. He was irked by my proposal but was trying to contain his anger.

"It's not so much what I think, Jason. It's what everyone else thinks. I don't claim to be a psychologist but I know something about the human psyche."

"So, as someone who knows 'something about the human psyche,' do you believe I'm unbalanced?"

His eyes fixed mine with defiance, as if daring me to answer affirmatively.

I hesitated, unwilling to push him too far. "Last night, you asked me if I thought you were a monster and I said no."

"Did you mean it?"

I hesitated. I hadn't been sure then and I still wasn't.

"I mean, as someone who knows something about the human psyche, what do you think?" he added wryly.

I wasn't sure whether he was looking for an honest answer or not. The irony in his voice suggested the latter. However, I was determined to remain calm. "Jason, how long have we known each other?"

"About thirty years. Why?"

"Well, until a week ago, I was totally ignorant of your private life. All

I knew was a talented, intelligent, sensitive actor and director called Jason B. Finding out about your...other life came as a shock to me."

"So, you frown upon my sexuality," he said accusingly.

"If you mean your homosexuality, no, of course not, as long as it involves consenting adults, but it seems to me that you have been taking advantage of young men's vulnerability, merely to use them sexually. If that is true, then I find it abhorrent."

Jason leaned back in his chair, which creaked ominously. "Patrick, there is a world out there you know nothing about, a world that has been pushed underground because of society's prejudices. It's almost like a clandestine society, the members of which know each other by secret signs and codes. We recognise who is gay and who isn't, who wants sex and who doesn't."

"So, you don't feel - for the sake of expediency at least - that it would be better to throw yourself on the sympathy of the courts and admit guilt."

"No, Patrick. It would be a betrayal of what I believe. Why admit to something that's not true, if I don't have to?"

"Maybe you will have to. You said yourself last night you see no hope of justice being done."

"Which is exactly why Victor S decided to get the case dismissed before it even comes to trial."

"Like it or not, this is a high-profile case. The public will be outraged if it doesn't go to court."

"Let them. If we can prove the allegations are false, they will have no option but to dismiss the charges."

"I'm glad you have confidence in your lawyer but the man is not infallible. It might be better to accept a mitigated sentence rather than face the unmitigated ferocity of the courts, egged on by popular outrage."

He suddenly looked downcast. "I wouldn't last a day in jail, Patrick, you know that. I'd sooner kill myself."

I realised I had been considering the situation purely from my point of view. Jason was not me. I would have found ways of spending my time in prison, writing, learning a language, reading, honing a craft, staying clear of my fellow inmates, but Jason was not a recluse. He needed people, space and sunlight to bloom. "When is your next meeting with Victor S?"

"He's preparing a deposition that will prove I could not have done the things of which I am accused."

What proof could he possibly come up with, I thought?

Jason's face took on a look of virtuousness, the eyelids drooping sanctimoniously. Was he already rehearsing for the judicial hearing? Or had he convinced himself that he was innocent? Either way, I was worried. "Where will you meet?" I had images of Victor S turning up on my doorstep in his chauffeur-driven Merc.

"He'll send me the draft by e-mail for my approval, but he has a whole team working on it. I doubt I will have anything to add."

"Would you mind if I had a glance through it?"

Jason gave me an uneasy look. "It's the best I can do, Patrick. I've decided that I must go along with Victor S. It's my only hope."

"I'd still be curious to see his skills as a fiction writer."

Jason's face contracted in a sudden onset of anger. "Patrick, if you'd prefer me to leave, I will."

"Jason, I didn't invite you here lightly. I want to help you, but you need to be one hundred percent sure this is the way you want to go."

"You're not a lawyer, Patrick. You don't know how the law works. There is no such thing as black or white. Good or bad. The edges are blurred. A good lawyer can make them seem so hazy even the judges and juries can't tell the difference between black and white or good and bad."

I realised he was right, but I was still not convinced this was the proper way to proceed. I believe we must always accept some guilt when our actions are reprehensible, not only for the sake of justice but for the sake of our souls. If he got away with it, what message would it send to society? What would it mean to Jason? Would it mean he could go on exploiting young men to satisfy his nefarious desires?

"I can't help feeling it would be much better to show some remorse. You publicly express your regret, accept punishment along with intensive therapy and, who knows, you might even be able to walk away with a clear conscience, even work again. The public is extraordinarily forgiving if they believe that there is genuine contrition. If necessary, fake it, as I know you can."

He sank back into his chair with a sigh of despair. "Patrick, I may be a monster, but I am innocent of the crimes of which I was accused."

The last piece of advice was not given blithely. I thought it might appeal to his Thespian nature, by providing him with a challenge to convince his audience of the depth of his remorse, even if it was pure charade. Now, he was saying he was innocent. I didn't know what to believe.

"I can see you've been living a very sheltered life, Patrick. Things don't work like that. My only hope of survival is if my case does not go to trial. I'll have to leave the country, of course. I will disappear for good, acquire a new identity, start a new life, but at least I will have a life."

Would he go on corrupting teenage boys? I was beginning to think maybe it was better he should be locked up. Then I thought of Andrew. I couldn't make the same mistake twice. Even though Jason was not my real son, I always felt he was the next best thing. I had to do my best for him, if only to appease my conscience.

Were Andrew and Jason so alike? No, not at all. So, what was it that fused their images in my mind? Alice would have known the answer. She would have set me right, as only she knew how. "You can't save Jason in the same way we couldn't save Andrew," I could hear her say. "You're going to get yourself embroiled in a nasty court case. Think about yourself for a change. This film Billy recommended will help you get out of the doldrums you've been in since I popped off. I don't want you to give up on life. I told you that the day before I died. It's been over six months now. That's long enough to mourn anyone. I know you'll do what you can for Jason but for once you must put yourself first."

"Patrick?"

I looked up, startled. I had completely forgotten Jason was still sitting next to me.

"I am a disappointment to you."

"Sorry. I was thinking about Alice. She was very wise. She always knew the best course of action."

"Don't I know it? She knew I was gay long before I fully realised it myself."

"She said so?"

"It was one Sunday after lunch, years ago now. You and Andrew had gone for a walk by the river. You know how I hate walking. So, I sat with

Alice, and we had a cosy cup of tea together in the conservatory. She said, 'You're gay, aren't you, Jason?' I was taken aback at first… Alice was not one to mince her words," he added with an amused smile.

"Yes," I said, remembering moments of embarrassment when she told a distinguished guest exactly what she thought of them.

"She changed my life. She made me admit who I truly am and not to be ashamed of it."

Yes, she had the knack of changing people's lives. I wondered in Jason's case, whether it had been for the better.

Jason's phone rang. He picked it up and looked earnestly at the floor. I knew it was Victor S. Jason was clearly in awe of him.

It was a short call. Victor S was not one to waste time chatting. He charged by the hour, which was worth more than what most of us mortals earn in a month.

"He's sent me my deposition. I need to look through it and sign off on it."

"Send me a copy. We can discuss it later."

"Sure, but I know Victor S. He won't change a word."

"Send it anyway."

I had very little chance of intervening in what would clearly be a skilfully woven conglomeration of lies. I was curious, nonetheless.

Chapter Five

It was a very astute piece of writing. Totally fictitious, I suspected, but the more I read the more I found myself being taken in by it. Victor S played around with dates and times that refuted the accusers' claims. The day on which Hassan maintained he had been abused by Jason supposedly coincided with Jason's presence at the Northern Theatre Festival, where he had greeted a number of people who could vouch for his presence there. Apart from that, the Young National Theatre group was putting on a play, which Jason had directed and acted in. Similarly, on the day the second accuser claimed he had been abused, Jason had ostensibly been on holiday with some colleagues and friends, who would be able to back up his claim.

After reading the fifteen-page deposition, I was almost convinced Jason was innocent, almost, but not quite. Could the accusers, under pressure of interrogation, have muddled up their dates? Could Victor S have shifted the time when Jason was allegedly absent from the city to make it look like the boys were making it up?

"What do you think?" said Jason, eyeing me warily.

"I must admit it's a very convincing screed, assuming that all the 'witnesses' will corroborate your story."

"Why shouldn't they? It's the truth."

I tried to interpret his body language. Did I detect a slight vacillation before he said, 'It's the truth?' However, there was no point in disputing something he would almost certainly deny.

"If it is the truth, then you have nothing to worry about."

"Well, it could be the truth."

"What do you mean? It isn't the truth?"

"With some adjustments."

I gave him an avuncular look. "You surely must be aware if they find just one flaw, it will discredit the whole deposition."

"Please, Patrick, stop trying to father me. You think Victor S would leave a chink in his armour?"

"Victor S is too clever by half. He believes he can pull the wool over anyone's eyes, but the prosecution will dissect every word, comma and dotted i to find a loose end."

"I'm sure it will pass muster," he said with an edgy chuckle.

"I honestly hope so," I said, not altogether sure of my own sincerity.

I poured him a cup of coffee and we once again sat down at the kitchen table. "So, what's your next move?"

"There's going to be a hearing. It can't be avoided. Victor S needs to grill me on how to answer their questions."

"Have you been given a date?"

"The day after tomorrow."

"Where is this 'grilling' going to take place?"

"Well, I was wondering…"

I looked up in alarm. "Not here, Jason, please."

"Victor S promises to be discreet."

"Discreet? He doesn't know the meaning of the word. The man draws reporters like dung attracts flies."

"It's my only hope of avoiding the mob. I suppose I can always get a taxi to his offices, but they're bound to be waiting for me," he said dolefully.

If Victor S was seen turning up at my home, I would be seen as a collaborator, at best an accessory. My reputation would be trashed in an instant, but could I let him be devoured by the wolves? No. I couldn't bring myself to do it. "Well, please tell him to come by taxi and not by chauffeur-driven Merc? The media would have a field day."

"I'll insist on it."

"Please stress the importance of his remaining as inconspicuous as possible, for both our sakes."

"Thanks, Patrick. I will."

I looked at him dubiously, wondering whether I was being incredibly foolish. Would Alice think so? I relied so much on her balanced judgement.

"So, how am I going to keep you entertained till this afternoon?" I said, trying to erase the thought of meeting Victor S again.

"I'm not a child, Patrick. I think I can entertain myself. Just being here is enough. I became so despondent alone in my flat with no one to talk to. Suddenly, nobody wants to have anything to do with me. I now realise how fickle all my so-called friends and colleagues were. Weird, isn't it? Yesterday's most ingratiating sycophants are today's most vehement critics."

"You can't blame them, Jason. If the skipper decides to scupper his own ship, the crew is hardly going to risk their lives to save him."

Jason understood my inept analogy and looked at me forlornly. "I don't remember you being so forthright, Patrick."

"Something of Alice rubbed off on me, it seems."

He studied me intensely, with a deeply furrowed brow. "You weren't even on the ship. Yet, you're jumping on board just as it's about to sink. It seems to me you have some kind of death wish, Patrick. I hope this is not true."

I smiled. He was always discerning but I was neither going to confirm nor deny his observation. "I'm going for a walk by the river. I'll pass by the shops on my way back. What would you like for lunch? I feel like Italian. How about spaghetti with tomato sauce *alla Patricio*?"

"Suits me, though after that enormous breakfast I can't guarantee I'll be hungry."

"We'll eat when you are. Since Alice passed, I often skip a meal. So, we might just have an early supper. I must say, though, it does make a difference having someone to cook for."

"Well, if all goes well, I will give you many opportunities to do just that. I have such vivid memories of meals here. Or was Alice the *grand* chef?"

"A combined effort. We did things together."

Jason stared at me with a look of regret. For what exactly, I wondered? I knew his parents did not have a happy marriage. His father had been an acclaimed writer and a renowned theatre critic. I had met him once or twice at different theatrical functions. He struck me as a rather taciturn man, with a hint of intellectual snobbery. Jason once told me as a child he had been kept at arm's length, 'so that Daddy can write.' Doctor Ares, as he was known, was also a notorious womaniser, though one wonders how he managed to find time to entertain his mistresses.

His parents finally split up when Jason was about to finish elementary school. They both remarried, leaving Jason to oscillate between two homes,

25

neither of which was a real home. In fact, from what he told me, both his parents treated him as an encumbrance, believing a boy of eleven, going on twelve, should be old enough to get on with life without them. Besides, they had formed new relationships leaving little time for the offspring of a marriage that was little more than a blot on their successful lives.

I always had the feeling Jason might have seen Alice and me as pseudo 'foster' parents, despite our belated entry into his life. During his student years and for quite some time afterwards, he spent many weekends with us, until his career took off and his visits dwindled to one or two Sundays a month. Was it regret for Alice's absence that he was feeling? Or regret that he had never received the love and attention from his real parents a young boy deserves?

Were we poor substitutes for uncaring parents? Did we enter his life too late to make a difference? Despite our efforts to make him feel like a member of the family, I always felt he was desperately trying to fill a void or at least cover it over. What was it that was missing from his life? Love? Attachment? Meaning? All three? Yet, I couldn't help thinking the void was like an abandoned well, hidden from sight by rampant undergrowth, yet still gaping and perilous, and that one day he would fall...or even throw himself...into it.

"Alice was not an easy woman to live with," I said, trying to divert my thoughts from my companion's troubled upbringing, "but we found a modus vivendi, as they say."

"You always seemed so perfect together."

"It required some effort, on both our parts. I think all relationships do. It's all a question of whether you think it's worth it."

"You were so—how can I put it?—harmonious together, like seasoned dance partners that know each other's steps instinctively."

"That can happen when you've been together a long time."

"How long was it?"

"Over fifty years. A lifetime, in fact. Look. I've got to go, or we won't have time to eat before Victor S turns up.

"I wish I could come with you," he said wistfully.

Well, why not, I thought? I looked out of the front window to check on the weather. It was overcast and rainy. Everybody was wearing anti-Covid masks. "Why don't you? Just put on your cat burglar's outfit and a long scarf. We should be able to avoid the paparazzi…but I thought you didn't like walking."

"I don't but I've been cooped up for so long I need to reassure myself there is a world out there."

I laughed, though I couldn't help thinking if convicted he would not see the outside world for a very long time. "I'd love to have you along. Someone to share my thoughts. I find conversations with myself distinctly hackneyed of late."

"I'll do my best, though I can't promise stimulating conversation. In the past we could have talked about the theatre and all the things I had planned for the National. Now my life seems terribly empty. What is there to talk about?"

"We can talk about the past then. It's what I think about most of the time, anyway."

"The past it is then. Until I'm certain that I will have a future."

He needed reassurance, like someone in a desert desperate to quench his thirst, but miles from an oasis. Yet, I couldn't in all honesty give him what he wanted without being hypocritical. So, I said nothing.

Chapter Six

I took him along my favourite path by the river. It was where I go to collect my thoughts and, if I am totally honest, to be with Alice, especially when I need her insight. She would say that I never listen to her advice, so what's the point in wasting her breath? I do listen to her, most of the time, even if I don't always give her the satisfaction of acknowledging it.

It was too early for the afternoon strollers and too late for the morning joggers. So, apart from the odd OAP being taken for a walk by their dog, we were virtually alone. We passed one hoary granny, who seemed vaguely familiar. I remarked how old she looked, though she was probably not much older than me. It's odd how glibly we paint a distorted image of ourselves in an endeavour to buoy our waning self-esteem. The old dear, who was about five foot tall and less than forty kilos, was being dragged along by an obese and extremely ugly bulldog puffing its heart out, spewing froth and saliva from its flapping jowls. "Patrick, isn't it?" she shrieked, as she scudded past. "I haven't seen you in ages. Is that Andrew with you? I'd hardly recognise him. I suppose it's these silly masks we have to wear."

I didn't answer, not that she would have heard me, as her single-minded bulldog had already whisked her some distance down the path. Then, I remembered who she was. We had been on a local committee together some years past. All I recalled about her was that she was a bit of a busybody. I was surprised she hadn't heard about Andrew.

Jason must have realised the subject of my ruminations. "Do you miss him?" he asked.

"Every day. It's not right for one's children to die before you."

"It was all over the news at the time," he said. He glanced at me, and no doubt saw a shadow darken my face. "Perhaps you'd prefer not to talk about it."

"It wouldn't help."

"Talk can sometimes be good therapy."

"Maybe, but however much I talk I can't escape from myself."

"From yourself?'

"The guilt."

"Why should you feel guilty? You were in no way to blame."

"Parents are always to blame for the way their children turn out. We … I let him down."

"I can't believe that, Patrick. You were such a close-knit family."

"In many ways we were, but he didn't turn to us for help when he most needed it. No doubt, he knew how we would react. I didn't do anything until it was too late. I felt he was to blame for the mess he'd got himself into and it was up to him to get himself out of it. I was wrong. One should never abandon those we love, no matter what they've done, especially our own children."

Jason laid his hand on my shoulder. It was a gentle hand. It was hard to believe it was the hand of a 'monster.' "And so you've been beating yourself up ever since."

"More or less. I had one child, Jason, a child I loved more than anything else in the world. So why did I abandon him?"

"I'm sure you had your reasons and no doubt at the time they were very good reasons. Perhaps you didn't realise the seriousness of the situation."

"You're right. I didn't, but that does little to console me. I sometimes wish I could do penitence, purge myself in some way. The monks in medieval times had the right idea. Self-flagellation."

"I reckon you've done enough of that, Patrick."

"I was brought up a Catholic, Jason, but I was never a religious man. There are times, though, when I wish I hadn't lost my childhood faith in Jesus and the Virgin. I so envy those who can find forgiveness in God."

"Forgiveness like so much else can only come from within. You need to have faith in yourself."

"That is the hardest thing of all."

A slight drizzle began to fall, which felt strangely comforting, like a placenta insulating us from the hostile world. It was only temporary, I knew, and like the soon-to-be born babe, we would shortly have to face the iniquities of harsh reality.

"Andrew and I were very close, even though we were of different sexual persuasion. We were very much into dope, as you probably know."

Why did he tell me that, I wondered? Was he trying to inure me to a truth I had been trying to avoid?

"I knew he partook but I had no idea it was serious, not until we found out how..."

"It wasn't. It was purely recreational...at first. In order to acquire it, you have to get in with a bad crowd. Even though they may only exist on the edges of organised crime, it's very easy to get sucked into the vortex and soon find you're unable to drag yourself out."

I must have given him an incensed look because he said, "I didn't think it was my place to tell you, Patrick. Besides, even I didn't know how deeply involved he was until it was too late."

"Was he an addict?" I asked reluctantly.

I had always had my suspicions but had preferred to recline in self-delusion and denial than confront the challenge of confirmation. It was something Alice and I never discussed. Neither of us wanted to face the truth about our son.

Jason eyed me probingly, possibly wondering whether I really wanted to know what he was about to tell me.

"It doesn't matter now, I suppose," I said untruthfully.

"I think you know that he was, Patrick. He told me how he had asked you for money and you had refused because you said you had no intention of funding his drug habit."

"That's true. I suspected something was not right. He didn't look well, and he always wore long-sleeved shirts, even in summer, which he had never done before."

The image of him, pale and emaciated, when one day he washed up on our doorstep, was heart-rending. Had he come to see us? To let us know he was still alive. Though he must have known how much it distressed us. Was it simply to wheedle some ready cash out of us? No doubt the latter. "How did he fund his drug habit, do you know?"

"I think you can guess, Patrick?"

"So, because of me he got involved in peddling drugs."

"It was his choice."

"What choice do you have when you're an addict?"

"You always have a choice. He was very strong-willed. He said he could quit whenever he wanted. He did eventually when he realised it was going to kill him."

"You mean he didn't die of an overdose?"

"I know that was the official verdict. The info I have is that fellow inmates killed him. Of course, no one wanted to admit it. It would have made the prison authorities look bad. It was easier just to sweep it under the carpet. You see, about a month before he died, when I visited him in prison, he told me he was clean, one hundred percent clean, and he swore never to go back to heroin."

"And you believed him?"

"Absolutely. When Andrew said he'd do something, he always did it."

I realised how little I knew my son. I had deliberately avoided finding out what would only upset us. I suppose I wanted to protect Alice. What good would it have done, anyway? He was as good as dead and there was nothing I could do to bring him back. At least that's what I thought. Now I suddenly had a burning desire to know everything, every detail of his death and what led up to it. I wasn't sure why I hadn't thought of asking Jason earlier. The truth is I had no idea they had remained friends. "So, how did he die?"

"I can only surmise."

"Well, what do you surmise?" I said brusquely.

"I suspect he displeased the big bosses and they saw the need to have him expunged. I'm sorry, Patrick. I know this must be very upsetting."

"Could I have done anything to help him?"

"I doubt it. When you get involved in organised crime, the only escape is with your life."

"So, you think he tried to disentangle himself and they had him liquidated because he knew too much."

"That's my theory. When he said he'd quit, he didn't mean just heroin. Once he told me when he got out of prison he was going to cooperate with the police and go after the drug bosses. I told him he was crazy even to consider it, but he was very pig-headed."

"Don't I know it," I said with a faint smile, remembering some of the tussles we had had as he was growing up.

He always knew best, acted like a man of the world, even before he graduated from school.

All this new information about Andrew was driving me crazy. Why was I so eager to learn more? To exonerate him or myself? Perhaps both. I realised that in all likelihood, I would never know the whole truth. Jason was clearly only in possession of part of it. I felt frustrated. I had been given a glimpse of a world I knew nothing about but all I could see were vague, flickering images with no means of gaining a clearer picture.

"And that's all you know. Surely there must be someone who can tell us more."

Jason looked at me apprehensively. "Patrick, you don't want to go there. First of all, the chances are you'll never find out more than I've told you. If you do, you will become a target. These guys don't mess around. There is too much at stake. Millions, in fact. Life is expendable in the circles Andrew moved in. They would think nothing of having you disposed of in the way they disposed of Andrew."

Jason's warning did little to put me off. I had nothing much to lose, except my life, which was nearing its end anyway. It was more important to me to die knowing that Andrew's death was not by his own hand but in the service of justice.

We passed the old lady and the bulldog again. Or should I say she passed us. "Andrew, what are you up to these days?" she managed to utter, as she was yanked along the path.

I remembered her name. "Home on holiday, Lily," I shouted, but I'm not sure she heard me.

We said little on the last part of our walk. I was thinking about Andrew, but Jason too was on my mind. Would he manage to survive in prison? I was beginning to hope that all Victor S's lies would save him from conviction, that all the witnesses would come forward and vouch for his innocence, that the charges would be dropped and that he would walk away Scot free. I wasn't able to save Andrew, but I knew I had to save Jason, one way or the other. I was almost certain he was not wholly innocent, but I justified my need to save him by convincing myself that he was not as bad as the media tried to make out. Whatever the result, I promised myself I would do my utmost to at least save his soul.

"Why did you resign from the National, Jason?" I asked, curious to know why he had not simply let things take their course.

"I naively thought that if I did it would all go away."

"You're too much of a public figure for them to let it drop."

"I know that now and it seems they're going to make an example of me."

"There's a lot of anger out there."

"Anger that is blinding them to the truth."

I still did not know what the truth was, so I said nothing.

As we turned the corner into my street, I saw what I had been dreading, Victor S's shiny black Mercedes parked outside my house, alarm lights flashing as if he was deliberately trying to attract attention. "So much for discretion," I said, expecting a convoy of paparazzi to appear any minute.

Maybe because the rain had kept them indoors or Victor S's driver had given them the slip, there appeared to be no reporters on his tail. One or two of my neighbours, however, were enjoying the spectacle, especially an obnoxious, upstanding member of the community and stalwart pillar of the church, with whom I had had differences over a tree on my side of our common boundary that had the impertinence to seasonally drop a portion of its leaves on his side of the fence. He had threatened to sue me if I didn't hack the offending tree back to its trunk, which would have left it maimed and mutilated on one side. I ignored his threats. I had still not received the summons but Victor S's flagrant appearance on my doorstep would provide him with a perfect opportunity to get his own back for my indifference to his leafy plight.

Victor S must have seen us coming. He got out of the back of his car and stood bolt upright like a visiting dignitary waiting to be led up the red carpet. Seeing him there in his glitzy suit looking self-important brought it all back; the battle to get the court's decision overturned and Victor S's ultimate failure to save my son.

The last time we met resulted in my behaving badly, unforgivably so, I must admit. I had the gall to accuse him of incompetence, Victor S, one of the top lawyers in the country. I blush at my arrogance, but I was angry, very

33

angry. I felt he had not played all the trump cards he had at his disposal. His rhetoric in court, though flamboyant, had failed to move the judges, which I put down to the fact he made no attempt to show Andrew was as much a victim as a felon. I lost my temper, said things I would later regret and stormed out of his office. Since then, we had maintained no contact. I was not looking forward to meeting him again.

As I approached, he fastened a penetrating glare on me, which was hard to interpret. "Patrick," he said with his deadpan expression. "It's been a long time."

"Not long enough," I wanted to say. "How are you, Victor?" I said aloud. "Thank you for taking on Jason's case."

"It's a tough one but I believe we are on top of it. I was sorry to hear about Alice. Very sad. A lovely woman."

It seemed that Victor S did not bear me any ill will, though I couldn't be sure. His civility may well have been mere legalistic diplomacy.

Without waiting for my response, he turned towards the house with a look of resolve on his face, closely followed by a cowed assistant carrying a Samsonite briefcase. "Now, let's get to it," he said. "We've got work to do."

Chapter Seven

Victor S took over my home in the manner of a Napoleon establishing his centre of operations, totally ignoring me and my privacy. He only interrupted his annexation to order coffee. I wanted to say that not every home has a maid, but I realised there was no point in being petty. So, I made it myself. In the meantime, he marched into every room looking for a suitable location for the mock hearing. He finally chose my office, which he deemed sufficiently claustrophobic and oppressive to resemble a small courtroom, though he would have preferred it to be more sparsely furnished. To my surprise, he agreed to let me follow the proceedings, on condition that I did not interfere.

He tut-tutted when he saw the clutter on my desk and ordered that it be removed at once. What seems like a clutter to some is a carefully ordered scheme of things to others, but I said nothing and cleared it anyway. He enthroned himself in my chair, assuming an imperial posture. All that was missing was the tricorne and the chain of the *Légion d'Honneur*. His silent assistant sat beside him, shuffling fretfully through papers, which he passed to Victor S with a tremulous hand when requested. Jason sat alone on a chair in the middle of the room, looking very much like a prisoner about to undergo torturous interrogation. I sat in a corner, making myself as inconspicuous as possible.

"Now, Jason, the charges against you are farcical," Victor S pronounced. "You are innocent of the charges and I want there to be no doubt about this in your mind. Are we clear?"

"Yes, Victor," said Jason meekly.

"Good, because I have no intention of anyone making a fool of me. You must answer the questions without hesitation. You will naturally deny any suggestions that you had intercourse with these young men. Whether you did or not is irrelevant. If asked, you will admit to being gay. Homosexuality is not a crime, but you have never had sex with a minor, male or female, ever. Understood?"

"Yes."

"The onus of proof is on them. Now, if you have any little peccadilloes like child pornography or videos of a dubious nature, delete any trace of them today. If the charges are upheld—which I believe is highly unlikely, given their tenuous nature - then they will turn your flat upside down, confiscate your computers and other material that might give them the evidence they need to convict you. I have used every influence I have at my disposal to ensure that things are delayed, to give us time to mop up, so to speak. Despite the accusations, your contribution to the theatre and arts still carries some weight, thank God, and there are those in high places who would like to see this whole mess disappear as quickly as possible. Now, let's begin. I want you to imagine that this is a film or play in which you are acting the part of the innocent victim. I am the intransigent, homophobic judge, who would like to see all gays put behind bars. All my innuendoes and insinuations are designed to trip you up, trick you into admitting something that might give me the rope I need to hang you. The populace is crying out for your blood, and this is putting the justice department under pressure to satisfy their lust. Don't think, Jason, that the courtroom is all that different from the Colosseum. Judges are not beyond giving a thumbs-down to a defendant unable to prove his innocence just to keep the masses happy. So, anything is possible. You understand?"

Jason nodded.

Victor S was good, I had to admit. He could have made a career as an actor, screenwriter or director, possibly all three. He had an eye for the dramatic. He knew what would move the audience, what they might or might not believe, all the time putting Jason through his paces, scolding him if he was too hesitant, too implausible or in any way suggestive of wrongdoing. "Jason B, you were a volunteer at a local refugee camp for unaccompanied adolescents. Isn't that right? What motivated you to volunteer for this work?"

"Well, I …" he began tentatively.

"No, Jason, no. You know exactly why. You felt sorry for them and wished to help them. Your speciality is theatre. So, your idea was to do therapeutic theatre. You believe in the cathartic effects of drama through the process of acting out pain, in this case of being separated from parents, of being violently removed from home and country. You did it solely to help them overcome the traumas left by exploding bombs and flying body parts. Drop in the term '*post traumatic syndrome.*' It will impress. Use your imagination. Your motivation was not only to improve their mental health but to help them adapt to a new culture, give them an opportunity to learn the language *interactively*, that sort of thing. These guys love jargon. It makes you seem as wooden headed as they are. Improvise, Jason. That's what you've spent your whole acting life doing. Now is the time to put it into practice, especially as it could determine how you will spend the next twenty years of your life. So, let's consider the question again; what made you volunteer at a refugee camp for unaccompanied minors?"

Jason did not hesitate this time. He spoke about friends who became volunteers and the work they were doing. He felt an urgent calling to help the refugees, as he believed that with his knowledge of theatre, he could provide support and relief for these unfortunate young people, deprived of parental care and support, stranded in an alien environment, unsure of their future, unable to return to their homeland. Jason said it all with such conviction I almost believed he meant it, even more so when he interspersed a bit of well-chosen pseudo-psychological jargon. Perhaps he did mean it. I never ruled out that possibility.

With Victor S's coaching, Jason acted beautifully. Only a very hard-hearted judge would not be moved by his apparent sincerity. Even Victor S seemed pleased. He smiled, which was rare for Victor S, who frowned on any form of gleefulness, however bland. "Good. The critics could hardly fault your performance. I think we've covered most of the topics, but don't be fazed by something unexpected they might come up with. They are bound to have a few tricks up their sleeve. Okay. Let's call it a day."

As we exited my insulated office into the living room, I thought I heard a commotion outside. It was coming from the front gate. I ran to the window and saw a mob of reporters and paparazzi outside. Some were attempting to scramble over the fence. Others were ramming the locked gate to burst it open.

"The bastards are here," I shouted. "And it looks like they're besieging the place."

I saw Jason hurrying towards the window but intercepted him just in time. They must have guessed he was inside but there was no need to give them the proof. A squad of photographers had their long-lensed cameras trained on the window where I was standing, ready to shoot, should Jason appear. I could already hear their shutters snapping on the off chance that Jason's ethereal image might appear in the background. For want of the real thing, however, I knew they wouldn't hesitate to use a photograph of me. I could guess the headline. PATRICK G PROVIDES HAVEN FOR ALLEGED RAPIST.

"I'll deal with them," said Victor S, who strode defiantly into the garden. "The rest of you stay inside and lock the door. Jason, I'll send my driver to pick you up on Friday an hour before the hearing. Wear your best suit."

Before he even reached the front gate he was bombarded with questions, most of them nonsensical and misleading, like 'Why did he do it?' or 'How many years will he get?'

Victor S had no intention of starting a dialogue with them. He merely repeated, "My client is innocent. The charges are a pure fabrication." The questions didn't cease, though, not until he and his assistant were securely in the back of the car and the driver was cleaving a passage through the crush of reporters and paparazzi.

I turned to Jason, who stood with drooping shoulders, supporting himself on the back of an armchair. "It looks as if we're back to square one," I said.

Jason looked at me apologetically. "I'm sorry, Patrick. I seemed to have landed you in it."

"It's not your fault. I knew Victor S would be unable to keep a low profile. Besides, there was never any question of my not helping you."

"Really, Patrick?" he said with a surprised look on his face.

Jason could not understand what motivated me to stand by him, no more than I could myself, though our walk by the river had made it a lot clearer in my mind. "I'm doing it for Andrew. You were friends and I know he would want me to do everything I can for you."

"I hope it won't have any repercussions for you."

"It might, but my main concern is you now. I've lived my life and a damned good one it would have been, if it hadn't been for Andrew's death. That's why I want to make sure you don't go the same way."

"I don't see why I should."

I was taken aback by his naivety. He must have had some inkling of what life in prison is like. The survival rate of child molesters is alarmingly low, but I said nothing. I thought it best that he not know what might be in store for him.

"It looks as if I'm going to have to face the mob," I said. "We got chatting on our walk and I forgot to go by the supermarket to get the ingredients for supper."

"I'm not hungry, Patrick. I'm happy to make do with whiskey and whatever bits and pieces you have lying around."

"Not a good idea. I've got to face them some time. Otherwise, we'll starve. This siege could hold out for days."

I took a coat and a shopping bag and headed for the door. "Just keep out of sight. I don't intend to give them the satisfaction of knowing for certain you're here, even if they have a pretty good idea that you are."

As I walked down the garden path, I had a feeling of *deja vu*. I was overwhelmed by the same gut-wrenching foreboding I had before Andrew's trial. Then later, after his death - or murder, if Jason's intelligence was correct—when I had to face the firing squad again and deflect their inane questions and the blinding flashes from their snapping cameras. It resulted in my being overcome by a sense of utter despondency that made communication with anyone, even Alice, almost impossible for some time afterwards.

I found myself being fenced in, as I tried to spot an opening among the multitude of scavengers fighting for a scrap of information that could be turned into something newsworthy. "Why are you hiding Jason B?" "Were you aware that he has sexually assaulted minors?" "Do you intend to be a witness for the defence?" I kept my mouth hermetically sealed and my temper in check, though neither was easy. I found their aggressive questioning infuriating. I had to exert immense self-control to stop myself from lashing out, though I knew if I had it would only further alienate me from the public. They had every right, it seemed, to use heavy-handed tactics on me but I had no right to retaliate, one of the paradoxes of a liberal democracy.

I finally managed to push my way through the throng but was dreading having to run the gauntlet again on my return. Then, it occurred to me. I didn't have to. I could approach the house from the street behind my house, cut through the neighbours' garden and somehow climb over the high wall that separated my garden from theirs.

In the end, I did a lot of shopping as I didn't know how many days we'd be holed up. So, I had the problem of getting three heavy bags over a two-metre wall. I just hoped none of the occupants of the house behind mine happened to be staring out of their back window. The sight of their elderly neighbour attempting to scale their wall into his own garden might arouse more than a little concern, as I had, so far, shown no obvious signs of insanity or dementia.

Fortunately, there was an upturned wheelbarrow lying next to the wall, which I used to reach the top, where I placed the bags of groceries. Then, with a great deal of scrambling, I managed to pull myself up, puffing and straining. I finally succeeded in straddling the wall, from which I was able to let myself drop into my garden below. With a broken ladder that had just enough rungs to allow me to reach the top of the wall, I retrieved my supplies.

Now I had the job of attracting Jason's attention so that he could let me in through the back door, which I always kept locked. I tapped on several windows without success. I reckoned he must have gone to Andrew's room to lie down, so I threw small pebbles at the window. I had no idea how he would react to this, possibly just ignore it, if he thought the paparazzi were trying to draw him out. Fortunately, it was still light when he eventually came to the window and cautiously looked down at my pitiful figure. With sign language, I indicated that he should come down and open the kitchen door, which he did.

"Patrick, what are you doing? Don't you have a key?"

"To the front door, yes, not the back."

He understood at once what I had done.

"So, you found a way to breach the siege."

"By trespassing on the property next door and jumping a few hurdles, yeah."

I entered the kitchen with the three bags and laid them on the table.

Jason stared at me in astonishment. "How long do you expect this siege to last? There's enough food here to keep us going for a couple of months."

"Better to be prepared," I said. "Though, with any luck it won't last more than a day or two. Those poor bastards out there are still expecting me to return. They'll think I've abandoned you to your fate. How long do you reckon they'll stay if they see no sign of life inside? What do you say we don't turn on the lights tonight?"

"Suits me. In that way we can spy on them and make snide remarks about their bedraggled appearance. I think we will call them *The Great Unwashed*. We can even take bets on how long they'll stick it out. How about doing a rain dance and hope the heavens open tonight?" he said with a mischievous giggle.

"Sounds like fun."

We both had a good laugh, possibly the last we would have for a very long time.

"Besides, I reckon there's enough light from the streetlamps to navigate the house without bumping into each other."

"Living in a city does have its advantages. You can save on electricity, if you're that way inclined. Alice would often turn up after work and berate me for not turning on the lights. She thought I did it to economise, but I like the semi-darkness. It has a certain serenity about it that reminds me of my childhood in rural Ireland when we still used oil lamps."

I set about making supper while I could still see what I was doing.

Chapter Eight

After supper, when I went to check my e-mail, I found that one of the assistant producers of the film Billy mentioned had sent me the script along with a very flattering letter, extolling my acting ability and my contribution to both film and theatre. Despite my age and the bad publicity surrounding Andrew's death, I was apparently still a saleable commodity. The part I was being offered was not a starring role—that would have been too much to expect—but it was certainly a challenging secondary role that had some interesting scenes.

Though I was not familiar with the scriptwriter's name, he was clearly very talented. It lifted my spirits enormously, as I felt it would help me to finally get out of myself, and maybe get over Alice. Though filming can be tedious at times - all the waiting around for the cameras and the set to be spot-on - you meet a lot of interesting, often bizarre people with strange backgrounds, who have chosen an alternative, unpretentious life over luxury and ostentation. There are others, of course, who, though well into their second or third quarter, never give up hope of one day hitting the big time.

In the meantime, Jason and I felt our way around the house, emitting the odd squeak in the manner of ambulatory bats, to make sure we didn't bump into each other. Yet, it's surprising how quickly one's eyes adapt to darkness. Reading was impossible, of course, though I did suggest to Jason that if he felt like it, he could do what we did at boarding school, take a book with a torch under the bed covers. Some of my most enjoyable reading was done in this manner, especially as it provided some respite from my farting, foul-mouthed fellow occupants of the dormitory.

So, we just talked, pretending that everything was hunky dory and that Jason had come to spend a night or two, as he often did in the past. It was difficult, though, not to feel the absence of Alice and Andrew. Yet, somehow it made his presence that much more vital and meaningful. He was standing in for both of them.

After a short silence, while we savoured the silvery light issuing in through the curtain-less windows, he said, "I've actually known you for nearly forty years. Did you know that, Patrick?"

"Really?"

"Yes, you wouldn't remember, but when I was about ten—or was it eleven? - my father took me to the Illysia, where you were playing Hamlet."

"Good god. Was that forty years ago? Yes, I must have been in my early thirties then, the apex of my acting career, you might say."

"My father was a great admirer of yours. He said, 'Anything Patrick G does is worth watching.' And it was. I was very young but I loved your portrayal of Hamlet; the tortured soul, torn between revenge and justice, love and duty. Even today I can't imagine there could be any other Hamlet but yours."

I laughed self-effacingly. I immediately assume that if a person heaps praise on me he must have some ulterior motive. True or not, it's a way of not letting flattery over-inflate my ego. "Are you trying to butter me up, Jason?"

"Why on earth would I do that? No, it's just something I've been meaning to tell you ever since I met you. I thought now that we were revisiting the past it was as good a time as any."

"Well, thanks. In many ways, Hamlet was the highlight of my career. Everything I did after that was bland. No other role demands as much of an actor as Hamlet. Except Lear perhaps, which I'd love to do before I shuffle off this mortal coil."

"Let's hope we'll get the chance to do that together. I'd love to direct you in that."

Again, he was showing his naivety.

"When I got to know you better, I always wondered how you got into Hamlet's skin. Rightly or wrongly, I have this idea that we can't portray emotions we've never felt. Were you very close to your father?"

"Not really. He was very much old school. Stiff upper lip and all that. Yet, I somehow always knew what he was feeling. It must have required great effort on his part to hide all that emotion. I only saw him cry twice, once when his favourite cat died and the second time just before my mother passed. He had a very strong sense of decency and believed in justice and equality, though he had his prejudices, of course, like all of us. So, yes, although he was not exactly my role model, he instilled in me certain principles that I have largely held on to throughout my life."

"I guessed as much."

I contemplated his grim face through the penumbral shadow that drifted in from the street outside. "You were not close to your father either, I know."

"I suppose I can sum him up in one sentence. He was an intellectual with an irrepressible libido. Nothing much mattered in his life except sex and theatre. As for me, I was an impediment. I had to be palmed off on to anyone who would take me so that he was free to pursue one or other, or both, of his passions, often together. He was not one to miss an opportunity."

"But you said he took you to the theatre."

"Occasionally. He couldn't shirk all his parental duties, though he would have liked to. Without me, he would have been able to seduce one of the actresses after the show, take her for a drink and then to bed. He was such a giant of a man in the theatre world. Well, you know that. Girls just swooned at the sight of him. He was not a handsome man, by any means, though he always gave the impression of being young. Even when his hair went completely white, he wore it long, sometimes in a ponytail, like an ageing hippy. He also had a beautiful voice, soft but manly."

"So, you didn't like your father," I said conclusively.

"On the contrary, I adored him. I wanted to be just like him."

"Even when your parents split up?"

"Oh, yes, I had little respect for my mother. She was arrogant and very sarcastic, always trying to put me down. Because she was my mother, I had to put up with her. I was glad when they separated, and I could choose where to lived. I often stayed at my friend Joseph's house. He was my first love in fact, though I never declared myself. Back then, I was not sure what love was all about."

The gloom seemed to have a strange effect upon us both, perhaps because we couldn't see or anticipate each other's reactions. It made it easier to open up. We felt anonymous, as if cloistered in a confessional, speaking to God, or his taciturn representative, sequestered in the adjacent booth. Jason told me things that helped me understand him better, why he had turned out as he did. I realised how much like his father he was.

"It was largely because of you that I became an actor, Patrick," he said, turning his head in my direction to see if he could discern a reaction.

"Oh dear, I'm sorry," I joked. "If I'd known you were in the audience that night, I'd have given a crappy performance."

He didn't seem to register my feeble attempt at humour. "It's not your fault, Patrick. It was in my blood, I think, but you were the deciding factor. When it came to choosing a drama school, I chose the one where you were teaching without a second thought."

"With no regrets, I hope."

"You taught me everything I know about the theatre, all the things that are not taught at other drama schools."

"Like?"

"How to be yourself, for one."

How can you teach someone to be themselves, I wondered? But I understood what he meant. Acting has to do with drawing something out of yourself that you don't even know exists. At least, that is what I used to tell my students. Some think it is a question of looking around for a suitable skin to wear, a skin that resembles the character you are portraying, and of course that is part of it, but a suit of clothes is not enough unless you marry it to that other self, deep within you, the residue of a past life perhaps or a doppelganger lurking in the depths of your soul.

"By the way, I've been offered a rather nice part in a film. I skimmed through the script this afternoon and I like it. The director sounds good, too."

"Are you going to take it?"

"I'm definitely considering it."

"You must take it, Patrick. You've been out of the limelight too long. I always regret we never did something together. But we will."

I wanted to say that if he had asked me, I wouldn't have said no. Why didn't he? Was he afraid of being accused of nepotism? I was his teacher, yes, but as far as the public was concerned, that's where the connection ended. "So do I," I said, trying not to make it sound too definitive. Whatever the outcome of the hearing, I knew that the chances of his ever regaining his former glory were very slim indeed.

I wondered how easy it would be to change Jason. At seventy, could I become the concerned, caring father he never had? Could I save his soul? It was not my job to do so, I knew. What can any father, real or adopted, do after the event? Any intervention will almost certainly be futile? I could not give up on him. I was not going to make the same mistake twice.

After a few drinks we both started to feel drowsy and groped our way to bed. I felt strangely optimistic that Victor S might pull it off. Victor S's overweening confidence was so redoubtable it was hard to believe he could fail.

Victor S failed miserably with Andrew. Yet perhaps Andrew had been a lost cause from the start. I tried to convince myself that his situation was different from Jason's. It was not based on tenuous accusations. There was no proof, only their word against his. Andrew's guilt was never in question, from a legal point of view at least. What had led him to a life of crime was another thing altogether. Jason, on the other hand, was on much more solid ground, or so I thought.

I decided to write back to the assistant producer that night and tell him I was interested. I suspected they wouldn't bother calling me in for an audition as they must have known what I was capable of, unless of course they wanted to see how I had aged over the years. Billy was so sure I'd get the part that I didn't even consider the possibility they might not take me. I found myself feeling more excited and alive than I had for years. This might be a new beginning, a way to start over, even at this late stage in my life.

I slept well, banishing thoughts of Andrew and Jason from my mind. I was back. I dreamt of all the great times Billy and I had enjoyed backstage and on set. It was almost like having my youth returned to me.

When I woke up the next morning feeling unusually bright and chirpy, I almost forgot about the reporters, the paparazzi and the mess Jason had got himself into. My enthusiasm was such that I even expected to look out of the window and see the peaceful suburban street purged of crook-necked vultures.

However, it was not to be. I was saddened to see that they were still there. Had they gone away for the night and returned the following morning? Had they camped on the pavement, or more likely perched on the branch of one of the maple trees that lined the street, waiting for the object of their bloodlust to crawl out of its burrow so that they could swoop down and take a peck at it? These guys had tenacity. I had to give them that.

I was in the habit of listening to the news headlines over breakfast. Jason had still not appeared, so I turned on the radio with the volume low. The news was still dominated by Covid, the vaccines and the number of cases and deaths. The government was cautiously optimistic that by the end of summer, we'd be more or less over the worst of it.

I was about to turn it off when the presenter started reading the headlines of the major newspapers. The quality newspapers led with President Biden's rapprochement with Europe and the revival of the Paris Agreement on Climate Change, all positive stuff. Then, he read a headline from a gossip rag that hit me like a bullet in the chest. JASON B FINDS SHELTER IN THE HOME OF PATRICK G.

The presenter found it necessary to explain to his listeners, to those at least who had been born in the last decade, who Patrick G was, the actor whose son had died in prison of an overdose. What he failed to mention was that Jason was as much a son to me as Andrew had been. The gist of the article was that I must have had some ulterior motive for shielding an alleged child molester and rapist. If not, he could only conclude that I condoned Jason B's monstrous actions. I suppose I shouldn't have been surprised.

Once again, I hadn't listened to Alice. She warned me and I ignored her. The die was cast, no backing out now. I would have to go the whole haul.

Chapter Nine

The next day Jason and I kept our heads down, avoiding windows or making loud noises that would indicate a presence in the house. I cooked a superb lunch with all the things I knew he liked. The thought of acting again and his presence in the house had an invigorating, uplifting effect on me, which felt very much like the old normality.

I was no longer pondering the question of his guilt. I accepted it as fact. What I was perhaps unable to grasp was the extent of his crime. Maybe it was because of my lack of knowledge of such things or my inability to admit to myself that Jason was an innately bad person that I was unable to accept the most vicious of his alleged crimes. It didn't seem possible that he could knowingly hurt or harm anyone. Was I so blind? Was I so capable of self-delusion? The possibility that someone can be two diagonally opposite people, angel and devil rolled into one, had not occurred to me.

As we relaxed after lunch over a cup of coffee, I asked him, "How are you feeling about tomorrow? Are you ready?"

"A lot more so since being with you, Patrick. Just to be treated like a normal human being for a change has done me a world of good. I was beginning to think that I really was a satyr."

"Maybe this is not the time to talk about it but how did you let it happen? I mean, how did you lay yourself open like that? You must have known there were many who would relish the thought of you being dragged through the mire."

"Foolishness, I suppose. You know how many men like me have their toy boys, young men after easy money and a good time, in exchange for sex. Yet, I was the one they chose to make an example of. Now, all my 'victims' will start crawling out of the woodwork. You'll see, in the next few weeks others will come forward claiming I sodomised them against their will. Look at me, Patrick. I am hardly a strong man. I have never done any manual work

48

in my life, and I can't walk for more than a kilometre without collapsing. Do you honestly believe I can force these robust, beefy young men to have sex with me?"

I glanced at his puny body and had to admit that he did look pathetically frail, possessing all the features of a malnourished hermit who spends his day fasting and praying to God, which was obviously not so in Jason's case. There was no doubt he had the physique of a non-athletic fourteen-year-old rather than a grown man. "You must say all this in court, Jason," I pleaded.

"Victor S is my lawyer. I must do what he thinks is best."

I could see I wasn't going to be able to change his mind. "Maybe you're right," I said. "He may not be infallible but he's the best person you've got at the moment. I just wish you could be more honest with the courts. I'm sure that if they saw some remorse they would be far more lenient."

"Remorse for what? Do you think I forced myself on these boys?"

I didn't know what to say. The truth is he hadn't admitted outright that he had. So, why did I assume that he had? I was no better than the scandal mongers and detractors that hounded him.

"I've got to follow his instructions now. It will all depend on my performance tomorrow. I may not be in the running for an Oscar, but it might determine how the rest of my life will pan out."

I leant across and put my hand on his arm. "If anyone can pull it off, you can. After all, you were my star student and, as you said yourself, you had a good teacher."

He smiled wanly. "That I did, for what good it's done me."

"A lot, I hope."

A sullen silence hovered darkly over us. I guessed we were both considering the worst, as one is wont to do before a first night. In Jason's case, however, it was not a first night but a first and last night rolled into one. There would be no second night to iron out those first-night glitches. He was going to have to do it cold, no warm-up, no real rehearsal, all ad-lib, and improvisation. One false move and it was all over.

~ * ~

That afternoon I thought I might do some writing, but I was unable to concentrate. Victor S's aura was still hanging in the air like the aftermath of a bad dream. I sat at my desk contemplating the scene of the previous day. It was so much like a poor play sponsored by a famous playwright who thought he had written the work of the century, yet it had all the makings of a flop. Everyone could see it, except the writer himself. Not that I hadn't seen badly written plays turned into moderate successes, thanks to the verve of the actors and the resourcefulness of the director, but they seldom became resounding successes. In this case, I had limited faith in my actor and even less in my director. All I could do was hope for the best and try and remain optimistic for Jason's sake.

That afternoon I retired to my room and tried to eke out a page or two of my current novel. Writing a novel is the easiest thing in the world. Writing what people want to read is another thing altogether. After becoming a tad disillusioned with theatre, I tried my hand at writing stories, but with only a modicum of success. It was enough, though, to give me the stimulus I needed to try and hone the art of writing. Yet, despite sending my work off to hundreds of publishers, all I got back was 'Sorry, but it doesn't fit our list,' which became a standard reply, as if they couldn't be bothered to find something more original to say. It was up to writers to be original, it seems, not the publishers.

Alice knew exactly what I was doing wrong. She would say, "You're a great writer, Patrick, but your themes are too obscure to appeal to the general public. And why do you insist on choosing such controversial protagonists? Write about someone people can sympathise with. They might be prepared to give your other novels a chance." She was right, of course, as usual, but in the same way I wished to play challenging roles I needed to write challenging books. As an actor, I must take what is offered to me. As a writer, I have the freedom to choose, and I suppose that's what I love about it. Rightly or wrongly, I see writing as a journey of exploration. It's a way to delve into the minds of others and my own. "In that case, you only have yourself to blame if you don't get published." *Oh, Alice,* I thought, *how little you understand me but how right you are.*

I suspect Jason spent the afternoon running over his lines, getting his story off pat in his head, not an easy thing when you know the story is a farce.

The question was, would he be able to make it sound spontaneous, from the heart, and not something he rehearsed for a lay audience? If the magistrates hearing his case were anything, it was not gullible. They saw too many people try to pull the wool over their eyes, prompted by smart Alec lawyers like Victor S, who considered everyone else a fool but themselves.

I wondered if Jason felt any guilt for what he had done. If he did, he had not shown it. Was it lack of sensitivity on his part? I would love to have known he felt some remorse, some change of heart, some urge to reform. I was still not sure the 'monster' within him was not pathological, a creature that could not be slain or even tamed. I wished Alice was around to enlighten me. She had a way of cutting to the chase, of disposing of all the bullshit, as she would say, and seeing things are they really are. Yet, I knew if she were standing before me, looking me in the eye, telling me I was deceiving myself, I would still be unable to accept Jason was a monster.

I couldn't write. I had too many voices in my head. Alice telling me that I must accept the truth, Andrew telling me in his new-age technobabble there is no such thing as a guilty person, just guilty circumstances. My mind spinning in the manner of a devout believer racked with misgivings but stubbornly refusing to doubt the religion that gives meaning to his life.

So, I decided to lie down for a bit and try to focus on the here and now. Separating the rays of light in the dazzling orange phalanx of arrows beaming through the milky windowpanes or trying to imitate the bird sounds dampened by the looming twilight or simply watching a spider soundlessly scaling its web in search of the day's catch. I had almost succeeded in detaching myself from my troubled biosphere when the phone rang. It was Billy.

I was in two minds whether to answer it. I knew what he was going to say. He must have heard the news. In fact, I was surprised he hadn't rung earlier. "Billy, hi," I exclaimed with overstated eagerness.

"Patrick, please tell me it's not true."

"What?" I said ingenuously.

"You know bloody well what. How could you do this to yourself? What in God's name do you owe this man? You know perfectly well he's going down and it looks very much as if he's going to take you with him. Get out now, this instant. Call a press conference. Say he turned up on your doorstep and you couldn't turn him away. Plead ignorance. You live an isolated life and never watch the news. You knew nothing about his private life. Find some way of disassociating yourself."

"I can't, Billy."

"Can't. What in God's name do you mean? There's no such thing as can't. There is only won't and you know it. If you have any respect for me and yourself, you'll leave now, face the TV cameras congregated outside your house—I saw them on the three o'clock news - and give an impromptu interview. Exonerate yourself, man. You're innocent. I know it and everyone who is acquainted with you knows it, but those who don't will have your guts for garters. Why, Patrick? Why? What has he ever done for you?"

The truth was he had never done anything for me. It had always been a one-way street. "He was Andrew's friend," I said meekly.

"I see," said Billy, like the blind man who couldn't see at all. "I know you feel guilty for what happened to Andrew but you did what you thought was right. Most fathers would have done the same. Of course, in hindsight, you realise you could have done more but what has this got to do with Jason? Jason is not your son."

"He has been very much like a son to me, Billy. Ares was a rotten father, if you could even call him a father. When Jason found Alice and me, he found a home."

"Well, it didn't do him much good, did it?"

That hurt, but I swallowed his accusation without gagging. "The damage was already done, Billy. He was like a wounded bird whose broken wing had mended badly. A part of him was mutilated forever."

"Very poetic and hopelessly romantic, my friend. Surely you must know after fifty years in the theatre that no one will show any understanding of what you are doing, even if some second-rate TV channel gives you the chance to spout all that sentimental bullshit. Don't tell me it's all bloody hypocrisy because I know it is but that doesn't make a scrap of difference. You will lose every friend you have left in the theatre world. You might as well take your typewriter and find a remote cave somewhere high up on a mountain top because no one will have anything to do with you. It's the name of the game, Bud. Once the world consisted of thousands of tribes roaming the earth. After being ousted from one tribe, you might have found another to take you in. The world is one big tribe now. If this one rejects you, you have nowhere else to go. There's no escaping it."

Despite my feeble attempts at defending my stance regarding Jason, I knew Billy was right. I had to give up Jason or condemn myself to a very lonely old age. Even the foreign gentleman who ran the corner shop would look at me with disdain. I would become a pariah, not for any crime I had committed, but simply by association with Jason. "Can we meet?" I asked. I don't know why I said that. Was it simply to buy time? Or did I believe I could bring Billy around to my way of thinking?

Billy hesitated. "I don't know whether it's such a good idea, mate. To be honest with you, Patrick, I don't want to be compromised. I cherish my career and my friends."

"So, that's it, Billy. I must choose between Jason and you?"

"Patrick, you must understand, I have too much to lose. As I said, have nothing more to do with Jason, talk to the press, make your excuses and you might get out of this unscathed."

"I don't think you have any idea what you're asking me to do, Billy. Would you abandon your own son?"

"Yes, if he had done what Jason has."

"But how can you be certain it's all true?"

"Does it really matter? Even if it's half true, it's just as bad. He's going down, Patrick. What's the point in being dragged down with him? Save yourself, for God's sake."

"I'll give it some consideration," but I didn't mean it. I said it simply as a means of reassuring him and maybe holding on to him for just a little while longer.

"Don't think, just do. Before it's too late. Look, I've got to go. Meeting the boys at the club for bridge. You should become a member. The company would do you good. Now, get out there and talk to the press. I expect to see you on the nine o'clock news denouncing the man. Good luck, my friend."

"Thank you," I said limply, wondering whether we would ever talk again.

Billy hung up and I felt unbelievably alone and defenceless. My heart started pounding and it felt as if my chest was about to implode. Was I having a coronary or was it the onset of a panic attack? I concluded it must be the latter and forced myself to take deep breaths. After about ten minutes of mind-numbing fear, I was breathing normally again.

I lay on my bed and tried to separate the sun beams into single threads but all I could see was one big blur of light splashing into the room like an unstoppable tsunami. The spider had gone back to its nest and the birds were silent.

The full extent of what I was about to do came home to me. I had lost my longest and closest friend, possibly my only real friend and I was about to give it all up to save someone I wasn't sure deserved to be saved.

Chapter Ten

It didn't take the tweeters long to start posting their self-righteous, hateful tweets, condemning someone without knowing the real facts. 'Patrick G. disappoints the world by providing refuge for a child rapist. He should be locked up along with the sicko.' 'Patrick G, the adored *jeune premier* of the eighties' theatre scene, reveals a shadier side to his character. A great shock for his loyal fans.' 'Will Patrick G finally come out into the open and admit his sexuality? Was he also involved in Jason B's nefarious activities? When will he be put on trial along with his protégé?' And so, it went on.

It quickly came home to me what I was in for. I realised I hadn't fully understood the implications of what Billy had said. It was more than just rejection I was facing. It was banishment, total ostracism. People would look upon me as a depraved, dirty old man, someone not to be allowed near children. Maybe Billy was right. I needed to exonerate myself. Could I do it and still stand by Jason? The two were completely incompatible.

I had been planning to go with Jason to the hearing, though I wasn't sure whether they would let me follow the proceedings. I knew, however, merely being beside him as he entered the courtroom would give him some moral support. If I were to disown him now, it would have a disastrous effect on his morale, and I know first-hand the effect this can have on an actor's performance. The more I thought about it, the more I realised I was yoked to his cart and could not unharness myself without letting the whole shebang hurtle down the hillside into the abyss.

Jason's appearance had reverted to the haggard, drawn look he had when he arrived on my doorstep two nights before. The bags under his eyes seemed even more bulbous than ever. If it had been a theatrical performance he was about to give, I would have advised him to go back to bed and try and get some sleep, but Victor S's chauffeur was due to arrive in less than an hour. I would have to try and fortify him in other ways.

"Coffee or tea?" I asked trying to sound cheery.

"Whatever you have, Patrick."

"You'll have some toast and marmalade, right? I gather you haven't really acquired a taste for porridge."

It was clearly an effort for him to smile. The most he could produce was a faint twitch at the corners of his unyielding lips. "Nothing, thanks. I already feel bloated."

"Alice always said that if you have a good breakfast, it'll set you up for the day. You need your strength. We don't want you fainting in the middle of the show."

I don't think he appreciated my reference to the hearing as a show, though that's how I saw it, and I wanted him to see it like that too. He had an audience to impress with his Thespian skills and powers of persuasion.

"I just need to be able to get through it," he said wearily.

"Jason, you said yourself, this will be the performance of a lifetime. Our aim here is not to just get through it."

"I have to believe in what I'm doing."

"You mean you don't?"

"Not a hundred percent. Maybe they're right. Maybe I should go to prison. I'm going on fifty and I like young men. Is it an illness, Patrick?"

"I'm seventy and I still like young women. I don't think that's an illness. It's just human nature."

Jason banged his fists on the table making the breakfast things leap perilously into the air. "But I'm not innocent, Patrick," he shouted. "For God's sake, can't you see that?"

I was taken aback by his unexpected outburst, but I held on to my composure. "Yes, but how many guilty people are willing to admit it? That means you want to change, and someone who wants to change can change."

"Patrick, please stop it. You don't know me. I am not the person you think I am. It's true what they say. I am a monster."

I didn't know how to react. His admitting that he was a monster somehow made me want to prove him wrong. "Of course, you're not, Jason. It's just you're worried about the hearing. Now, sit down and force some toast down you. You're going to need it."

I wish I had been able to ask him what he was guilty of. Had he had sex with underage boys or not? I still wasn't sure. If not, why did he consider himself a monster?

I pulled my chair closer and put my hand on his arm. I tried to get him to look me in the eye but he was doing everything he could to avoid my gaze, as if some blinding light was radiating from my forehead. His stare remained doggedly downcast. I had no idea what to do. He had clearly sunk into a deep depression.

"So, what are you going to do? Let them lock you up and throw away the key?"

He suddenly looked up as if what I proposed was a great idea. "Why not? My life is over."

I felt like taking both his arms and shaking some sense into him, but I knew that would do no good. "Your life is over only if you want it to be. There are ways out of this. It's true that things are never going to be the same. There will be a life of sorts when this is all over. If the worst comes to the worst, you can join me in my remote cave in the mountains."

He gave me a puzzled look.

"Billy says that after this I might as well retire to a remote cave with my typewriter. Perhaps it's for the best. I might finish my latest novel."

"So, I'm ruining your life as well as my own."

"You don't have to ruin either of our lives. As Cicero said, 'While there is life there is hope.' Now is the time to believe that. It's going to be an uphill battle, but it is worth fighting for."

Jason sighed but I felt that something I said had got through to him.

"We'll do this together because I believe in you. All you must do is believe in yourself."

I poured him a cup of tea, prepared a piece of toast and marmalade and put it on his plate.

The sweet milky tea seemed to do him some good. Eventually, he looked up and smiled wanly at me. "How can I ever repay you, Patrick?"

"You can repay me by going out there and knocking them for six. You know you can, if you believe in your worth as a human being. Now, can you do that? For my sake. I don't want all this to be in vain. I can't bring Alice back. I can't right the wrong I did to Andrew, but I can do my best to save you. That would be reward enough. So, if you don't want to do it for yourself, do it for me."

We stared at each other for some moments, trying to gauge the extent of each other's sincerity and willingness to see this through.

"I will," he said at last. "For your sake, Patrick, not for mine. I'm not worth it."

"Go on now and smarten yourself up. You'll find a couple of good suits in the cupboard in Andrew's room. You and he have the same build. Then, come down and we can do some warm-up exercises."

When he left the room, I collapsed into an armchair. I had been living a very sheltered life. This sudden advent of distress was taking its toll. I knew I would have to conserve my energy, as I had a presentiment that this would not be over any time soon. Even if it was, I had committed to taking a very sick man under my wing, and I wasn't sure even Hippocrates himself could concoct a cure for what Jason had.

For a moment I thought it was Andrew when Jason entered the living room in Andrew's suit. It fitted perfectly. Both he and Jason were slim and of slight build.

"What do you think?" he said doing a full-circle twirl.

"Amazing. For a moment I thought you were Andrew."

"I'm sorry, Patrick. I wish I were."

"No. I'm just glad it fits. So, let's start with a few body exercises. You don't want to look too stiff. You need to appear relaxed and confident."

After he loosened up a bit, I gave him some tips on body language. "Now Victor S's advice was good but when asked a question, don't look down or away from the interlocutor. That is a sign of guilt. On the other hand, try not to appear arrogant or over-confident. That could have the opposite effect. Always look the magistrate in the eye, though. Be polite and show humility without grovelling. That irritates them. A groveler is asking to be punished. What you are trying to create between you and the magistrate is a rapport of mutual respect. You want him to say, 'Here is a decent, honest man. He can't be what they claim he is.' Got it?"

"I'll do my best."

"Break a leg," I said, putting my arms around him and drawing him towards me. "Think of it as just another performance. It'll be a difficult audience, but you know how to play them. I always found that the fun part, in the first scene trying to suss out their predilections. Do they like slapstick or subtlety? Is it the boohoo that moves them or the elusive, subcutaneous emotion? They will do their best to hide their reactions, so you must observe their body language too to ascertain the effect you're having on them."

"Aren't you asking a lot of me, Master?"

"I never ask of my students more than they can give. I know what you're capable of. Besides, it's second nature to you. How many parts have you played anyway?"

Jason shrugged his shoulders. "I've lost count."

"I like to keep a record of all the parts I've played. I try to recall them sometimes when I'm in need of inspiration or a particularly apt line used by one of my characters."

"You mean you remember your lines?"

"The best of them. People like you and I play so many parts in our lives we sometimes forget who we are. I think that's what happened to you. When this is all over, together we are going in search of the real Jason B. If necessary, we're going to dismantle the present one block by block and piece him back together again. This time making sure that the pieces are in the right place. How does that sound to you?"

"Do you think such a thing is possible?"

"Of course, it's possible. I was married to a therapist for fifty years. Alice used to say anything is possible if there is a will."

"I'll take your word for it, Patrick."

My phone rang. It was Victor S. "Patrick, I don't like the look of things. There has been another claim of rape. Only someone of your calibre and prestige can sway the courts. You're going to have to take the stand and give Jason a character reference."

"I won't lie. You know that."

"No need to. Just tell the court what you know. You're very fond of him, I can tell. You could be our only hope."

"Can I think about it?"

"No. My chauffeur should be outside your door in five. I'll tell him to give you a call."

"I hate having things sprung on me, Victor. If you'd…"

"I wouldn't have, if I didn't think it wasn't crucial. I can count on you, right?"

I said nothing.

"Good," said Victor S and hung up.

Jason looked at me with some concern. "What did Victor S want?"

"He wants me to take the stand."

"And you agreed?"

"Did you hear me agree?"

"No, but I didn't hear you disagree."

"Shit."

"So, it looks as though the teacher has to put his own precepts into practice."

I suddenly felt overcome by stage fright. The increased heartbeat, butterflies in the stomach and the fear of fluffing my lines. It now looked as if I too would have to give the performance of a lifetime.

Chapter Eleven

I realised I had to crystallise in my mind what my real feelings for Jason were. It wasn't easy. I too had been influenced by what I had heard and seen over the past few days. I couldn't divorce all that from the Jason I knew and loved before the events now monopolising the media became public knowledge. Strange though it may seem, it was Andrew who helped me to see him in the light I knew I would have to portray him in.

I called to mind images of him and Jason as young men in their early twenties, both still a bit immature, both experimenting with life, both playing with fire, both on the verge of something great. I recalled their laughing together, sharing jokes that were supposedly unfit for the ears of us oldies. It's funny how young people find it hard to imagine that the older generation were ever young, profane, reckless, that they too once believed that the world in all its glory belonged exclusively to them.

I had no idea what to wear, formal or casual? In the end, I opted for something in between. I looked at myself in the mirror and wondered whether Alice would approve. She would have said the shirt was a bit too flamboyant, too gay perhaps. 'We don't want them to get the wrong impression. Magistrates are people too, you know. Though they may like to think they're resolutely unbiased and unswayable, they will also have read the tweets.' So, I changed my shirt to something plainer. 'That's a lot better.' She would then raise herself on tiptoes and give me a peck on the cheek and say, 'How could they not be bowled over by such a handsome young man?'

The phone rang. "Mr. G. It's Paul, Mr. S's chauffeur. I'm parked a bit down the street from the reporters. Mr. S. would like us to get to the courtroom as soon as possible."

"Okay, Paul. We'll be with you in a couple of minutes."

I let Jason choose whatever clothes took his fancy. He looked good in the semi-formal khaki suit Andrew wore to auditions and job interviews.

Even the brown bootees were still quite modish. Andrew had good taste, like his mother.

"If it were a fashion show we were going to, we'd certainly pass muster," I said, trying to lighten the atmosphere.

"I think even Alice would approve," he said with a restrained smile.

I remembered how close Jason and Alice used to be, far closer than he and I ever were. They always had their heads together, sharing some intimacy or other. Or was that Andrew and she? I sometimes get them confused. She always found time for them in her busy schedule, maybe because she realised how much they needed her. They both confided in her, though she never relayed these confidences to me, for fear of how I might react. Was it her therapist's insistence on confidentiality? Maybe it was much simpler than that. She just thought I wouldn't care to know what they were up to.

"So, let's face the mob," I said, unlocking the front door.

The waiting pack had not been fooled by our going to ground or the self-imposed blackout. Or had they decided to wait it out anyway on the off chance of our re-emergence?

They must have seen Victor S's car pull up a little way down the street and prepared their cameras and notepads in anticipation of our appearance.

Microphones darted out like dragons' tongues licking hotly at our faces. "Jason, do you expect the charges to be dismissed?" "Patrick, why are you standing up for Jason B, given the barrage of accusations against him?" "Patrick, do you think he's innocent? Or is there some other reason why you are harbouring him?" "Jason, what do you have to say in your defence?" "Jason, are you sorry for what you've done to these boys?"

It was the sheer force of their will to condemn that I found so hard to accept. In their minds, there was no question that he was not guilty. Soon, the whole country would be represented by what they wrote. Few people think for themselves, which is understandable. We rely on the media not only as a means of obtaining information but also to form opinions. How reliable are the media? Where do they get their facts from, given that there is no such thing as a *well of absolute truth*; a source of information of indubitable provenance or an opinion of unquestionable veracity? Even police statements can be biased, and medical reports flawed. So-called truth is often based on inference, speculation, prediction or at best dubious fact. Yet, we believe what the members of the press tell us. They are our shepherd-priests, leading us to the true faith, depending on which sect they happen to belong to; right, left or centre. In Jason's case, however, I was certain that all the media denominations would join forces to present a united front, because sometimes the truth is simply what the people want to hear.

We valiantly pushed our way through the vultures, who were determined to tear a chunk of flesh off us, around which they could construct a theory, a conspiracy, a scenario to suit their purposes. One innocent phrase would have been enough, but both of us decided to give them nothing, not a single word. I put my arm out and pushed aside a photographer, who withdrew hastily to protect his camera. I rushed for the gap and hoped that Jason would follow before the tidal wave closed back in over us.

We set off down the street with the horde in our wake, firing question after question. By the time we reached the car our backs were riddled with smarting pockmarks.

Paul had the doors open and we shambled in. As he drew away, I threw a glance back at them and saw that their feathers were ruffled and their wings drooping. I almost felt sorry for them. We had left them empty-handed and ravenous.

~ * ~

There must have been at least two hundred people outside the courthouse. Some were waving banners and chanting slogans, exhorting the state to bring back capital punishment or, better still, pass a law sanctioning castration.

"Is there a back entrance, Paul?" I said, dreading the thought of having to fight our way through another crowd of fanatics.

"I'm afraid not, Sir. Even if there were, they'd quickly cotton on."

"You mean this's the only way in?"

"I believe so, Sir."

"We're going to need police protection."

"There are usually a few officers on standby in case things get nasty."

Behind the crowd, I could see the heads of some uniformed officers, looking hopelessly docile and ineffective.

"I don't like the look of that crowd. I think their mind is set on lynching us."

"I've seen worse, Sir. They make a lot of noise and may appear threatening but they're pretty harmless."

"You could have fooled me."

"The police will intervene if things get out of hand."

"Great. Where the hell is Victor S?"

"He thought it best to meet you inside."

Paul drove as close to the marble steps as he could without knocking someone over. Within seconds protesters and religious fanatics were crowding in on us so that all we could see were myriad contorted faces glaring in at us. The car began rocking back and forth as they pushed from all sides. Some were shaking fists or wielding makeshift weapons - it was hard to believe they had no intention of using them. Others spat on the windscreen or pounded the glass with their fists.

Paul managed to open the door for us. Jason got out first and ran as fast as he could up the steps. A tumult of foul language and abuse was showered on us, followed by plastic bottles, rotten fruit and anything that could be used as a non-lethal missile. Our only protection was our arms, which we held as tightly to our heads as we could. "Where the hell are the police?" I muttered. I looked up and saw them standing apathetically at the top of the steps, a look of sardonic detachment on their faces. So, even the authorities were indifferent to our plight.

We scrambled up the steps and through the heavy wooden doors, on which were embossed the words *animus in consulendo liber*. From my rudimentary knowledge of Latin, I guessed what it meant and hoped that it was true. Thankfully, once we were inside, the doors were closed and barred behind us.

Victor S was standing in the hallway, his jittery henchman by his side. "It's become a high-profile case," he said. "It wouldn't even merit a mention in the papers in normal circumstances, but you have the misfortune of being a celebrity, Jason."

That did little to console either of us. "What now?" I inquired.

"We've been allocated a small room, where we can wait until we're called." He turned and looked at us. "How are you feeling?"

His question, which I could only assume was rhetorical, was directed more at me than Jason, though I wasn't sure which of us was in a worse state.

Victor S ushered us into a room, where he seemed to feel at home, but Victor S had a knack of making himself at home anywhere. "Right. I don't think either of you need any last-minute coaching. There's no need to tell you that we're all under pressure here, including the magistrates. Remember, this is not a trial, just a hearing but it is important. They will be ascertaining whether they can bring a case against you. It will also determine whether they believe you are a threat to society, to yourself, or whether there is a risk you might try to leave the country, in which case you will be remanded in custody until the date of the trial. I have reassured the chief magistrate - in private - that you are not a threat and have no intention of leaving the country. I also promised on your behalf that you will present yourself at your local police station every day, should they decide the case has to go to trial. But that is the worst-case scenario. I am optimistic they will find no cause to take this any further. The evidence against you is tenuous at best."

Chapter Twelve

Nobody spoke. Jason looked uneasy and I was worried that he might break down under questioning. However, there was little I could do to reassure him. I paced, as I always do before a performance. I need to hype myself up, so that the first scene does not seem like a beginning but a continuation. Victor S revised his notes, every so often putting a hand out to his assistant, expecting him to know, through some form of osmosis, I imagine, what it was he wanted. If the wrong item was produced, he would rebuke the browbeaten secretary for his ineptitude or, more precisely, his inability to read his mind.

At five minutes to the hour, a steward came and led us along wide corridors to Room 8. For some reason, I expected it to be almost empty, but quite a few seats were already occupied. I found out later that a limited number of members of the public are allowed to attend such hearings on a first-come first-served basis. We were ushered to the front. To our right was a small group wearing gowns I assumed were the prosecution. On the bench sat two robed individuals, a man and a woman, with an empty, slightly elevated, seat between them.

We were asked to stand while the magistrate entered in all his finery and sat at the head of the bench. From his sagging jowls and bloodshot eyes, I suspected he was on the cusp of retirement, which was evidently none too soon, judging by the resigned air of apathy on his face. He cleared his throat and pushed out his chin pugnaciously, scanning the assembled company in an endeavour to warn off any potential rabble-rousers.

After the summary introductions, the prosecution was asked to present its case. They said nothing we didn't know, that is, which had not already been leaked to the press. Then, Victor S was asked to present his case for the defence. He made references to the written deposition in which he disputed the allegations made against Jason. It soon became clear to me these presentations were mere formalities. It was the questioning that took place later that would sway the court one way or the other.

Jason denied all the charges in the way Victor S instructed him. The problems arose when the prosecution claimed that none of the witnesses Victor S quoted in the deposition were prepared to state categorically that they had seen Jason at the time he was supposed to have raped the young men in his flat in the city. Yes, they saw him at the Northern Theatre Festival, but only on the day the Young National gave their performance, not on any other day, which theoretically meant that Jason could have travelled from the city that morning and left the same day. Similarly, regarding his holiday with friends, although they were holidaying in the same location, they said he kept to himself, so much so they hardly saw him, and on the night on which he was supposed to have raped Hassan he did not turn up to a gathering at a restaurant where two tables had been booked for a party of six, which included Jason. Nor had he rung to inform them he wouldn't be coming. However, they were not unduly concerned, as it was apparently quite common for Jason not to keep an appointment. Naturally, the lawyer for the prosecution pointed out these discrepancies to show the deposition was flawed.

The chief magistrate stared at Jason over the top of his glasses, a look of defiance on his pinched features. "Jason B, do you have any way of proving that you were where you claim on the two nights in question?"

"What kind of proof, your honour?"

"You must have stayed somewhere? At a hotel or lodgings? Can you produce a receipt of some sort?"

"During the Northern Theatre Festival, I didn't stay at a hotel. A friend who was on a film shoot let me stay in his apartment. As for the night I didn't turn up at the restaurant, I was not feeling well. In fact, I had a high temperature, most likely due to exhaustion. It had been a very hectic time at the National, preparing for festivals around the country and abroad."

"Why didn't you call your friends to inform them you wouldn't be going to the restaurant?"

"I intended to but fell asleep and didn't wake up till the next morning. I rang them later that day and apologised."

"Can anyone confirm that you were in your room all night?"

Jason thought for a moment. "I don't think so, unless I ordered a drink from room service."

"The hotel should have a record of that. Now..."

Jason answered the magistrate's questions calmly and confidently, never failing to look him in the eye, as instructed by Victor S, who seemed pleased.

The magistrate shuffled through some papers he had on the desk in front of him and seemed satisfied everything had been covered. "Right, well, it seems..."

"Your honour," interrupted Victor S. "There is one piece of business you have overlooked. I made a late petition to allow a close friend and colleague of Jason B's to make a brief character appraisal."

"Very late, it seems, Mr. S, as I don't seem to have any mention of it here. Therefore, I'm afraid..."

One of the assistants raised a hand to draw the magistrate's attention to a piece of paper that was separated from the rest. The magistrate showed signs of disapproval but, after more discussion, he nodded in resigned agreement. "All right, Mr. S, we will accept your belated petition on this occasion but in future I would advise you to be prompter with any such requests. So, would Mr. Patrick G please come to the stand?"

My turn came and I felt slightly lightheaded, but I knew for Jason's sake I had to speak with confidence and conviction.

"What is your relationship to the accused?"

"I was Jason's teacher at drama school. He was a brilliant student. I could tell from the word go that he would do great things in the theatre world. We quickly became friends and would often go for a coffee or a drink after class. When our friendship grew, I introduced him to my wife and son. After that, he became a regular visitor to our home."

"Is it common for a teacher to befriend one of his or her students?"

"I know teachers who form very close friendships with their students but in my case, Jason was an exception. It is difficult to say whether we adopted him, or he adopted us but he quickly became a beloved member of the family."

"So, why did you make this exception?"

"Apart from the fact I found him an extremely stimulating person to be with, he was very keen to meet my family. I believe that as a child he did not enjoy a secure, loving home environment and he yearned to be part of a real family."

"So, your interest in Jason B was purely altruistic?"

"Absolutely."

"Mr. G, what is your sexual orientation?"

I was momentarily fazed by his insinuations, but I tried not to show it. "I am heterosexual."

"Have you ever had relationships with young men or boys?"

I could only guess the magistrate was trying to provoke me into revealing a darker side to my character. I did my best to contain my rising anger. "No, your honour, I have not," I said coldly.

"Were you aware that Jason B was homosexual and had intercourse with minors?"

"I was aware that Jason was homosexual, yes. However, the accusations made against him came as a shock to me."

"Do you believe that they are true?"

"Knowing Jason as I do, I find it highly unlikely. Jason has always struck me as a very kind person. I do not believe that he would knowingly hurt or harm anyone."

"Even in a state of extreme sexual arousal or under the influence of drugs?"

"I cannot answer that, but I do not believe so."

"Are you aware the police found drugs in Jason B's apartment?"

"I think this was mentioned in an article I read."

"Were you aware he used drugs?"

"No, I was not."

"How well do you know Jason B?"

"We have been close friends for nearly thirty years. As I have already mentioned, he was also very close to my late wife Alice and my son Andrew. However, I should also mention that we are of a different generation and in many ways, he was closer to my son than he was to me."

"How well did you know your son, Mr. G?"

"I beg your pardon, your honour?" I was momentarily flustered by his question and had to struggle to recover my composure.

"I believe he was convicted of drug dealing," continued the magistrate, "and died while serving a five-year prison sentence?"

I could feel my blood boiling. How dare he bring my son into this? I knew exactly why he was doing it. He wanted me to blurt out something that might incriminate either me or Jason. I clenched my fist in a supreme effort to exert self-control.

Victor S must have seen that I was on the brink and intervened. "Your lordship, with all due respect, I cannot see how Patrick G's relationship with his son has any bearing on the case of Jason B."

"Mr. G claims that he took Jason B in—'adopted him' I think he said - as he felt Jason B needed to feel part of a happy, caring home environment but the so-called family environment Patrick G provided for his own son can't have been all that happy and caring given how he turned out."

"Please forgive me, your honour, but I know from personal experience Patrick and Alice G were a devoted couple, who gave more than the usual amount of love and attention to their son Andrew, no doubt to Jason B as well."

I didn't like the way things were going. The magistrate was almost blaming me for Andrew's involvement in drugs, implying Jason too turned bad because of his association with Alice and me.

"In my experience, Mr. S, good families do not produce drug addicts and hardened criminals. But that is as it may be. I have always admired and respected you, Mr. G...as an actor, that is. So, I am prepared to give you one minute to tell us who Jason B is."

I panicked. I realised I had no idea who Jason B was, not the present Jason B, anyway. I tried to recall the one I thought I knew and loved best. "As a student, Jason stood out for his incredible sensitivity and understanding of people. It was not just his ability to analyse a complex character and reproduce it on stage. He was capable of great compassion and empathy. Throughout the years I have known Jason he showed immense kindness to both my wife and my son. During my wife's prolonged illness, he visited her in hospital, even at a time when he was extremely overworked as an actor and director. He also did everything in his power to help my son, both before and after he was convicted. Therefore, I cannot believe Jason could have committed the heinous crimes he has been accused of. It is just not in his nature."

"Was it in your son's nature to sell drugs to the vulnerable youth of our city?"

Again, my son. I gritted my teeth and closed my eyes for a moment to keep my anger in check. "My son, it appears, was one of the vulnerable youths of our city," I uttered between clenched teeth. "Like many others he resorted to selling drugs to maintain his habit. Therefore, I would not describe him as a hardened criminal. If your lordship is implying that I was in some way to blame for his addiction, I am not able to deny it. No doubt a psychologist would link it in some way to failings in his upbringing. If, as you seem to imply, I am also to blame for the way Jason has turned out, then possibly it is I who should be sitting in the dock, not he. However, it is not up to me to decide whether Jason is guilty or not. That is the function of the justice system, of which your lordship is a member. My concern for Jason is that he does not become a victim, like my son, of a state correctional system that is unable to protect its inmates." I almost spat the final words at the magistrate.

"Your son, Mr. G, committed suicide, if I remember correctly. It was hardly the fault of the correctional system."

"You no doubt read the papers of the time like everyone else, your lordship, but I have it on good authority he was murdered. I intend to make it my business to find out why and under what circumstances."

"I would seriously suggest you leave well alone, Mr. G. Your son died two years ago. The prison report stated quite categorically that he took his own life."

"It would not have been in their interests to admit that my son had been murdered. That, however, is beside the point. My interest in knowing exactly what happened to my son is purely personal. I want to set the record straight. As much as I would like to, I cannot bring him back. Jason, on the other hand, is still alive, which is why I am going to do my utmost to make sure he does not go the same way as Andrew."

The magistrate had allowed himself to get embroiled in a peripheral discussion that had little bearing on Jason's case and it was not going in the direction he would have liked it to go. Now, he was keen to wind up the proceedings. "I am impressed by your concern for Jason B, Mr. G, and as much as you would like to believe the best about your protégé, the allegations against him are damning and cannot be glossed over. We will now adjourn to consider the case in the light of today's hearing."

"All rise," said the bailiff.

We all stood until the magistrate exited. Then, we slowly drifted out into the corridor. We looked around aimlessly wondering what to do next. It was obvious to all of us things had not gone as expected.

We re-assembled in the room allocated to us. Fortunately, some kind person made coffee. I helped myself and sat at the end of the table. I was not happy with my performance. I allowed the magistrate to stir me up and make me say things I would have preferred not to.

Victor S seemed subdued.

"How do you think it went?" I said, cautiously looking over at him.

He didn't answer. He just sat at the other end of the table biting his lower lip and looking pensive. I suspected he didn't want to admit how badly things looked for Jason. Eventually, he said, "The deposition would have been watertight, if your so-called friends hadn't ratted on you, Jason. Why didn't you tell me you didn't go to the restaurant that night? It totally scuppered the whole deposition."

"I saw them that morning and the following day. They must have known I hadn't left the hotel."

"Well, it seems they didn't want to give you the benefit of the doubt. If this goes to trial, we've got to find some proof that you were in your hotel room that night?"

"If not?"

"It's their word against yours."

"So, the onus is on them, surely?"

"Not exactly. If they can establish a pattern in your behaviour, based on multiple testimonies, it could be enough to convict you. Each testimony will have to be invalidated with counter evidence and I'm not sure how easy that's going to be. For instance, no one can vouch for your being in your hotel room and you're not even sure if you ordered something from room service that night… Let's not jump the gun. I know the magistrate likes to put his defendants through the mill. His decisions, though, are usually fair. Let's hope he didn't get out of bed on the wrong side this morning."

"Why did he go after me like that?" I asked, still a bit shaken by the magistrate's insistence on bringing Andrew into the discussion.

"It was a mistake putting you on the stand, Patrick," said Victor S wistfully.

I looked at him in surprise. That was the first time I heard Victor S admit making a mistake or was he questioning my ability to present Jason in a favourable light?

"I should have realised he'd try and draw a parallel between Jason and your son. I was relying on your charisma to win him over…but you seem to have lost your lustre, Patrick," he added bluntly.

I knew he'd find a way of putting the blame on someone other than himself.

After half an hour of waiting, Victor S's man brought us more coffee, which provided some relief. The waiting went on and with every minute that passed we became more apprehensive. What was causing the delay?

~ * ~

It was nearly midday when they finally called us back in. We sat in our places and waited for the magistrate to appear. The silence was absolute. Not a paper stirred. Not a breath could be heard. All eyes were on the magistrate as he took his seat at the bench.

"The court has come to a decision," he began, stretching his scrawny chin in an involuntary twitch. "Given the gravity of the accusations against Jason B and the inability of the defendant to prove that the charges of rape brought against him were unfounded, the court has unanimously decided that this case should go to trial. Furthermore, given the seriousness of the crimes, we believe Jason B may be a threat to society and therefore we have no choice but to order he be remanded in custody until the date of the trial, which should not be more than four weeks hence. Will the custodians of the court please take the defendant into custody? Provisions will be made for him to be transferred to the female wing of Penal Institution 5 B and to be kept in a cell with no more than three others to await trial. This hearing is now dismissed."

Things went much worse than any of us anticipated. "I'm sorry, Jason," I said, putting my hand on his arm.

He shrugged and gave me a wan look.

I did my best but I knew it wasn't good enough. "But it's far from over," I added. "We will fight this."

"It's a relief really," he said placidly. "Maybe the press will leave me alone for a while. I might at last get a bit of peace."

"I'll visit you, of course, make sure you've got everything you want," I said lamely.

Victor S said nothing. He was not good at handling defeat. He took it as a personal affront.

A policeman took Jason by the arm and marched him out of the courtroom. I waited, expecting him to look back for some reassurance, but he didn't. Had he lost faith in me? Lost faith in life? Had I failed him as a surrogate father in the way I failed Andrew?

Then, I thought maybe the time in prison would do him good. It would give him time to reflect on the injury he had done to his young victims. I pulled myself up short. I was beginning to think like the rest of the country. I was assuming his guilt before his case even went to trial. One way or the other, I had to go on believing in him and in myself.

Chapter Thirteen

Victor S had his back to me as he headed for the door. "Victor," I called out.

He gave no indication of having heard. Only when I called a second time did he reluctantly half-turn towards me, just enough to reveal a choleric scowl.

"I'm sorry about today. Is there anything I can do?" I said apologetically.

"I think you've done enough. It's best if you don't get involved."

"I told you I was not going to lie. Not that I think I said anything that compromised Jason's case. As you said yourself, the deposition was not watertight."

"Thank you, Patrick, we shall not be requiring your assistance in the future," he said with a patronising sneer.

"I'd like to visit him in prison."

"That can be arranged," he said coolly, instantly turning and hastening towards the door.

As we descended the steps, reporters, cameramen and paparazzi folded in on Victor S like loose sand sliding into a pit. I took advantage of the commotion to slip around the back of the teeming crowd.

There was great jubilation in the air. People were smiling gloatingly and hugging each other. Some were even dancing, frenziedly shaking their crudely daubed banners in the air. Had justice been done, I wondered. Or had the court simply buckled under popular pressure? It was true Victor S had been unable to produce any solid counter evidence to the claims against Jason, but they were still only claims. Rightly or wrongly, Jason had been vilified and no one, not even the unbiased agents of justice, were going to believe he could be innocent.

Just when I thought I escaped the reporters, I heard someone calling me. "Patrick G. Patrick G." I turned to see Valerie F, a popular TV presenter, running after me. She was clasping a bulky handbag that seemed to be discharging its contents on to the pavement. I stopped while she retrieved the spillage and waited for her to catch up with me.

"That was clever of you," she gasped.

"I'm sorry?"

"To escape like that. Everyone was so keen on getting a statement from Victor S they completely ignored you. Can we go somewhere? To talk? Off the record?"

It had been a tiring morning, and I hadn't eaten. I was in two minds about sharing my lunch with someone I hardly knew, and a reporter at that. Still, she always struck me as a pleasant enough person and, as journalists go, she was quite objective in her views, so I thought it wouldn't do any harm. Apart from that, the idea of having lunch by myself, rehashing the same old thoughts and ideas that always led to a dead end, did not appeal to me. "If you don't mind having lunch with a harbourer of child abusers," I said cynically.

"On the contrary, I want to hear your side of the story."

We continued walking down the street.

We must have been walking for at least five minutes, talking idly, when I realised we had no clear destination in mind. "Do you happen to know a quiet restaurant around here? I'm famished," I said.

"I know a little place just down the next street that does business lunches. We won't be disturbed. They will be too busy making deals to notice us. I assume you've been vaccinated."

I nodded.

"Me too. Who would have thought the day would come when we had to prove we were healthy to be allowed into a restaurant?"

It was a smart little place called the King's Retreat. Fortunately, they had a table for two next to a window looking out on a quiet side street.

I sat down and looked across at Valerie F. She was still an attractive woman, though well into middle age. "So, why me, Valerie?"

"Because I know you'll tell me the truth. All I'd get from Victor S is the official version. I want the real one."

"I'm afraid you won't get much from me. I don't know the real version."

76

"Yes, but you know Jason, possibly better than anyone."

"I know a side of him, but I can't say I know him, in the same way I didn't know my own son, it seems. Children have a way of hiding things from their parents - things that we don't wish to see perhaps."

"But they still remain our children."

I liked Valerie. She was not pushy like most journalists, or, if she was, she was pushy in a gentle way.

"I'm not sure I'll be able to enlighten you," I said. "Since my wife died, I haven't seen much of Jason."

"He didn't attend her funeral."

It was not a question. I looked at her in astonishment. "How did you know?"

"It's my job to know these things. Why didn't he?"

"I don't know. It hurt at the time. I had to mourn Alice alone. I thought about it a lot. I even considered giving him a piece of my mind. Then it occurred to me that he was probably suffering as much as I was. I don't think he could have endured seeing her put in the ground. She was more than just a friend to him. She was a mother and mentor too."

"I thought you were his teacher?"

"I instructed him in the art of theatre. Alice instructed him in the art of life. My guess is he went off the rails a bit when she died. That's my guess. I could be wrong."

"Why didn't he contact you? It doesn't show much compassion on his part."

"It's been a strange time. Covid has kept us locked up in our homes."

"Not even a phone call? Sounds like you're trying to make excuses for him."

"It was after Andrew's death that his visits started dwindling, though he used to visit Alice at her office on a regular basis. He liked to talk to her privately, not as a client, of course, but as a friend."

"Have you any idea what they talked about?"

"No, Alice didn't share such private conversations. She treated their little sessions with total confidentiality. She would say, 'Jason came to see me today' and I would say, 'Oh, yes,' pretending to be blasé about it, though I was very curious to know what it was she had to be so secretive about. I could tell by her dark looks that he was of great concern to her, but I didn't want to interfere. She was the mind healer, not me. I asked her once what they talked about, but she just said, 'The poor boy is going through a difficult time.' And I left it at that."

"Do you think it had anything to do with Andrew?"

"It's possible but it may have been something more personal."

"Did she keep notes?"

"Of sessions with her clients, yes, but Jason was not her client."

"Are you sure she didn't?"

"To be honest, it never occurred to me. If she did, the notes are still there. Everything happened so quickly, though I believe she handed over most of her on-going clients to colleagues. Her office is exactly as she left it. I haven't had the heart to clear it out. I suppose I still haven't completely come to terms with her death."

"I can imagine…when you've lived with someone practically your whole life."

"There are nights when I sit blankly on the sofa watching the black screen of the TV, waiting to hear the key in the door and see her warm smile. Crazy, isn't it?"

Valerie smiled. "No, not at all." She waited a moment before saying, "Wouldn't it be interesting to find out what Jason talked to her about?"

"I would feel very bad about going through her private notes, if that's what you're suggesting. Besides, I very much doubt she kept notes on him."

"It might help to understand Jason, if she did."

"Yes, but it would go against all her principles, and mine too, for that matter. Besides, it's all in the past now."

"Is it, Patrick? I may call you Patrick."

"Sure, go ahead."

"So, is it in the past? Jason is about to go on trial. If he's convicted, the charges carry a very heavy sentence. Maybe you need to find out more about the man you're going out on a limb for. To find out if he's really worth it."

"Worth it or not, Jason was like a son to us. When Andrew died, he became even more precious to us. We were immensely proud of him, as one is of one's children."

The waiter came and gave us the menus.

"By the way, I can put this down on expenses," she said cheerily.

"So, it's a business lunch then. What a pity."

"It doesn't have to be all business."

"I know you journalists. Everything is business. So, I hope it will be worth your while," I said with a chuckle.

"It will be. I assure you."

"How can you be so sure?"

"Well, as we're about to have a free meal in a cosy little restaurant you're hardly going to sit there saying 'No comment' for the next hour. I'm bound to wheedle something out of you."

I laughed. I liked her manner. "You know, this is the first time I've had a meal out since Alice died."

"You have become quite the recluse, Patrick G. It has not gone unnoticed."

"Does anyone really care?" I asked.

"You underestimate yourself. You have a very large following. People can't wait to see you in another film."

"I wouldn't count on it," I said. "I haven't done myself any favours standing by Jason."

Valerie looked thoughtful. "It's true. There are those who will condemn you for it, but I believe they are in the minority. Most will respect you for not abandoning an old student and friend."

"I wish that were true."

The waiter came and we ordered. Valerie insisted we have wine, even though I wanted to keep a clear head. I am wont to become rather talkative with a bit of wine taken. A sign of old age, no doubt.

"Patrick, I'd like to do an interview with you. I want you to tell the world about Jason B."

"I'm afraid you're not going to get much dirt from me. I'm in no position to confirm or deny the allegations against him."

A waiter arrived and poured some wine into our glasses. Valerie chose it, a very expensive French wine.

We chinked glasses. "Cheers."

I took a sip. It was delicious.

"It'll be more about you than him, though I think people would like to know why you are sticking your neck out for him."

"I'll do it then, as long as it's not live."

"That's fine with me. We can get you into the studio one day and rattle it off. Do you have anything in the pipeline? A film or a series or something?"

"It's a bit premature but I have been offered a part in a film. It hasn't been confirmed yet, so please keep it under wraps."

"That's excellent news!" she exclaimed with what I felt was genuine glee.

"I know this is a business lunch," I said, "but I only know the public Valerie F. Are you married? Do you have children?"

"Divorced. Currently not in a relationship. I have two grown-up boys, one a film producer, the other a lawyer. Both doing well. Both trying to hang on to shaky marriages. The rest is the public Valerie F. I have virtually no private life at all. It's all work, work, work. Now you know everything about me."

"I'm sure there's a lot more to find out. I can see you must be very enamoured of your job."

"Moments like this, yes. The rest of the time is spent trying to catch up with myself." She gave me a winning look.

For a moment, I almost forgot it was a 'business' lunch.

The food was delicious, and we were both hungry. "Why did you come yourself, Valerie? You could have sent a minion."

"What? And miss this opportunity to drink top quality French wine," she said with a deadpan face, then laughed "Well, the truth is I've always wanted to meet you, to see if the image of the deep thinker and sympathetic actor has any relation to the real Patrick G. I was also intrigued when I saw that Jason B was staying with you. I admired your courage. Not many would have taken him in."

"It had nothing to do with courage. Weakness, or a guilty conscience, more likely."

"Really?"

"I think all parents think they could or should have done more for their children."

"So, you really do see Jason as your son?"

"In a way, yes."

The waiter brought our food, which looked mouth-watering. I had forgotten what a decent stew tasted like.

I told Valerie how Jason became part of the family and his close friendship with Andrew. I told her a little about their parallel careers, how they both started making names for themselves in the theatre at about the same time. "I think there may have been a certain amount of rivalry between them. Andrew was very good looking and had access to more leading roles than Jason. Jason, on the other hand, was very good as a character actor."

"I know. I saw him as Shylock. He was incredible. Very villainous. Still, they remained friends, despite the rivalry?"

"The theatre world is very cutthroat but, as far as I know, they remained close. Andrew did tell me once Jason went behind his back on one or two occasions, but I didn't take it too seriously. They were like siblings and siblings are always quarrelling about something, especially when they're vying for the same thing. But, yes, there was some jealousy, all right. In fact, now I come to think about it, Jason had a bit of the adopted child syndrome. I remember his complaining once that he could never be as close to Alice and me as Andrew was, because he wasn't our son, we may have overcompensated a bit, but I don't think Andrew felt relegated in any way."

"Surely, that was a bit immature of him. After all, they were adults not children."

"In a way, yes, but some people never really grow up. He still sees the world rather like a child, despite his erudition. It can be a charming combination, you know. His plays are very insightful, as are his commentaries. Yet, there is a naivety about them that makes them very endearing."

"Yes, most people know him as an actor/director. Few are aware of his literary side."

"Someone can be immature in some ways and very mature in others. Who said, 'The human soul is an abyss'?"

"Ah, that was Fernando Pessoa, but the ancient Greeks said it as well, I think."

"I'm impressed."

She ignored my compliment. "So, when Andrew died, he had you all to himself?"

At first, I wasn't sure what she was getting at. It was only afterwards that I gave it some thought. After Andrew's death, Jason became like an only child. He could monopolise Alice. I wondered if she was aware of this and indulged him. Did she try and wean him off her? Was she simply indulging her own need to replace the son she lost?

"I can see this is painful for you, Patrick. Would you like us to change the subject? Talk about the weather or something?"

Yes, it was painful. I hadn't talked to anyone about their deaths, which were still so fresh in my mind. "As long as you don't mind listening, I don't mind talking. Alice was a great believer in talk therapy."

"More wine?" Valerie filled my glass up. "So, what happened to Andrew?"

"I can't be sure. In many ways, he was a very sensible boy, but his private life was a mess. He was very sensitive, with a tendency to think the world was about to cave in when something untoward happened. Young people tend to change partners frequently these days, more so than in my day at least, which can be a problem for people like Andrew, who need stability in their lives. About ten years ago, I think it was. He got involved with a young actress. A lovely girl, very pretty, very vivacious. He was head over heels in love. He would have given up everything for her, even his burgeoning acting career. They talked about marriage and naturally we were very happy for him. Then, out of the blue she decided she wasn't ready to settle down and accused Andrew of trying to ensnare her in a marriage. Maybe he was. Who knows? Anyway, she left him and went off with another guy. Classic story really, but it had a disastrous effect on him. He became deeply depressed and lost all confidence in himself. He gave up. It was as if something broke inside him."

"Was it at about this time he started taking drugs?"

"He always indulged in recreational drugs. It helped him to relax, he said. It didn't worry us unduly. We all indulged a bit in our youth. Andrew was rather weak in many respects, easily led. It may have been around this time he started doing harder drugs. Jason mentioned something about it the other day, but he wasn't clear when it all started."

"Where was Jason during this time?"

"As far as I know, they still saw each other. The difference was that Jason was getting on in the world while Andrew was destroying himself. I know that now. I didn't at the time."

"If Jason was like a son to you and Alice, why didn't he warn you about the way Andrew was going?"

"Maybe he didn't want to worry us. I don't know. The truth is if we had known, we would have got involved before things got out of hand."

"He was an addict, and you didn't know it?"

"We suspected. We just didn't know what to do. He was not very approachable. I know Alice did her best, but Andrew hated it if we tried to interfere. He kept asking us for money, saying he'd pay us back when he got his next part. I refused but I think Alice gave him some on the sly. She never told me, but I suspected. She thought she had enough influence over him to get him to give up drugs, but on this occasion, she overestimated her therapeutic powers."

"Surely Jason could have done something?"

"For all we know he did."

"I've always been fascinated by people. I think if I hadn't chosen journalism, I would have been a psychologist. I've been thinking a lot about Jason lately. Do you think he was abused as a child?"

I looked up at her in surprise. "It never occurred to me."

"The abused often become abusers, so they say. Did Jason ever mention anything that might have indicated he had been abused sexually?"

"To me, no. Alice would say that those who have been traumatised repress the memory, even obliterate it from their conscious minds. So, it's something he wouldn't have talked about."

"To you perhaps. But to Alice? She was a therapist, after all."

"She always had a policy of not taking on friends or relations. So, it's unlikely."

"Yes, but they weren't real sessions she had with him. You said it yourself. They just talked, like mother and son."

Valerie had opened a whole new perspective on Jason and his relationship with Alice. If only Alice had told me about their conversations, I might have been able to understand Jason better and possibly help him. "My wife had incredible intuition, particularly about people. I think you share that intuition. Or is it something women have that we men lack?"

"I hate to differentiate between men and women, but it is true we women seem to have more sensitive antennae than men. Men tend to rely heavily on logic. They have an innate fear of the intangible."

"I think you may be right."

"Mm. That food was good, almost as good as your company, Patrick."

"I enjoyed yours too, but did you get what you came for?"

"I came to persuade you to do an interview with me. I thought I'd need to get you a bit drunk before you'd agree, but you gave in after one sip."

"So, you wasted a good meal on me."

"It was certainly not wasted."

"Yeah," I said with a smile. "I thought I could hear those antennae humming."

"They certainly were. Now, tell me, Patrick, when will they let you know about the film?"

"Soon, I hope. I need to get stuck into something. I've been wallowing in self-pity far too long."

"And Jason?"

"Victor S wants me out of the way. Blames me for the fiasco today but I'm certainly not going to give up. I'll visit Jason in prison as soon as I'm allowed. What good it'll do I don't know."

"You must do what you feel is right."

I nodded.

"How about dessert?" she said, perusing the menu.

"If it's anything like the main course, it's not to be missed. Let's go for it."

"Why not?" she said, smiling guiltily. "But how am I going to work after this? I'll end up falling asleep at my desk."

Chapter Fourteen

That evening, I sat on the sofa thinking about the day that was nearly over. Waves of conflicting emotions washed over me. I was disheartened by the way the court hearing went. I felt the circumstantial evidence against Jason did not warrant his being detained pending trial. Nor was there any risk of his fleeing the country. He was too prominent a figure to disappear. Yet, at the same time, I felt that maybe it was for the best. It would give him time to rethink his life and relinquish some of his errant ways. If he really was innocent, it would almost certainly come out during the trial.

I missed Alice but my extended lunch with Valerie F made me realise I was not beyond enjoying female company. In fact, it was quite a revelation to me that I could still find a woman attractive, even exciting. Just the unarticulated thought that something might come of it was enough to give meaning to my life. Yet, the idea of being unfaithful to Alice did nag at me, preventing me from entertaining too vivid a notion of a prospective relationship.

After a light supper, I decided to check my emails and saw that the film producer, or his assistant, had replied. I was surprised, as I hadn't expected to hear from him for at least a day or two. 'Were they so keen to have me?' I thought optimistically. I opened the email with some palpitation and was dismayed to see a curt reply, reminiscent of the rejection letters I receive from prospective publishers. 'Thank you, Mr. G, for your interest in participating in our film but after due consideration it has been decided that we cannot offer you the role. Thank you again. X.'

It was an enormous comedown and I decided to ring Billy to find out exactly why they changed their mind, though I guessed it had to do with Jason.

Billy didn't answer at once and I thought he too had cut me off. Eventually he picked up. "Patrick, I expect you're calling about the film. I'm sorry, mate. I did my best to get them to reconsider but they were adamant. They say that having you in the cast could jeopardise the whole film. You know how prudish people are."

"But that's crazy. Anybody's think *I* was a bloody rapist?"

"I warned you, mate. I always said Jason was bad news, but you wouldn't listen to me. You insisted on making excuses for him. Even when Andrew died, you wouldn't consider the possibility that he might have had something to do with it."

"Billy, that's absurd. How on earth could Jason have been connected to Andrew's death?"

"It's not just his death I'm talking about."

"What then?"

"Do you really want me to spell it out?"

"Not if it's just hearsay."

"Of course, it's hearsay. I wasn't there in person, for Christ's sake. People talk, people I trust. Some of it may be balls, but not all. Anyway, I can see you don't want to know. You never saw that side of him because you never worked with him. I won't say any more, only that Jason can be quite ruthless when it comes to saving his own ass."

What did Billy mean by that? I knew he never liked Jason. For a start, he didn't share his right-wing politics. He once called him 'a dyed-in-the-wool blue-blooded narcissist,' which was absurd. Jason was self-confident, that's true, could sometimes be a bit smug, but definitely not narcissistic. I always put Billy's contempt for Jason down to the scathing review Jason had written about a play Billy had directed once. Jason described it as 'an insult to classical theatre.' I assumed; therefore, it was just sour grapes on Billy's part.

"So, I've lost the part, even if I get down on bended knees?" I asked despondently.

"Look, mate. It was a sure thing. You'd be brilliant in the part but you're a liability now. What production company is going to risk losing ten million or even half that?"

"There's no way you can put in a good word for me, is there?"

"Only if you publicly renounce Jason B."

"Well, you know I can't do that, Billy."

"I don't understand you, Patrick. You're prepared to destroy your sparkling image for someone like Jason when you did little for Andrew, who everybody said was more of a victim than a felon."

"I did my best for him, Billy."

"Not by my book, you didn't. You were too damned moralistic for your own good."

To all intents and purposes, Billy was saying I was in part responsible for my son's death, which I couldn't accept, of course, but it hurt, nevertheless. Now he was asking me to sacrifice Jason.

"Which is worse? Sacrificing someone who is like a son to me or sticking to my principles?"

"It's a hard one, I'll admit, mate. If I thought Jason was worth it, I'd say the second. But he isn't. You've got to see that. If I can't convince you, ask around. There are colleagues and friends of his who know a lot more than they're letting on. That's all I can say. Look, mate, you can call me whenever you like but I've got to go. The guys are waiting. It's the boys' night out."

"Sure, Billy. Enjoy yourself."

It was always the boys' night out for Billy. How I envied his lack of attachment to wife and family. Or did I? I wasn't sure.

I poured myself a strong one and turned on the TV. It was halfway through an episode of a rather contrived and highly predictable cop series. I quickly lost interest. I needed to talk to someone but could only think of old actor friends I hadn't been in touch with for years. I thought about ringing Valerie. I didn't want to disturb her at that hour of the night, but in the end, I decided I'd take a chance on it.

She picked up at once. "Hello."

"Hi. It's Patrick. I just wanted to thank you for lunch."

"Patrick. I didn't expect to hear from you so soon."

"You must be exhausted so I won't keep you."

"No. I'm glad you called. I would have phoned you in the morning anyway. We can do the interview tomorrow afternoon if you're available. We need to get it out there while Jason is still newsworthy. I don't want you to say anything that would compromise him or you, but people respect your opinion. I think they would be interested to know more about the Jason you know."

"Okay. I'll do it. Just tell me a time… They don't want me in the film. They say I am a liability."

"Oh, I'm sorry. I understand their reasoning. Your association with Jason could be detrimental."

"At least, I'll be free to devote myself to helping Jason. First, I need to find out for sure if there is any truth in these accusations."

"Do you want to know?"

"Yes, Valerie, I must. I need to know whether I've got a blind spot where Jason's concerned. Is it possible to be close to someone for thirty years and not know them?"

"I can't say, Patrick, honestly. I suppose it is possible, but we would usually have some inkling of another side to them, I guess."

"I'm considering trying to find out what really went on in Jason's flat. I'm not sure it's the right thing to do. What do you think?"

"As long as you're prepared to face a truth that may be very different from what you are hoping for."

"I am. I need to find a reliable source."

"If you do, can you be sure they'll tell you the whole truth and nothing but the truth?"

"I can only try. Look, I won't keep you. You must be shattered."

"Not more than usual. It's nice to talk to someone who isn't from work for a change."

"Anyway, you'll let me know what time you want me for the interview."

"Yes, I will. When this is all over, I'm going to allow you to take me to your favourite restaurant, and I promise we won't talk about Jason or work."

"Really? What a pity," I said with a laugh. "Anyway, I'll look forward to it."

~ * ~

I should have gone out like a light but there was a lot on my mind. I hated having doubts about Jason. However, I had to find out more, even if it meant going behind his back. I justified it by saying that I was able to uncover things that Victor S was not, things that could be used in court to mitigate or even invalidate the accusations.

I wondered whether I should ask Jason's permission. Yet, if he refused, it would be worse. So, I decided to do a bit of investigating on the quiet. I knew the names of people he'd worked with. He had spoken warmly of an actor called Marcus V, who made his name in a popular soap and was living it up on the proceeds. In fact, they had already started filming the fifth season. If anyone would know about Jason's secret life, it would be he. I suspected he was gay, and the gay community is rather like a village - everybody knows everybody else's business.

I had no idea how to approach him unless I waylaid him at Mercury studios before or after a day's shooting. I used a bit of influence to get one of the sound engineers a job there and he owed me one. He could tell me the times Marcus V was there and when they knocked off. It was worth a try.

Of course, there were Alice's notes. Could she have kept notes on Jason? Did he visit her as a client or a friend? I knew that one of the reasons she kept notes on her clients was to build up an accurate picture of them. Why should she not do the same for Jason? Yet, the thought of going through her private papers was such a violation of confidentiality I could hardly contemplate it. Yet, if she were alive, wouldn't she do everything in her power to help Jason, even if it meant revealing information given to her in confidence?

It was past midnight. I was still weighing up why I should or should not contravene the rules of confidentiality. Was it not a question of life or death? How long would Jason survive in a real prison? He was all right for the time being, isolated in a wing of a female prison, but he wouldn't last long among coldblooded homophobes, who would think nothing of having him wiped out. And even if his life was not in actual danger, how long would he be able to stand the stagnation of prison life? No, desperate circumstances required desperate measures. I had to find out if Jason revealed anything to Alice that could provide important insight into his life.

I tiptoed downstairs in the half light and unhooked her keys from where she left them the last time she came home from work, over six months previously. Just handling them felt like a violation. They could open up a world that should have remained forever forgotten, tucked away in the dark, dusty drawers of her office. Clearly, Jason did not wish me to be a party to what he imparted to Alice. Yet, I was about to crack open a safe that contained his darkest secrets. In doing so, I would commit a double crime, against both Alice and Jason. Yet could it be considered a transgression, if it saved Jason from imprisonment?

It was a cold, dark night in late winter, rain clouds scudding across a moonless sky. Feeling like a cat burglar about to go on the prowl, I wrapped myself up in a scarf and overcoat and set out for Alice's office, which was a twenty-minute walk from the residential suburb where we lived. The streets were deserted, apart from screeching cats scurrying out from under cover or a lone car hissing by over the rain-spattered asphalt.

Alice's office was in an old three-storey building overlooking a busy square. Fortunately, I knew the code that opened the downstairs door. As I entered, I was hit by the familiar smell of leaking drains, a constant source of vexation for Alice. I turned on the light and wondered whether my presence would be noticed by a passing patrol car. How would I justify my presence there in the middle of the night?

I didn't bother taking the lift. Alice's office was on the first floor. Reaching her door, I fumbled with her keys and found the right one on the third attempt. My heart was pounding inexplicably. I felt like I did the day a boy at school dared me to sneak into the headmaster's office and retrieve his confiscated Swiss penknife.

I opened the door cautiously, not knowing what to expect. The second I entered I breathed in her distinct fragrance, a subtle blend of Lancôme Jasmin d'eau natural and a rose-scented cream she used to soften her skin. It felt as if a warm, wet blanket had been placed over my face. It was at once comforting and stifling, precipitating an irrepressible urge to weep. I must have stood there in the dark for at least ten minutes sobbing uncontrollably, gagging for breath, taking in her spirit in voracious gulps. I didn't dare turn on the light for fear of dispersing her presence.

When I came to pick her up after work, I would often find her in her office writing up her notes. Knowing it was me, she wouldn't turn as I entered. Her notetaking required all her concentration, as she interpreted scribbled phrases taken during her sessions. It was something that couldn't wait till the next day, she said. So, I would sit there watching her or pottered around tidying up as best I could so that we could go directly to our favourite restaurant or, alternatively, straight home to a drink and TV. Sadly, I could hear no rustling of paper, no quiet mumbling. The air was hollow and silent.

I eventually turned on the light. Everything seemed so unremarkable. Nothing had changed. It was exactly as she left it, a mausoleum without a body. A shrine to her memory. She lived for her work and no doubt would have gone on working until she dropped, if death hadn't taken her first. I wondered if her intuition told her on that last day she wouldn't be coming back. Did she turn perhaps and take a final look before exiting for the last time? Did she still entertain the hope that the Herculean doctor could slay the Lernaean Hydra that was fast devouring her viscera?

For a moment I almost forgot why I was there. She completely eclipsed my thoughts, as she was wont to do, especially in those last months before her passing. Suddenly, I remembered my nefarious task, steeled myself and tried to recollect where she kept the files on her clients. I found them without much searching. I knew she would have them somewhere to hand. I pulled open a deep drawer next to her desk and saw a row of neatly arranged files in alphabetical order. I assumed she would have Jason under J rather than B and feverishly drew back each file one by one until I reached the letter I. I hesitated, overawed by fear and respect. Would it be there? If so, should I take it?

"Alice, it's up to you. Just say the word," I said aloud.

At that moment I heard a muffled voice downstairs outside the main entrance. "Who's there? Is there anyone in the building?"

I grabbed Jason's file and made for the door.

Chapter Fifteen

I sauntered down to the front door, pretending to be surprised at the officer's agitation. I didn't recognise him but suspected he had been acquainted with Alice.

"I came to get something from my wife's office," I said ingenuously.

He eyed me warily.

"It was urgent," I added.

"A strange time of the night to be retrieving things from your wife's office, isn't it? Do you have any form of identification, Sir?"

I searched in my pockets but was not in the habit of carrying a passport or ID. I raised my arms in a gesture of emptyhandedness. As I moved into the light, I saw a hint of recognition on his face.

"Are you Mr. Patrick G, Sir?" he said with deference.

"As a matter of fact, I am."

"A delightful lady is Mrs. Alice. I haven't seen her for a while now. I've been on night patrol. How is she?"

"She passed away six months ago."

The officer's face went flat. "I'm very sorry to hear that, Sir. I used to have some lovely chats with Mrs. Alice."

"Yes," I said, remembering how easily she struck up conversations with people from all walks of life. A casual bystander would think they'd known each other all their lives.

"I saw Jason B here a few times too. I think she was trying to cure him but it didn't do much good by all accounts."

"It appears not," I said dismissively.

"You're trying to help him too from what I read in the papers. I don't know whether he deserves it, though. He should be locked up for good if you ask me."

"Well, that's up to the courts to decide, isn't it?"

"I don't always trust the courts, Sir. With a smart Alec lawyer like Victor S, he might get off. Walk away Scot free and start molesting other young men. Sick that's what I call it. There's no cure for perversions like that."

"My wife wouldn't agree with you."

"She didn't help him much, though, did she, Sir?" he said with biting frankness.

"Maybe she didn't have time."

The officer pursed his lips and tilted his head in doubt. "Anyway, you'll make sure to close the door securely when you leave, won't you, Sir?"

"Don't worry, officer, I will."

It seemed like a very long and tiring walk home, exacerbated by the light rain that came at me in gusts soon after I set off. I hadn't brought an umbrella. As a result, I was soaking by the time I reached home. Fortunately, I had brought a briefcase for Jason's file if I found it. So, that at least remained dry.

Though curious to see Alice's notes, I was too tired even to cast an eye over them. I also knew that a cursory reading would not give me the answers I was looking for. I needed to study them thoroughly from beginning to end to find out exactly what had been going on in Jason's life.

~ * ~

I was awakened late the next morning by my phone ringing. It was Valerie to tell me the interview was scheduled for that afternoon at five. It would be broadcast the same evening on a programme called *Today's People*. We said little. I was still a bit groggy from my night's exploits and she was about to go into an urgent editorial meeting.

As I came down to a late breakfast, I saw Jason's file lying on my desk winking at me enticingly. I looked at it charily, wondering what I should do with it. I was in possession of stolen property and, though not an indictable offence, I was tempted to put it in a drawer and forget about it. Out of sight, out of mind. In the end, I prevaricated and put it under some bills that needed my attention.

My first concern was arranging to visit Jason. Whether he would welcome my visit I wasn't sure. He hated being in situations he had little power over, and this was one of them. The tables had turned. I wondered how he would take to being bossed around by brusque guards. I suspected it would be anathema to him. The new prison policy was to treat inmates with respect, but I seriously doubted they would show much respect towards a rapist, especially one whose alleged victims were teenage boys.

From our experience with Andrew, I knew that visiting someone in prison involved a lot of red tape. We had to get on a list and then fill in an application form to be approved by the prison authorities. I found a phone number online and was surprised at how polite the lady on the other end was. Yes, I had to fill in a form, which I could download and send by email. Yes, I had to have the prison's approval to be put on the visiting list. Was I a relative? When I told her I wasn't, she asked if I was involved in his defence. Here I lied, though it was not entirely untrue. After all, I was unofficially working on his defence. "So, you will be accompanying Mr. Victor S."

I replied that I wouldn't, as I was operating independently. I was a kind of guardian, I said artlessly.

"Are you a legal guardian?"

I had to tell her that I wasn't but that both his parents were dead, and he had no close relatives.

She hesitated. "It will be up to Mr. B then. You will need to contact him by email and ask him to put you on the list."

I asked how long this procedure was likely to take.

"It shouldn't take more than a day or two."

It appeared I could at least communicate with Jason by email until I was given the go-ahead to visit. So, I immediately wrote informing him of my intentions and asking him to make sure I was on the visiting list. I racked my brains to think of something reassuring to close the email but whatever I came up with sounded empty and meaningless. So, I merely said, 'Always in my thoughts. Patrick.'

I sat at my desk wondering what to do next. Should I pay the bills that had stacked up? It seemed like a good idea, if it weren't for Jason's file hiding underneath. However, there was one thing I needed to do first. I sent a message to the sound engineer at Mercury Studios in the hope that he would be willing to repay his debt. I didn't state specifically why I wanted to speak to him, though he would probably guess it had something to do with Jason.

Surprisingly, I got a reply almost at once. "Sure, Mr. G. Will call you during the break in about one hour."

I then paid the bills online, which took me much less time than I expected. I was now at a loose end, with Jason's file staring doggedly at me. I could procrastinate no longer. I put out my hand and tentatively drew the file towards me. I stared at the cover for some time, pedantically studying each letter of his name, still uncertain whether to enter Jason's secret world. Finally, I opened the file and was overtaken by Alice's distinctive handwriting, with its odd curls and twiddles. The image of her sitting at her desk assiduously writing up her notes immediately came hurtling back, nearly setting off another round of mawkish tears.

As I read the first few lines, I could hear her voice speaking to me in that quiet assured tone she had. It began, *"Jason came to see me today. He wished to be treated as a client not a friend. I suggested I recommend a colleague, but he insisted I was the only one who could help him. He appeared extremely troubled, so I said we would give it a go and see how things went.*

He told me he contemplated suicide on several occasions. He was in a very depressed state, though unable or unwilling to tell me why. He described his life as 'empty.' Only the theatre gave it meaning but even that had lost its appeal. I asked him how long he had felt like this but again his answer was evasive. I could see we had a lot of work to do.

I decided I would treat him like any other client and asked him to tell me his life story, beginning with his early childhood, a period I genuinely knew very little about.

He set about this task as if it was an unavoidable chore. I could tell he had no desire to go back there. His parents were distant, he said, and spent little time with him. He recalled a few relatively happy moments when he was about five or six, when they shared a house by the sea with some friends during the summer holidays.

He felt his mother was indifferent to him and made no effort to show love or affection. He believed she regarded him as a burden she had to shoulder. She found children tiresome and seldom played games or read to him. On the other hand, whenever he was around, which was seldom, his father was not averse to spending time with him, though he treated him like an adult from a very early age, talking above his head, using long, complicated words that he didn't understand. However, he didn't mind because he felt there was a sort of bond between them, even if very little real communication took place.

He was about seven when his parents' arguments got worse, often violent. At the time, he didn't understand what it was all about, but he remembers finding it very distressing and crying himself to sleep at night. Later, he realised it probably had to do with his father's extra marital affairs, which he made little effort to hide. He would often turn up at the house with a young female student he was overly affectionate with.

Then, came what he described as a period of hell. It reached a point where his parents could not be in the same room together without clashing. He remembers them throwing objects at each other, plates, cups, glasses, anything that came to hand. After such a fracas, neither would clear up the debris. So, he had to do it himself or else be stepping on fragments of crockery every time he went into the kitchen. He remembers making himself breakfast and being unable to find any plates or cups—they had all been smashed - and having to use a paper plate and mug left over from a birthday party. He was nine or ten.

During this time, his parents were so absorbed in their animosity for each other that they almost totally ignored him. His father would be away a lot of the time, which meant there was relative peace in the home. However, he hated being with his mother, as she was permanently bad-tempered and irritable and would snap at him if he dared even open his mouth. It was at about this time that he realised he was totally alone in the world and decided he could rely on no one but himself.

Jason was keen to talk. He said it was the first time he had spoken to anyone about his childhood and was surprised at the relief he felt confiding in someone he could trust. He was impatient and wanted us to meet again tomorrow. I explained that our meetings would have to be at regular times and days. They would also have to follow the usual therapeutic process. We arranged to meet the following week at the same time."

I was aware Jason had experienced an unhappy childhood, but I had no idea just how bad it was. It explained a lot; his self-sufficiency, his periods of self-doubt, his constant need to boost his self-esteem and his bouts of deep depression, which I had known little about until I read Alice's notes. Having crossed the threshold of his secret life, I wanted to continue, but my phone rang.

It was Tony, the sound engineer from Mercury Studios. "Mr. G. How can I help you?"

"I'll be honest with you, Tony. I believe there's a slur campaign going on against Jason B. I'm not saying there isn't some truth behind it but I don't want him to be convicted for something he didn't do."

"You're right, Mr. G. It wouldn't be the first time. Once the media get a bee in their bonnet, there's no stopping them. I have to say I quite like him myself. I filled in for a bloke at the National once. Jason B was directing the play. I found him very patient and understanding, even though I was a bit of a rookie at the time. It's hard to believe he did all those things they accuse him of."

"That's it, Tony. The media hype this whole business has received will make it very difficult for the courts to acquit him or even give him a fair trial."

"So, how can I help, Mr. G?"

"Jason has talked warmly of Marcus V. They were once good friends."

"Still are, as far as I know. Well, maybe not since…you know. No one wants to admit to being a friend of Jason B now."

"I know he won't agree to meet me. So, I was thinking of nabbing him as he leaves the studio one of these days. Do you have regular shooting hours?"

"We usually knock off at about five but if things haven't gone according to plan, we sometimes do over time to finish a scene. Look, Mr. G, I can text you the approximate time we'll finish. Just tell me a day that suits you."

"That would be fantastic. Does he leave alone?"

"Usually. If we finish late, he often goes to a gay bar a couple of streets from the studio, called Bright Lights. There's a good chance you'd bump into him there, if you're willing to risk being hit on."

I laughed. "I'll take my chances. I'm doing an interview on Today's

People at five today, but if you finish late just let me know and I'll pass by Bright Lights this evening."

"Will do, Mr. G. Good luck. I hope you find what you're looking for."

"So do I."

I looked at my watch. I still had plenty of time before heading off for my interview with Valerie. I decided to read the highlights of another of Alice's sessions with Jason.

"*Jason looked tired. He said he had been sleeping badly. He feels there is a lot of antagonism at the National. The feeling among the actors and Board of Directors is that they should only be doing avant-garde theatre, while he believes the primary function of the National is to put on classical plays, though he was not opposed to experimental theatre per se.*

In the previous session I became aware of the deep hatred he still harbours for both his parents, particularly his mother, which clearly continues to fester within him. I asked him to play the part of his mother after one of the fights with his father. I would take the role of the young Jason. The dialogue went more or less as follows (abridged):

Jason: What was the point of shouting and throwing things at him? You know he's not going to change.

J's Mother: I'm just so angry with him. He treats me like dirt. It's as if he deliberately wants to rub my nose in all those young women he brings into the house.

Jason: Why do you care, Mother?

J's mother: Because I still love the bastard.

Jason: Why do you love someone who doesn't deserve to be loved? Perhaps you need to let go.

J's mother: You think that's easy?

Jason: But isn't it a bit like hitting your head against a brick wall?

J's mother: You'll understand when you get older what it's like to love and not be loved back.

Jason: I already understand, Mother.

J's mother: How can you understand?

Jason: I love you and Dad, but you don't love me back.

J's mother: Don't be silly. Of course, we love you.

Jason: Why do you never show it?

J's mother: Everything is not just about you, you know. There are other people in the world too.

Jason: Yes, Mother.

I asked J how he felt being in his mother's shoes and if it helped him to understand her better. He said it was not a pleasant feeling, but he understood better why she behaved as she did. Her pride had been severely battered and she was fighting for 'moral survival.' He could not forgive her callousness towards him, but he realised how much she must have been hurting.

I asked if he felt my portrayal of him was accurate. He hesitated before answering and said simply, "I wish I could have been so logical."

We then played out a scene with J as young J and me as his father. (abridged)

J's father: Your mother and I should have separated years ago. We're totally incompatible.

Jason: Why haven't you, Dad?

J's Dad: We decided to try and stay together for your sake.

Jason: But you just fight all the time.

J's Dad: But at least we're still together.

Jason: I hate watching you fight.

J's Dad: If we split up, who's going to look after you?

Jason: I can look after myself.

J's Dad: But you're only a child.

Jason: No longer, Dad.

J's Dad: What age are you, anyway?

Jason: Ten, Dad. Remember? I had my birthday last week.

J's Dad: Yes, of course. I wasn't sure whether it was ten or eleven.

I asked Jason whether my portrayal of his dad had any resemblance to reality. He was surprised how accurate my portrayal was. His father never remembered how old he was. He also thought it was typical of his father to claim he was doing something for someone else when in fact he was doing it for himself. He wanted to have girlfriends and expect his mother to grin and bear it. His conclusion was that both his parents were very self-centred and selfish.

I asked if he understood anything about himself from his portrayal.

He said it reminded him very much of dialogues with his father in which there was very little communication. He tried to understand his parents, but they made very little effort to understand him.

I believe Jason left with a greater understanding of his parents, though it did little to change his feelings for them. Nevertheless, I believe it was a fruitful exercise as it helped him compartmentalise his parents, an important part of coming to terms with his dysfunctional childhood, which I hoped would eventually lead to some closure."

Alice told me something about her methods, but I was fascinated seeing them in practice. I couldn't wait to read the next session as I felt I was already well on the way to discovering the real Jason B. Little did I know then how much there was to find out.

Chapter Sixteen

I had to get ready to go to the interview. I needed to be there an hour in advance for make-up and a briefing. I still had time to check my emails. To my surprise, Jason had answered.

"Thank you, Patrick, for your concern. However, I feel there's very little that can be done. Nothing will ever be the same again. My reputation is in tatters, whatever the outcome of the trial. I will be shunned and feared wherever I go. My only hope of a life is to join a monastery, if they'll have been.

"Of course, I'll make sure you are on the prison visiting list but please let's not talk about the future, just the past, when Andrew and Alice were still alive. As I lie in bed in this hell hole, I imagine that she is sitting next to me. I can hear her calm, reassuring voice telling me that there will be life after hell.

I look forward to your visit.

All my love, Jason."

I didn't bother replying. There was very little that hadn't already been said.

I arrived at the TV studio early, where I was greeted by an overly smiley girl in her early twenties, whom I suspected was an intern, trying to make a good impression. She ushered me upstairs to make-up and hair. Why do they insist on embellishing their interviewees when their stated intent is to present the truth?

I was given the VIP treatment, a comfy chair, a cup of Earl Grey and a sticky bun. I hoped Valerie would not be too disheartened with her poor ratings, as I couldn't imagine people eagerly turning on the TV to watch an interview with a has-been actor, unless it was to glean more dirt on Jason. In that case, they would be disappointed.

Valerie came to greet me shortly before the interview was due to begin, apologising for not meeting me at the door, but as usual things were hectic. She took my hand in what struck me as an over-familiar but rather engaging manner. She led me into the interview room, which was surprisingly stark. This, she said, was deliberate, so the background designers could be more creative with light and shade.

"So, Patrick, how do you feel?"

"I can't deny that I'm a tad nervous."

"There's no need to be. I want you to imagine we're sitting in a quiet corner of the King's Retreat drinking top quality French wine. Would you like a glass, by the way? It will help dispel those nerves."

"I'd better not."

"I believe people are keen to hear about the real Jason."

"Are you sure, Valerie?"

"It's true they are outraged by his alleged crimes, but it is our duty to present as balanced a picture as possible."

I couldn't help feeling that she had some ulterior motive, beyond ratings. "Why are you doing this, Valerie? I can't believe it's just to help Jason."

Her eyes dropped for a moment. There was something she wasn't letting on. "Well, I believe in justice and…"

"Is that all?"

"I can see there's no fooling you, Patrick. Yes, there is another reason, but it isn't the right place to make confessions." She glanced at the cameraman and crew preparing for the interview. "Another time…when we are alone."

I wasn't particularly happy with her answer, but she was right. It wasn't a good place to divulge secrets. You never know when a microphone has been turned on or an apparently benign figure is taking down every word you're saying to sell to a tabloid.

We were checked to make sure not a hair was out of place and our clip-on microphones worked. Valerie made me feel relaxed at once and through her natural charm and ease of manner a kind of intimacy was established on set, which I quickly realised could be insidious. So, I remained on my guard, just in case. Yet, I was never aware of her trying to trick me into saying something that might provide fodder for the social tattlers. She appeared genuinely interested in knowing the other side of Jason.

I talked about his outstanding student years and his subsequent contribution to theatre. Then, she asked more personal questions; how he became part of the family and his friendship with Andrew. I was careful not to even hint at what I found out from Alice's notes. I merely mentioned that he had a rather turbulent childhood. Then, towards the end of the interview, she asked me the most difficult question of all. "Patrick, do you believe Jason is guilty of the crimes he is accused of?"

For the first time I hesitated, even though I thought I was prepared for such a question. I wanted to be honest but at the same time did not want to commit to a hard and fast opinion. "Valerie, the human soul is an abyss. People we've known all our lives can surprise us, but it is rare. I have seen many sides to Jason, and I am sure there are many I haven't seen. He is a complex personality, which no doubt goes a long way to explaining his genius. All I can say is that it is my belief that the Jason I know could not, even under the influence of alcohol or drugs, commit the heinous crimes he has been accused of."

"Thank you, Patrick, for coming on the show tonight and sharing your life with Jason B with us. Sadly, we didn't get the chance to talk about you and your plans for the future. Another time perhaps."

"There's not much to talk about but it would be my pleasure."

The interview lasted a little over an hour. Valerie seemed pleased. "That's the first time an interview went so smoothly," she exclaimed jubilantly. "The people in editing will be happy for once, which means I'll be clocking off early tonight. Any plans, Patrick?"

I looked at my mobile phone. Tony had sent me a message. 'Should finish at around seven."

"It looks as if I have," I said, indicating my phone.

"A date, Mr. Patrick G?"

"Not exactly. It's a kind of blind date. At Bright Lights."

A look of dismay came over Valerie's face. "I didn't realise you were that way inclined."

I quickly realised the misunderstanding and chuckled. "I'm not. I'm trying to track down a close friend of Jason's to see if he can open a door or two."

She looked visibly relieved. "Oh, good. So, you're determined to go ahead with your investigations."

"As I said when we first met, I have to."

"The other day at the King's Retreat I tried to discourage you but I'm glad I didn't succeed," she said with an enigmatic smile. "You'd never forgive yourself if you didn't at least try."

"Quite."

I was warming to Valerie. I felt her deferential treatment was not simply because I was a minor celebrity. Her empathy was genuine. At least, so I believed. "So, when are you going to tell me about your mysterious interest in Jason B?" I asked teasingly.

"I see I've roused your curiosity. What are you doing after your meeting at Bright Lights?"

"What I always do, go home to a cold and empty house."

"In that case, why don't you come around to my place? It's at least warm and not completely empty, and we can watch Today's People together. They say there's this rather interesting actor by the name of Patrick G being interviewed by Valerie F."

I smiled. "The first proposal sounds good, the second not so much. I hate seeing myself on screen."

"Your loss, but I suppose I shouldn't have expected anything different from the modest Mr. Patrick G. Why not come round anyway and not watch Today's People? After all, who wants to know about Jason B?"

"Just about the whole country."

"Who cares? We can embrace our individuality and listen to music instead? What do you like? Blues, jazz or something a little funkier?"

"I have pretty eclectic tastes, but I suppose I like just about anything that's been around for over thirty years."

"Oh, dear, are we showing our age, Mr. G?" she said playfully.

"Afraid so."

"Well, as it so happens, I also like the old hits, Sting, Phil Collins, Jethro Tull…"

"Ah, now you're talking."

"I can rustle something up or we can order out, whichever takes your fancy. I might even make a confession if you promise not to tell anyone."

"I promise. When it comes to secrets, I'm as silent as a Trappist monk."

"That should be interesting. I must confess I've never spent an evening with a Trappist monk. Will communication be limited to sign language then?"

I laughed. I could see we were going to get along fine.

"Good. It's a date then. Come whenever you finish. No need to rush. I can sleep in tomorrow. I've got the day off. Yeaaaa. The first time in weeks."

~ * ~

It was a little after seven thirty when I arrived outside Bright Lights. From the boisterous mishmash of voices and laughter, I realised the bar was already filling up. I suddenly felt uneasy. What would I do if Marcus V was with someone? Would I even recognise him? People look so different off camera.

I pushed open the bar door, feeling very self-conscious. I was the oldest and probably straightest person there. However, they were all too engrossed in light-hearted banter to notice the passage of an old man scrutinising faces. I slowly inched my way through the motley crowd, trying not to make it seem too obvious I wasn't there for the beer.

I was just about to give up when I saw Marcus V entering the bar, a look of bright anticipation on his face. The remains of make-up were still evident on his forehead and around his eyes. I was surprised how similar the screen character and the real Marcus V were. People were already hailing him. I had to act fast before he got settled in. I darted through a cluster of beer drinkers, nearly barging into an outstretched hand holding a pint of lager. I intercepted him just before he reached a group of revellers in the corner.

"Marcus," I said. "Can we have a word?"

He looked at me indignantly, questioning my intrusion into his fun time. A reporter perhaps? A plains clothes policeman? "Do I know you?" he said irately.

"Of me perhaps."

"I've had a long day. This is the last thing I need. I'm here to relax.

You people have no respect for a person's privacy."

"I'm Patrick G," I said, ignoring his protests.

He leant back to get a better look at me. The scowl softened slightly when recognition hit in. "Patrick G," he said as if to himself. "I'm a great admirer but you're hardly the person one wants to be seen with these days."

"I want to see justice done. As a friend of Jason's, I expect you do too."

He looked over my shoulder to see if the group in the corner were observing our discussion, but they were too busy exchanging repartee to show any interest in who Marcus V was talking to. "Look. Can we go somewhere?" he said in a hushed voice. "This is not the best place to talk."

I agreed and we made for the exit. Someone shouted, "Hey, Marcus, where are you off to? It's your round, mate."

Marcus pretended not to hear.

The door swung shut, strangling cackles of raucous laughter.

"Do you know somewhere we can talk?"

"Let's just walk."

It was dark and quite cold, but I had no objection to walking, as long as I found out more about Jason.

"I need to get a bit of fresh air and stretch my legs," he said. "It was a long day at the studio. How did you know you'd find me at the Bright Lights?"

"A birdie," I said cryptically.

"Right," he said, rolling his eyes.

Marcus V was very good looking. He had a youthful Jude Law face. I could see him in myriad roles. It was obvious why he was so popular with directors. *The camera must love him,* I thought.

"I'm sorry for ambushing you like this but I need to find out whatever I can about Jason. If I don't come up with something, I'm afraid he's going to go away for a very long time. I know you were once good friends. He talked warmly of you."

"Friendships in the theatre world are often shallow and short-lived, as you no doubt know. But, yes, he was—is—still a friend."

"Was your friendship with Jason shallow and short-lived?"

He didn't answer at once. "No, I suppose not. We used to hang out a lot together."

"No longer?"

"Not now, for obvious reasons."

"So, you can tell me if it's all true or not then?"

He scratched the nape of his neck and looked vacantly down at the pavement "You'd have to ask the guys involved," he said evasively.

I could tell he knew much more than he was letting on, perhaps for fear of incriminating himself. "Let me ask you straight out. Is Jason capable of raping these young men?"

"It depends on your definition of rape, Mr. G."

"Okay then. Did he have sex with these 'boys' against their will?"

Again, he hesitated. "Well, there may have been a bit of inducement involved."

"Please, be specific. I need to know."

"Money, drugs, promises."

"Promises he had no intention of keeping?"

"No, I think he genuinely wanted to help these boys. He had the power to influence people."

"But he didn't, did he?"

"Oh, he tried, but no director is going to take on someone who has no talent."

"So, Jason made empty promises?"

"Kind of."

"Kind of?"

"You know Jason. He gets carried away with good intentions. Let me tell you something, Mr. G, something you probably already know. Talented people like Jason are not always aware of their genius. They put their success down to hard work. Yes, you cannot succeed without hard work, that's true, but Jason has always thought that's all it is. He believes anyone can be an actor if they make enough effort. That's why he has the reputation of being a bit of slave-driver with his students."

"So, let me put it to you straight. You don't think Jason actually tied up his victims and raped them."

"I find it unlikely. He did confess to me once that he found great release in sex, especially when he was down in the dumps. It's a bit like a drug for him, an upper. It makes him aware that he's alive. That's what he told me once, anyway."

"Did he use drugs?"

He looked at me askance as if to ascertain whether I was a recently-arrived alien from outer space. "Of course, he did, Mr. G. Everybody does. It's all underground, of course. But taking libido-enhancing drugs these days is as common as going to a bar for a drink."

I heaved a sigh of frustration. I felt I was getting nowhere. "Did Jason rape these 'boys'?" I asked insistently.

Marcus V understood my frustration. "I'm sorry, Mr. G, but I don't know."

"Did Jason volunteer at the refugee camp for the sole purpose of picking up likely sex partners?"

"No, definitely not," he said without hesitation. "I can state that categorically. He gave me a long spiel once about how he wanted to help the refugees, not just the boys, but particularly the boys, because he said he could empathise with them. He understood their despair, their feeling of abandonment."

"Would you be prepared to state that in court?"

Marcus V stopped in his tracks and stared at me imploringly. "Mr. G. you are asking me to throw away my career."

"But if it's the truth. Are you going to let Jason be destroyed because the courts are not in possession of the facts?"

"I don't trust the courts and I don't trust the media. They will destroy me. I might even be taken off the series."

"You? Surely not?"

"Mr. G, I have the feeling you're a bit out of touch. It's all about money these days. I'm sorry. I can't do it," he said adamantly and continued walking.

I understood and was not going to push him any further. "Is there any other way you can help? I get the feeling that you also think Jason is being wrongly accused."

"I'm not sure, Mr. G. Honestly. All I can do is give you the number of someone at the refugee centre - but don't say you got it from me. They may be able to help you get in touch with the victims or one of them at least.

Good luck there, because it won't be easy getting them to change their story. You don't want to be accused of coercion. You might end up in court yourself."

"I would appreciate that. I'm sorry if I was a bit pushy earlier."

"I understand what you're doing, Mr. G, and I admire you for it. I'd probably do the same if Jason were my son."

"He's not my son," I said in surprise.

"He told me that you were his 'real' father. I didn't quite understand him at the time because I always thought Ares B was."

I walked Marcus V back to a dark corner a block away from Bright Lights. He promised to send me a number and the name of someone at the refugee camp who was 'pliable,' whatever that meant. I suspected some financial inducement would be required to ensure cooperation.

Chapter Seventeen

Valerie lived in a very elegant apartment on the top floor of an old block in the city centre. The building had immense character; a lot of old varnished wood and a lift that made clanging noises. I could tell she had had time to cook by the rich aroma of basil and garlic issuing from the kitchen, along with the familiar voice of Sting singing 'I'm an alien.' She took my hand and led me into what was clearly the hub of the flat, a kitchen-cum-dining room equipped with a fifty-inch TV and an old-fashioned fireplace that was blazing cheerily.

"You are amazing!" I said admiring her handy work. "How on earth did you have time to do all this?"

She placed a glass of chilled white wine into my hand. "I'm just well organised," she said with mock immodesty. "I hope you're hungry."

I hadn't thought about food all day but the mere mention of it set my stomach rumbling. "Famished."

"Great. I hope you like Italian," she said, giving me an anxious glance.

"I adore it."

"Fantastic. Just make yourself at home while I put the finishing touches to the salad. Everything is ready. So, we can eat at once if you like."

"Why don't we have a glass of wine first? I'm a believer in deferred pleasure."

We sat down together on a settee opposite the log fire. It felt strange being in someone else's house about to have dinner alone with a woman who was not Alice.

"Am I being a bit forward, Patrick, inviting you to dinner? It's just we get on so well together. It seemed the right thing to do."

"No, absolutely. I'm glad you did. Were you happy with the edited version of the interview?"

"Yes, I was. I thought it gave a very balanced view of Jason. It was quite moving, in fact. Your concern for him really came across."

"Do you think it will help to influence public opinion in his favour?"

"Probably not, but it was worth a try."

"So, Valerie, why your interest in Jason?"

She took a sip from her drink and looked at me circumspectly. "Patrick, I hope what I am about to tell you won't affect your opinion of me."

"I very much doubt it, unless you're going to confess to being the head of a drug cartel or a hit squad."

She didn't laugh. "Neither of those but…"

"Valerie, I may give the impression of being a bit stuffy but really I'm quite open-minded, if that's why you're hesitant."

"It's always been my policy to trust no one. What I'm going to tell you has been a skeleton in my cupboard for a very long time and it's about time I brought it out into the open."

"I promise that whatever you tell me will remain between us."

"Thank you, Patrick."

She took another sip of wine and stared at the burning logs. I guessed she could see vivid images of someone or something from her past hovering over the flames.

"Ares B and I were lovers," she blurted out, turning at once to gauge my reaction.

What she saw was a look of stunned disbelief.

"I knew you'd be shocked," she said. "Perhaps it was a mistake to tell you."

"No, no, not at all," I said, shaking my head in an endeavour to take in what she told me. "I just wasn't expecting something like this."

"Well, I can't take it back now, can I?" she said with a wan smile.

"No need to. In fact, I'm very glad you told me. It appears that we have much more than a TV interview in common."

"I was one of Ares' students at university,' she continued, ignoring my remark. "I think it was his mind I fell in love with," she added reflectively. "I was going through a big intellectual thing at the time, with a passion for theatre, modern and ancient. You see, contained within the walls of that extraordinary brain was everything I adored. When he started flirting with me, I didn't see his age—when you're on a philosophical high you convince yourself that thirty years is nothing. I was twenty. He was fifty-two."

It was all beginning to make sense now. "So, your first son is Ares'?"

"I was wondering how long it would take you to work that out. I hadn't intended to get pregnant. In fact, it was the last thing on my mind. I must have forgotten to take the pill one day. Ares already had a wife and child, and he certainly didn't want another of the same. He conveniently denied the child was his and left me shortly afterwards. Well, 'left me' is hardly the right term, as we'd never been officially together."

"He had a reputation for bedding his female students, I believe."

"Oh, I knew it too but in my youthful naivety - and arrogance, I suppose - I thought I was special, the chosen one. He had found his match, a mind equal to his. Besides, he could be immensely charming. I must have been the easiest lay he'd ever had."

"I met him once or twice. To be honest with you, I didn't like him. He was rather condescending and opinionated. He made no effort to listen to what I or anyone else had to say."

"Oh, he was like that. The truth is he was incredibly knowledgeable. His books on theatre have become classics, standard reading for every student of the theatre."

"It must have been difficult being in his classes after you split up."

"It was extremely awkward. Mind you, he was very good at ignoring me and I did my best not to make myself too conspicuous. I'm pretty sure he had a guilty conscience, though. He gave me a distinction in my end-of-semester thesis, which I'm sure I didn't deserve."

There was a long silence, while I endeavoured to take in the implications of what she had just told me.

She gave me an apprehensive look. "Say something, Patrick."

"Sorry," I said, collecting myself. "It's been such a mind-blowing revelation."

"I'm here to be judged, you know."

"I make a point of not judging anyone. It's far too fashionable. We have become a society of self-righteous critics. And I certainly wouldn't judge you. It's quite obvious you were the victim of a rapacious satyr."

"No, Patrick, I wasn't. I was twenty years old. I knew exactly what I was doing. Yes, he turned out to be a disappointment, but it was a lesson in

112

life, and he gave me a wonderful son."

"I just can't get over the weird connection we both have to Jason and to each other. I'm his 'adoptive' father and you're his 'circumstantial' mother. It's almost as if we were related."

"So, you see it was not by chance that I hunted you down after the hearing. I'm so glad you hadn't had breakfast that morning. I think it was the prospect of a hearty meal that tipped the balance."

"You underestimate your charm, my dear."

She blushed into a bashful smile.

"Did it take you a long time to get over Ares?"

"I bore no grudge, if that's what you mean. I understood that he wouldn't want to be burdened with another child. I did consider an abortion, but I felt overwhelmingly attached to the unborn baby. I said to myself, 'Okay, you may have lost Ares, but you've still got a part of him growing inside you. Hang on to that,' and I've never regretted it. I didn't tell anyone the child was Ares,' not even my parents. I think I wanted to protect him. Crazy really. I didn't want his reputation to be marred."

"Did he ever show any interest in the child?"

"No. That would have been a tacit admission of fatherhood. Ares was the most beautiful man in the world but it was all about his mind, nothing else. People were tailor's dummies, as far as he was concerned. They had no heart, no emotions. So, he was incapable of feeling compassion. I was foolish enough to become impregnated by him. Quite rightly, he believed that I was responsible."

"In other words, he was a callous bastard."

"Great artists are not like you and me, Patrick. There's nothing worse for a true artist than lack of freedom, to be shackled, tied down."

"In other words, artists are self-centred, heartless people, who only care about themselves and their artistic creations."

She laughed at my indignation. "Yes, but the world would be so dull without them. So, we must put up with their egocentric single mindedness. Like most great artists, Ares was self-destructive. None of his relationships lasted and he died alone, mourned only by those who admired his work. I went to his funeral, without telling anyone. I've never told my son who his father is. Perhaps I should have. I'm not sure I've done the right thing."

"Jason didn't want to go to his father's funeral, but Alice and I managed to persuade him. Alice felt he might regret it later if he didn't."

"Yes, I saw him there. I remember thinking how dry-eyed and dour he looked."

"Jason had very little to do with his father after he reached adulthood. I suspect Ares didn't approve of his son's homosexuality. Paradoxically, he was ultra-conservative in many ways. Jason loved his father and wanted to be loved by him, but it was impossible. They were unable to communicate, on any level, even though their raison d'être was the same, the theatre."

"Ares was not an easy man to love. How can you love someone who sees life as an idea? He was incapable of real love. Love requires commitment, accepting that a person is more than just flesh and blood."

"Do you still love him?"

"His mind, yes. I have yet to meet anyone with a mind like his."

"Has your son...? What's his name, by the way?"

"Dory, from Theodore."

"Has Dory ever met Jason?"

"No. Neither has any idea they share a parent. I daren't think of Dory's reaction if he found out now. He's rather conservative like his father."

"Does Dory look like Ares?"

"Not in the least, thank goodness. Ares was not a good-looking man, though Dory certainly has his brains. He's one of the city's top lawyers now, married with a wife and three children."

"Oh, so you're a granny."

"Let's not dwell too much on that, shall we? Oh, my goodness, we must eat. Come on. Help me get things on the table."

~ * ~

The meal was superb, as was the wine. I didn't want our conversation to be dominated by Jason, though it was clearly going to be a regular topic between us for some time to come. At least now I felt I had an ally. Valerie didn't know Jason in person, though they had met once or twice at official functions, but I could see she had his interests at heart. Was it for Ares' sake or to atone for her believed transgressions? Did she feel, like I did, that Jason was somehow a victim of circumstances?

She had told me on the first day we met that she had a second son. I was curious to find out who his father was. "Can I ask you a very personal question? You have a second son. Who was the father?"

"My second son is Declan. His father was Irish, an actor, a charming, soppy man, who sadly fell in love with drink. I couldn't take it, I'm afraid, and we split up quite early on. He eventually drank himself to death." She sighed and looked again into the fire, which seemed to contain many poignant images from the past.

"I'm sorry," I said. "I shouldn't have pried."

"On the contrary, I've divulged my darkest secret. What is there to tell you that can be any darker?"

"What does Declan do?"

"He studied film and theatre at university and with a little help from yours truly he's managed to find a niche for himself in production. He's doing very well but he's often away. Tell me about Alice. I get the impression you were very much in love."

"Yes, I suppose we were. We met when we were very young. We kind of grew up together, became like each other in many ways, though this is not always a good thing. We managed to find plenty to fight about, though, but nothing that led to serious disagreements, just enough to keep the marriage interesting. I think our main difference was in our attitude to Andrew. She believed I was too harsh on him and maybe she was right. I think he was in awe of me, which made me rather unapproachable. It's one of my big regrets."

"It's so easy to be self-critical in retrospect. We think we know what we should have done but at the time we did what we thought was right."

"The truth is life never ceases to be a learning process. We must live with our mistakes and try not to make the same ones again, if we are ever given the chance."

"Quite."

"Is it possible," I said vacantly, "that Jason is like his father, that he lacks compassion? And that he sees people as objects to be used?"

"Don't dwell too much on it now, Patrick. Let's see what your investigations turn up." Valerie put her hand on mine. It felt awkward. I still had not got used to being with another woman.

"I think it's time I was heading off," I said.

"But the night is young."

"The night may be, but I'm not."

"Okay, I'll let you off this time, but I hope we can do this again soon."

"Of course, we can. I just need to focus on Jason for the time being."

"I want you to feel that we are a team. I don't know how I can help but I want you to know that you can share things with me in the way I shared my secret with you."

"Just having your moral support is all I need, Valerie. I don't want my concern for Jason to interfere with your work."

"It won't. I'm always home by nine and seldom leave the house before ten in the morning. So, feel free to call me whenever, even at work, if necessary. And if I don't pick up, I'll always get back to you when I have a free moment."

I got up to leave and we stood facing each other like two shy adolescents. She smiled, came up to me and held me in a gentle, non-intrusive way. It felt good to have someone who appeared to care whether I lived or died.

Chapter Eighteen

I woke up the next morning surprisingly late, feeling unusually euphoric, which didn't seem right, as Jason was still uppermost in my mind. I remembered my evening with Valerie and her intimate revelations. Was it possible I was the first person she had told about Ares and her son? Did Dory never ask who his father was? If so, what did Valerie tell him? These were some of the questions I would have liked to ask her but felt our relationship had not yet reached that level, despite the confidences we exchanged. Yet, for the first time since Alice died, I felt that I had someone I could talk to who understood—and cared—how I felt.

I had still received no notification from the prison about whether I had been put on the famous 'list.' So, I decided to ring the contact at the Juvenile Refugee Centre. I was unsure how to approach him. His name was Asif. So, I assumed that he was, or had been, a refugee himself.

I considered using a false identity, then decided it was best to be up front from the beginning. I would have to tell him at some point what I was doing. My only fear was that he would clam up as soon as I mentioned Jason's name, especially if he was involved in a male prostitution ring, which would almost certainly be under investigation now. In the end, I thought it wiser to ingratiate myself with him before getting down to brass tacks.

Asif picked up at once. "Hello."

"Hi," I said in a cheery voice. "Marcus V gave me your number and said you might be able to help me."

"Who is Marcus V? I do not know him." I detected fear in his voice. He was being chary.

"Marcus V, the actor. You must have seen him on TV," I continued in the same jolly vein. "I believe he occasionally does volunteer work at the centre."

"Oh, yes. I know. He comes as a volunteer sometimes."

"I'm an actor myself and I was wondering if you could help me."

"I just work at camp. How can I help you?"

I suspected that after Jason's arrest those who had been involved in introducing teenage boys to prospective clients might be under suspicion and so he was being extra cautious.

"I need to find someone. It's rather important, as it concerns a very close friend of mine, who is in a bit of trouble."

"Why do you ask me? Go to the camp manager. She tells you what you want to know."

"It's like this. Marcus V said that you are someone I can trust, someone who is not going to ask too many questions."

He hesitated, possibly wondering if there was anything in it for him. "I do not want trouble."

"Don't worry. All I want is some information and I'm prepared to pay well for it."

"How much you pay?"

"It very much depends on the information I get."

"All right. We meet but not at camp."

"Sure, wherever it suits you."

"We meet in the town centre, outside the War Memorial train station. Tonight, at seven thirty."

"How will I recognise you?"

"I wear red baseball hat."

"Okay. Fine. I'll be standing at the entrance to the coffee bar just behind the station sign. I'll be wearing a dark overcoat. I'm quite tall with short greyish hair. You can't miss me."

"Come with nobody. Otherwise, I leave."

"Don't worry, I'll be alone. See you there then."

I was surprised at how easy it had been. I had never bribed anyone in my life but I realised how powerful a tool money can be. It may not be able to buy you love but it can certainly buy you just about anything else.

I looked at my watch. I had quite a few hours to kill before I set off. I'd walk to the station and take the train, allowing myself plenty of time. In the meantime, I would delve once again into Alice's notes. I still felt guilty about it but I could see no other way of finding out about Jason.

I made myself a cup of coffee and went into the study. I had put a marker in the file to show where I had left off.

"Jason was full of a play he was directing and acting in by Hugh Leonard called Da. He considered Patrick for the main role but was afraid of being accused of nepotism. He said he understood so much about his own father from the play and regrets not making more of an effort to bring about some reconciliation before he died, 'confronting some of those ghosts.' He now realises how important it was for him to attend his funeral and at least face the ghost of his father.

I asked him to continue with his life story. The year after his parents separated was the worst year of his life. He felt he belonged nowhere. They seemed to be fighting over him as if he were 'a possession' but ignored him totally. He now realises that neither really wanted him. He was simply a means for them to 'get at each other.' His mother was in a state of collapse and was incapable of looking after him. So, she sent him to stay with his uncle and aunt. At least, here he found relative peace. He liked his aunt, who was caring and paid him some attention, but he didn't like his uncle. I asked him why, but he evaded answering (this needs further investigation). He ended up living with his aunt and uncle for three years.

I asked if he had had any friends of his age at the time. He said he hadn't. He admitted to being very shy and had difficulty making friends. He found escape in reading. He read anything he could get his hands on, from comic books to his father's text books on theatre. By reading books written by his father, he felt some connection with him, even though he didn't always understand what he was reading. He remembered reading them aloud and imagining he could hear his father's voice, which he described as 'two long arms reaching out to embrace me but never quite touching me.' He said his father had a perfect actor's voice, deep, yet full of warmth, which always struck him as such a contradiction."

It was strange that Jason never told me about the years he spent with his uncle and aunt. Yet, it spanned a significant part of his early adolescence. There had been talk of his mother spending some months in a psychiatric clinic to overcome severe depression. Jason never confirmed this either. I wondered whether he mentioned it during his sessions with Alice. I decided to read on.

"I realised that talking about his work at the National gave him great joy and so I did not stop him. He talked again about the play Da and said that if it hadn't already been written, he would have written something similar. Through writing, he felt he was able to sort out some of the chaos in his 'psyche' (he used the word psyche 'because it included soul, mind and spirit'—he said the chaos was 'in his DNA'), which he described as 'a tangled ball of string that had been dragged through the dirt.' His world was 'a house built on sand, with no proper foundations, constantly in danger of collapsing.'

I wanted to find out more about his uncle and aunt, whether he formed a close relationship with them and what kind of substitute parents they had been. At first, his aunt showed great love and affection, which he liked, something his mother had never been able to give him. Then, something happened that came between them. I asked what it was. He was hesitant about telling me. Then, he said, 'She was angry and jealous.'

'Of what?' I asked.

'Of my relationship with my uncle.'

'You mean you were very close.'

'No.'

'You said you didn't like him. So, why did your aunt think you were close?'

'Because he would come into my bedroom at night.'

'What did he do to you?'

'At first, he would just lie beside me. Then, he started feeling me. Trying to arouse me. I was only twelve.'

'This happened every night?'

'Many nights.'

'And your aunt must have known about this?'

'Yes.'

'Did he do anything else to you?'

I could see him gritting his teeth. 'Yes, he wanted to penetrate me from behind.'

'How did you react?'

'I half wanted it but tried to stop him at first.'

'So, he forced himself on you?'

'Yes, in a way.'

'How did you feel?'

'Guilty but gratified.'

'Why were you gratified?'

'There was something about the intimacy of the sexual act that made me feel something like affection for the first time.'

'How did you feel exactly?'

'Wanted, I suppose. Someone held me, kissed me, penetrated me, hurt me.'

Have I touched on the heart of Jason's depression? Is it here I will find the way to release his 'tangled psyche?' Love, sex, guilt, desire, self-hate, physical and emotional pain all intertwined, a complex and highly destructive amalgam of emotions. I realised he had never known true love, innocent love, the love of a friend, parent or sibling, and this forbidden love he experienced with his uncle had become confused with real love.

'How long did this go on for?' 'For some time.' 'You didn't tell anyone?' 'No.' 'Did you feel any love for your uncle at the time?' 'It was hardly love. There was no real tenderness, no overt expression of affection. It was a physical act. I hated him because I wanted him to come to me, even though I knew that what there was between us was fickle.' 'And your aunt accepted it?' 'Yes, but she resented it too. I had taken her place in the home. Maybe she found it convenient, but she hated me for being the object of his desire and not her.'

How can I go about healing such a deep-rooted trauma? Can he ever feel real love? Is it possible to describe to someone who has never experienced true love what it should feel like? I will work on it in our next session.

I was in a state of shock. In all the years I knew Jason I would never have suspected he had undergone such a trauma. He managed to hide it well. Valerie's female instinct was right. Jason had been abused. It all became so much clearer now. Had he abused young men and, feeling overwhelming guilt, come to Alice for help? It was all supposition, but it made sense. Was he afraid of himself, afraid of what he was capable of doing? I knew he did not lack sensitivity, but were his nefarious urges stronger than his ability to control them?

I was eager to see how Alice would go about 'healing' Jason and wanted to read on but I realised I needed to grab a bite to eat before setting off for the station.

Was my meeting with Asif redundant now? It seemed highly likely Jason abused these young men but I still needed to have it confirmed. If it turned out to be true, I would certainly make no attempt to get them to retract. Jason would have to do his time and hopefully continue the therapy he had begun with Alice.

I was about to open the door when my phone rang. It was Billy. What could he want?

"How's it going, mate?"

He sounded friendly.

"Busy," I said equivocally.

"Good to hear it. I just rang to say I watched your interview on TV. Quite impressive."

I wasn't sure whether he was being ironic or not. It was hard to tell with Billy. "In what way?"

"The way you stood up for the man. After what happened, it's easy to forget his good side."

"Did it do any good?"

"The interview? I don't think it will help Jason much. It will all depend on the outcome of the trial but I think it went a long way to revamping your image. You made it very clear why you're trying to help him."

"You mean they might consider me for the part in the film, after all?"

"I wouldn't go that far. At least, they know you don't condone child abuse. Look, Patrick, everybody knows you would be the best person for the part. They're just too scared to commit at this time. It will all depend on whether they can find someone as good as you for the role. They've been auditioning all week. From what I hear, they're not all that enthusiastic about what they've seen. Don't get your hopes up."

"There's still a chance then?"

"I wouldn't bet on it. So, what are you doing these days?"

"Trying to find out who my 'adopted' son is."

"Are you sure you want to know?"

"Absolutely. I don't think he's a lost cause."

"You sound like Alice."

"I suppose I do. She didn't believe there was such a thing as a lost cause. Look. I've got to go. I'm meeting a guy in town."

"Work?"

"No. Nor pleasure, either. I'm seeing someone from the Refugee Centre."

"Careful, mate. You don't want to be accused of witness tampering. It could make things even worse for Jason. It won't do you much good either. Though, I must admit I admire you for it. You always were a stubborn old fool."

"Thanks for the compliment. I'm doing it for my own peace of mind, for no other reason."

"That's a good enough reason, I guess. Take care, my friend. We'll be in touch."

~ * ~

It was almost dark when I emerged from the train station. It was a quiet time. The evening rush hour was over and it was too early for the night crowd. There was the odd stroller and a few lone window-shoppers, but no one wearing a red baseball cap who looked like a middle eastern refugee. Lights were coming on all around the square, neon signs started flashing, promising titillating entertainment or wild dancing. I took up my position outside the coffee shop behind the station sign, as agreed.

It was nearly eight and still no one had appeared. I was about to give up when I saw a dark-skinned young man eying me from a 'safe' distance across the square. He wasn't wearing a red baseball cap so I couldn't be sure it was Asif. I decided it was better to let him approach me. I wondered how long he had been watching me. Had he seen me exit from the train station and was waiting to make sure I was alone? I pretended not to see him and idly glanced at my watch. Then, I caught a glimpse of him slowly coming towards me.

"Are you Patrick?" he said timidly, his voice only just audible above the rumble of traffic. He was much younger than I expected. I guessed he couldn't have been more than eighteen. He was smartly dressed, with shiny jet-black hair. His lips were tight, and his eyes narrowed in mistrust.

"Thanks for coming," I said, putting out my hand.

He didn't respond immediately but eventually took my hand and shook it firmly. "You alone?" he said, looking around.

"Completely."

"What you want?"

"As I said, information."

"What information?"

"I want to talk to the guy Jason B is supposed to have raped."

He looked at me in disbelief. "Why you want?" he said at last.

"Let's talk," I said, pointing to an empty bench on the edge of the square.

I set off across the street, wondering whether he would follow. When I reached the other side, I looked back and saw that he was dithering, half turned in the other direction. I walked on to the bench and sat down. A couple of minutes later, I felt a presence beside me. "Sit down," I said gently, not looking up at him.

After a while, he sat at the other end of the bench. I looked across at him. He had a frightened, but canny, look on his face, a dog not sure whether to trust someone about to offer him a bone. I could see, however, that the prospect of a reward was a powerful enough incentive to get him to grab at it.

"You know Jason B, don't you?"

"Yeah, he come to Centre. Do theatre."

"You know he's in prison now, awaiting trial."

"I know. Everybody knows."

"Well, I'm his father."

A startled look softened the edges of his sharp face. He understood the significance of family, a father wanting to do the best for his son.

"I believe my son may have committed a crime, but it is important for me to determine what the crime is. Do you understand these things? Did he simply have sex with these boys or did he rape them? Or neither? It could make all the difference to the outcome of the trial. You see why I want to talk to these boys."

"Not easy."

"Why? Aren't they allowed out of the Centre?"

"They will not want to talk to you. They be afraid. They will think you want to kill them."

"Why would they think that?"

"Revenge. 'Cos, they say he raped them."

"So, it's not true?"

"Maybe, maybe not. I don't know."

"Can you arrange for me to meet them or not? I will pay you well."

"How much?"

"You tell me."

"Five hundred."

"Five hundred?" I screeched. "You must be out of your mind."

"I need five hundred. I must to go to family in Germany. They wait for me. I try to save money but everybody rob me."

"Like you're trying to rob me. Okay. I'll give you one hundred now and the rest when I've talked to these guys and got some answers."

"Two hundred now."

"One hundred fifty."

"All right. I do my best, no guarantees."

"Well, for one hundred fifty I expect results. Where and when might I meet them?"

"Same time. Same place. I tell you day. I like you, Mr. Patrick. I hope you not try to trick me."

"Why would I do that? It wouldn't be in my interests. I need to know the truth, even if I can't get them to change their testimony. I'll pay them well - not to lie but to tell the truth. Okay? I suppose they have family they want to reach too."

"Germany. They all want to go to Germany."

"Germany, eh? What's so great about Germany?"

"Work, Mr. Patrick. Work. We want to live honest. Here no future."

I handed over the one hundred fifty. He grabbed it and stuffed it into the pocket of a pair of scruffy black jeans.

I watched him disappear into the night, wondering whether I'd ever see him again or Jason's alleged victims.

Chapter Nineteen

Next morning, while checking my emails, I was pleased to see that the Prison Authorities had acceded to my request to visit Jason. This lifted my spirits enormously. I don't know why, as I wasn't sure my visit would do him any good. I could only hope that my presence and obvious concern for his plight would help to alleviate the isolation of prison. I wondered if there was anything I might bring him but couldn't think of anything that seemed appropriate. A book? On what subject? Grapes? He wasn't a convalescent. What else was there? Everything I could think of seemed to carry a negative message.

I tried to imagine what prison life was like. The endless hours of idleness, alone, to think, to regret perhaps. To what purpose? I realised how much of our life is spent planning; a new project, a holiday to some exotic location, an outing with friends, repainting the apartment. In prison, the future is so vague, so distant, practically non-existent. There is nothing to plan for, other than to stay alive.

So, once again I was waiting. I had little hope that Asif would get back to me unless the boys were desperate to get their hands on money to leave the country. Yet, how could they, if they were to act as witnesses in Jason's trial? At least, I would see Jason, which was something to look forward to. What state would he be in? Could I cheer him up? What could I offer him that would be of any use? I became hopelessly aware of my own impotence.

I went to my office and opened Jason's file at the point where I left off the previous day.

'Jason was extremely excited. The play Da will go up on Friday. He is confident the reviews will be good. He has put so much of himself into the play, both as actor and director. The actors bonded well, essential for a play like this. It was hard to get him to talk about anything else, but for therapy to

proceed we needed to confront his abuse and start to resolve the issue of his dysfunctional perception of love.

His mother managed to get her life back on track after a period in a psychiatric clinic. He visited her once there, but she gave no indication of being pleased to see him. Nor did she appear interested in knowing how he was getting on at school or whether he was happy living with his uncle and aunt. They had nothing to say to each other and spent most of the time in complete silence. He decided not to visit her again. Nor did she make any effort to see him. Sometime after this, she remarried. It was a small registry office marriage with only a few close friends. He was not invited. In fact, he never met her new husband.

When he was about fifteen, his father went through yet another separation and was alone. He asked Jason to go and live with him. Jason was overjoyed and accepted. It was a chance to get away from his uncle and aunt and bond with his father, whom he never really got to know. His uncle voiced some reservations. His main objection was Jason would have to adapt to a new environment and make new friends. Ares didn't see this as a problem. Nor did Jason, who had almost no friends at school anyway, and so he went to live with his father.

What he hoped would be a chance to get to know his father turned out to be a profound disappointment. They saw very little of each other and once again Jason had to fend for himself. If Ares was planning to bring a woman home, he would tell Jason to stay in his room. Having a boy around the house was apparently not conducive to the seduction process. This happened frequently. He only remembers two or three occasions in the two years he lived with his father when they were alone together and were able to have a proper conversation. His father avoided talking about personal matters and they mainly discussed the theatre, or politics, which Jason knew very little about at the time.

Again, we didn't do any therapy proper, but I believe we took another small step towards 'untangling his psyche'.'

Jason's file read very much like a story in which I knew the ending but not the events that led up to it.

I needed to set off early for the prison, as it was some distance from my home. I had to do a Covid test too before being allowed in. Still, I had time to read one more of Alice's sessions with Jason.

'Jason was over the moon. The reviews were good. "A sensitive portrayal by Jason B,"

"Never a dull moment in Jason B's insightful direction of Da"

"One of the best productions this season."

He was in such high spirits I wondered whether there was any point in continuing with therapy, but I knew that his euphoria would only last as long as the play did. When it was over, he would once again have to face his demons.

I asked him how he felt about leaving his uncle and aunt's house. Were there any regrets? He didn't hesitate to reply. He said it was an enormous relief. In retrospect, he wonders how he put up with it for so long. He considered running away on several occasions but didn't have the courage. 'The atmosphere in the home was like a sodden blanket weighing down on us, making the atmosphere heavy and asphyxiating. We all felt guilt but did nothing to change the situation. I think if I stayed any longer, I might have killed someone or myself.' I believe he meant it.

I asked if his aunt and uncle were still alive. His aunt died from a rare form of cancer. He told me he believed his uncle was living abroad. He didn't say why he left the country. I asked if he felt anything for his uncle. He said nothing except anger and repulsion.

I asked him to imagine I was his dying uncle suffering from dementia, trapped in an internal world, unable to communicate with anyone. He (Jason) came to visit me at the clinic for the last time, what would he say to me as he sat facing my impassive, vacant eyes?

He concentrated for a few moments as he tried to metamorphose me into the empty carcass of his uncle. A strange look transformed his face into something almost unrecognisable. Was it hate, disgust, pity, love? I wasn't sure. "Uncle, I hate you more than I could hate anyone else in the world. I thought many times of taking that carving knife that you keep in the dining room cupboard and driving it straight through your heart just at the moment when you were shaking in the last spasms of your ejaculation. Why didn't I? Because you weren't worth it. You were nothing. You felt nothing, showed nothing. You were a worthless human being, just as worthless as you are now. Dying in such a spectacular way would only have given you dignity, a dignity you didn't deserve."

Slowly the look of hatred changed to pity. "If only you had the decency to show me some affection but you couldn't do that. Your guilt wouldn't let you. You wanted to pretend that I was to blame. I, the child, seduced you, not the other way round. I hated your hypocrisy, your inverted self-righteousness, your lack of feeling for Aunt Eva, your inability to truly love. I hate you with all my heart and I hope there is such a thing as hell in which you will burn for all eternity. Perhaps then you will understand my pain, my longing, my despair, my unfulfilled love..."

Jason was by now sobbing uncontrollably. Would that it could bring about the catharsis he had been yearning for all his life, the catharsis that theatre had paradoxically been unable to give him.'

I was beginning to understand how therapy worked and what Alice was trying to achieve. Yet, she told me herself that in difficult cases therapy is a long and often painstaking process, a constant fluctuation between progress and retrogression. On the point of making a significant breakthrough, the client withdraws, unable to break free from the trauma, which has become an integral part of their being. They are afraid to let go of the self they have struggled so long and hard to live with, for fear of discovering that an alternative does not exist or is even more intolerable.

I could have stayed there all afternoon reading Jason's file, but I had to leave for the prison.

~ * ~

Being allowed into the prison involved a lot of red tape, filling in and signing forms, which I didn't bother reading. Then, I had to have a long stick with cotton wool on the tip stuck down my throat and up my nose. The nurse in charge of testing for Covid went about her job with the insensitivity of a mechanic checking the oil in the sump of a car engine. She didn't seem in any way concerned when I nearly choked as the end of the baton hit my tonsils or surprised when I started giggling hysterically as it tickled the inside of my nostril. I was told to stand outside the Isobox in the cold and wait until the results came out.

Fortunately, I didn't have to wait long. I was frisked and scanned and told to wait for a guard. Then began the long haul through sliding doors and blinding corridors. I was finally ushered into a depersonalized, sterilised hall with a number of metal plastic-topped tables sparsely scattered around the room, with cheap-looking folding chairs on either side. Guards were standing around, as they do in museums, ready to intervene should a visitor dare to get too close to the exhibit. I couldn't help feeling that they did everything they could to make us feel unwelcome.,

A door snapped open, and Jason entered. I was glad to see he was not wearing stripes or arrows but a plain beige uniform and brown clogs, which made him look like a hospital orderly.

I observed him standing there. He looked like a frightened deer, edgy, flighty, as he tried to locate me among the other visitors. For an instant, I saw the timorous adolescent boy, as he described himself to Alice, beardless, skin still unblemished, the despair of 'unlovedness' in his eyes. I stood up and waved. He acknowledged my presence unsmilingly and shuffled over to my table.

We sat staring blankly at each other for a few moments, not knowing what to say. Neither of us cares to indulge in small talk or superfluous questions like, 'How are you feeling?' What was the point, anyway? I could tell how he felt. Like anyone would feel at the bottom of a black hole with no way of climbing out. He looked worse than ever, his skin sallow and dry, his eyes sunken. He was old before his time. I wasn't sure whether he was pleased to see me or not. What did he feel? Shame? Humiliation? Frustration? All three perhaps.

I had not prepared for this. I thought that conversation would come easily, as it always did with Jason, but it was as if we were strangers, sitting opposite each other on a commuter ride to work, feeling an obligation to exchange pleasantries. "How are they treating you?" I said at last.

"The food is crap. The guards unfriendly," he said monosyllabically.

Silence.

"I didn't know what you might want. A book or something?"

"Nothing, Patrick."

Silence.

"What do you do all day?"

"Do what I'm told."

"That's all?"

"And think."

"About what?"

"Everything and nothing."

"I can imagine."

"I feel like a mule tied to a pole, going round and round in circles. After a while, the brain goes numb, which is not a bad thing, I suppose."

"Let's hope they set a date for the trial soon, so that you can get out of here."

"Get out of here. You must be joking."

Silence.

"We must be positive," I said pathetically.

He laughed ironically. "Patrick, you know as well as I do that I'm fucked, well and truly fucked. They have sworn statements from two 'poor defenceless refugees' claiming I raped them. That's enough to condemn me for life. After all, they have all the 'concerned and compassionate' NGOs clamouring for my head on a platter."

"What is Victor S saying? Does he think there's any hope they might change their statement?"

"Not a hope. They are being actively encouraged to stick to their guns. I'm being made an example of. I will be the legal precedent that will 'deter others and *clean up* the theatre world'," he said with a sneer.

"What is Victor S doing?"

"I get the impression he's given up on me. He thinks I'm a lost cause. I reckon he regrets taking me on and would withdraw if he could. He's afraid I'll damage his reputation if he loses my case."

"Should I speak to him?"

"What good would that do, Patrick? It's obvious he doesn't like you."

"The feeling is mutual. His defence of Andrew was pathetic."

He seemed to perk up at the mention of Andrew. "Ah, yes, this might interest you, Patrick. They've moved me and I'm sharing a wing with three guys who work for a drug cartel. They avoided me at first but we've exchanged a few words. They quite like the idea that I'm a celebrity. They think some of it might rub off on them. They don't seem to care about the rest."

I looked at Jason quizzically.

"You wanted to find out what happened to Andrew. I'm going to find out for you."

"Do you think they might know?"

"Of course they know. When someone is bumped off, it's an event. People hear about it. They make sure of it. It acts as a warning to others."

"I don't like it, Jason. It seems like you're playing with fire."

"At least it gives me something to do. If I do get burnt, so what? I'd sooner die doing something worthwhile than live a life worse than death."

"Please, Jason, leave it alone," I pleaded. "I don't want you to put your life in danger for my sake."

"Patrick, believe me, it's not just for you. I need to know too."

"I know you and Andrew were friends but why is it so important for you to know why he was killed?"

"I have enough on my conscience. I don't want to die believing that I might have been in some way responsible."

I was flabbergasted. "But how…?"

"It's a long story, Patrick, one that it's best you don't know about."

I felt a surge of anger rising inside me. "Damn it, Jason. I have the right to know. I have been blaming myself for Andrew's death all these years. You cannot keep this from me."

He looked down, avoiding my fiery stare. "I'm sorry, Patrick. You're right. I will tell you everything one day. I just wanted to preserve the image you might have of Andrew. I don't care what you think of me. I am not your son." He looked away briefly.

"Andrew was our birth son but you have been no less a son to Alice and me."

He looked up at me, his eyes still red. "Do you mean that?"

"Of course, I do. I'm going to fight for you in the way I should have fought for Andrew."

"But you did, Patrick. You did. The tragic thing is he was innocent."

I stared at him in disbelief. Andrew was innocent. What was he telling me?

A bell rang. Our time was up. I still had so many questions to ask. What did he mean when he said Andrew was innocent? Why did he think he might have been to blame for Andrew's death? Were Andrew and he like brothers or enemies? I realised I was just as much in the dark now as I had ever been.

Chapter Twenty

I was about to settle down to another of Alice's sessions with Jason when Valerie rang. In many ways I was relieved. I needed a window on normality. I was becoming too involved in the turmoil of Jason's 'psyche.' I was hopelessly confused and frustrated. I wished Alice was still with me. I knew she would be able to see the two ends of the tangled twine. She would have the patience and the skill to unravel it.

"How was your day?" I asked.

I was genuinely interested to know what an ordinary day at work was like.

"Hectic, as usual, nothing world-shattering. I'm more interested in hearing how yours went. I knew you wouldn't ring me, so I rang you."

"I'm sorry. I visited Jason today."

"You didn't tell me you were going. How is he?"

"Not good. I think he's lost hope. It's going to be hard to overturn the rape charges."

"I'm sure Victor S will come up with something. He's a wily fox."

"If someone could be paid, I'm sure he'd do it, but I think it's impossible in this case."

"How are your investigations going?"

"I'm afraid I may have hit a brick wall. I haven't heard from Asif."

"Asif?"

"The connection at the Refugee Centre?"

"Right. Perhaps it's for the best."

"I just don't know what else to do."

"All you can do is be there for him."

"Whatever good that will do."

"A lot more than you realise."

"I wish."

"Do you fancy coming over for a drink later?"
I thought about it, but not for long. "Yes. I'd love to. About eightish?"
"Perfect. See you soon then."
I still had some time to read another of Alice's sessions with Jason.

'Jason was still on a high. The good reviews were bringing in the audiences. He wished his father could have seen the play. He believes he would have been proud of him, though he might not have shown it. Ares didn't believe in praise. He used to say that 'praise cannot be trusted.' The only praise worth its salt is self-praise, 'when you truly believe in your work.'

I needed to capitalise on the huge breakthrough of the previous session. It was clear that his feelings for his uncle were ambivalent, a volatile symbiosis of love and hate. It was important that he should be able to find some closure for this period of his life. I asked him if it would be possible for him to forgive his uncle. He said categorically no. Then, I asked him to posit a hypothetical situation in which he found out that his uncle had been abused as a child, would it then be possible to at least partially absolve him? He gave it some thought and decided that it would be easier. So, I proposed that he write a letter to his uncle, with the knowledge that he too had been abused. He agreed and produced the following letter.

"Dear Uncle,

Last week I cursed you to high heaven and hoped that you would suffer for all eternity in hell. That was before I found out that you too were abused as a child. I cannot forgive you for what you did to me but I understand you better. You thought you loved me, even though you were unable to show it. You thought you could find rebirth in me. You could have, if you knew how to express love. Yet, I understand that too. How can you convey something you have never felt? You have never been truly loved either and can therefore never love someone else. You could never love Aunt Eva because you can only love the abused, the violated, the emotionally extinct. You saw that in me, I know. But you were unable to make that leap, that superhuman leap out of the emotional void, conquering shame and guilt. You could not believe in the myth of love. If you had, we could have saved each other. Now you are dead, Uncle, dead to me anyway, I can do nothing for you. No doubt your life was hell, as will be your afterlife, if there is such a thing. Maybe that is punishment enough. I, on the other hand, am alive. I still must face life. Where can I look for salvation? Where? If you have an ounce of affection for me, just give me the nod, point the way, my sixth sense will pick it up.

Goodbye, Uncle. I will not write to you again. I cannot forgive you, because you should have known you were damaging me in the same way you were damaged, but I can at least understand. I no longer hope that you burn in hell. Life on earth was hell enough.

Yours, Jason

As he read it out to me, I saw the rabid hate on his face slowly change to clemency. All he needed was a pretext to excuse and now he found one. Real or not, it did not matter. While he read, it was real, as real as the words of Da or any other piece of theatre he had performed, which for him was more real than reality itself. I did not discuss the letter with him. The writing and subsequent reading of it was enough to produce the desired result. Had I achieved my initial goal? We would see.

I now had a clearer picture of what Alice was trying to do. Jason needed to externalise what he repressed all these years. That alone would give relief. To find closure he needed to come to terms with his abuse and its perpetrator. By postulating that his uncle had also been abused, she was providing an escape route, a way out, a board to cling to as he floundered in the churning waters of his inner tempest. It remained to be seen whether he could 'play the game' and allow himself to be taken in by the hypothesis.

~ * ~

I decided to walk to Valerie's. I knew she wouldn't mind if I was a bit late. I needed the fresh air to clear the fuzz in my head and let the icy north-westerly wind pinch my cheeks and bite into my skin. Sometimes physical pain is a good antidote to mental pain. This spell of cold weather was the sting in the winter's tail. Soon spring would bring renewal, revival, renascence to the northern hemisphere. Would that rebirth include Jason, I wondered?

I felt Alice's notes tugging at me, drawing me back. How far had she got in the therapeutic process before her illness prevented her from continuing? Had therapy done Jason any good? Would things have been different if they had completed the therapeutic process? Alice's death must have been an enormous blow to him.

I stopped at an off-licence and got a couple of bottles of expensive French wine. I knew she would appreciate that more than flowers. Besides, I didn't want to give her the impression that I wished to begin a courtship. For the moment, we were just good friends. Time would tell if either of us wanted to take it a step further.

She seemed happy to see me, even though I arrived nearly half an hour late. She kissed me on both cheeks and led me to the settee in front of the fire. A bottle of red wine was open on the table and she poured us a glass each.

"What is that delicious smell?" I asked.

"Boeuf Bourguignon."

My choice of wine had been correct.

"You do eat meat?"

"Anything French I adore."

"Then, I think you and I are going to get along very well, Mr. G."

We talked about current affairs; the possibility of elections - no one seemed happy with the government's handling of the Covid crisis. We touched on the situation in the Middle East and America's defeat in Afghanistan. Would this mean the Western allies, Europe and the US, would be on the defensive against the Russian and Chinese superpowers? It helped to take my mind off Jason for a short time but despite the obvious dangers of shifting world forces, Jason remained uppermost in my mind.

"By the way, we got a lot of positive Tweets about the interview," she said chirpily. "It appears you haven't lost your charm, Mr. G. There are many loyal fans still out there hoping that you'll make a come-back."

"It's flattering to know but my priority is Jason for now."

"Do you think he's innocent?" she asked, eying me warily.

"I wish I knew. What I do know is that he was doing therapy with Alice?"

"Really? Well, that is certainly something in his favour."

"He had an abominable childhood. Totally ignored by his parents. Growing up, he never knew what it was to be loved."

"If only the court could take this into consideration. Surely it counts as mitigating circumstances?"

"You were right. He was abused."

Valerie had her hand out to take her glass. A look of horror distorted her face. "How do you know? Did he tell you?"

"I don't think he ever would."

"So how…?"

I looked away in shame. "I found her notes," I said at last.

She gave me a reproachful look.

"I know I shouldn't have, but it was the only way I could find out about Jason."

She held her glass to her lips for some time, trying to take in what I said. "I think you did the right thing," she said at last. "If Alice were still alive, I'm sure she would want to convey her deeper knowledge of Jason to the courts. Do you know why he went to her in the first place?"

"It hasn't been stated clearly in her sessions with him, but I have the feeling it had to do with self-loathing and the resulting chronic depression. The theatre is the only thing that seems to give him a sense of worth. As long as he is involved in acting or directing a play, he can block out the traumas of his childhood. I think that may be the reason why he is so obsessed with his work. A hiatus of inactivity would be hell for him."

"You must go on reading Alice's notes, Patrick. I know you feel bad about it but it's the only way you are going to get a clear picture of Jason. It may even reveal the extent of his guilt."

Again, we had a lovely meal. I tried to steer clear of Jason in our conversation, but we inevitably came back to him. Still, it was a comfort talking to her, knowing I had someone I could share my thoughts and anxieties with.

~ * ~

I got home late but, despite the wine and the large meal, I was not sleepy. So, I decided to read another session with Jason.

"Da was becoming a routine for him now but after three weeks into the play he was still finding elements of his father that he had not noticed in rehearsal. I could see he was beginning to get tired. Doing the play night

after night was taking an enormous emotional toll on him. It was like having to confront his father over and over, with the knowledge that he would never have the chance to have it out with him. As a result, at the end of each performance he felt somehow cheated, despite the marked satisfaction of the audience.

I asked him if he had ever experienced what he thought was real love. He said he was no longer sure, as he believed he confused love with lust. I said that he was not the only one. Then, he said he thought he had been in love with a boy at the age of sixteen. I asked him why he thought it was different from lust. He said it had to do with how Rafi appeared in his dreams. They were never naked together, just talking or walking hand in hand by the river. I asked if his love was requited. He said everything was fine between them until one day he made the mistake of declaring himself to Rafi. After that, Rafi avoided him because he didn't want the other boys to think he was gay.

I asked Jason to paint a life-size portrait of Rafi. Despite his protestations of artistic incompetence, he produced a 'passable likeness,' so he said, of Rafi. He was clearly a good-looking boy with blue eyes and longish light brown hair. He dressed him in colourful summer clothes. I asked him to sit cross-legged by Rafi and tell me what it was he liked about him. He mentioned his gentleness, his tenderness, his smile, his confident way of walking, his magnetism (he was attractive to both boys and girls, who adored him), his teasing sense of humour, etc. I then got him to lie beside the portrait and feel the love he felt for Rafi without expressing it in words or actions. He lay on the ground for quite some time, apparently staring into Rafi's eyes. I think he may have stayed like that forever if I hadn't asked him to stand up and go back to his seat.

I asked him to tell me what he would have liked to say to Rafi.

He stared at his friend for some time breathing life into the rough image until Rafi stood before him exactly as he had been thirty years before, untouched by time, still perfect in every detail. "Rafi, I think I love you. I'm not sure what love is but what I feel for you is more than just sexual attraction. I want to become a part of you. I'd like us to melt together and become one so that we will always be together, inseparable. Yes, Rafi, I'm gay and I think you may be too, but you possibly don't realise it yet or don't want to admit it. Please do not reject me. I demand nothing of you, only that you remain my friend, because I want nothing more than to be with you, to see your beautiful person, to hear your tender voice, to watch you walk across the school yard, to feel your breath on mine. Is that too much to ask, Rafi? If it is, then I will just have to love you from a distance. You are my first real love and at this moment I think I will love you forever."

This exercise took an enormous amount out of him. He was on the point of emotional collapse, so we did a de-rolling exercise in which I asked him to dispose of the portrait of Rafi. At first, he didn't want to touch it. Then he carefully rolled it up and asked me to keep it in a safe place, even though he said he would probably never want to look at it again. After some discussion, he said that he believed the act of rolling Rafi up was symbolic of his closing this chapter in his life.

Was Jason slowly putting up the shutters on episodes of his life that remained semi-inhabited shells he had been unable to fully abandon, their vacant 'unshuttered' eyes drawing him back, forcing him to relive disillusionment repeatedly?

The progress I was making with Jason was an indication that he was highly motivated, though I was still unsure of the reason why he came to me in the first instance. Was it something more personal? A confession perhaps? Yet, I believe it will all come out in the end. The process we are currently going through, however painful, is an inevitable part of therapeutic progression.'

Alice's description of their sessions was so graphic I almost felt I was there watching Jason relive moments of his life. I could almost see the metamorphosis taking place and Alice's keen awareness of it. I could tell by the tone of her writing that she was pleased with the way therapy was going but I also felt that her optimism was cautious, restrained. She somehow intuited bigger things ahead that would determine the outcome.

I could have skipped to the end, I suppose, if in fact there was an end, but I did not want a half picture of Jason. I needed to see the whole to arrive at a complete understanding of this complex but deeply disturbed individual.

I could have gone on reading, but I felt my eyes getting heavy and was afraid I might miss something. I needed to be wide awake to take in every moment of every session.

There was also a selfish reason for not wanting to rush through her notes. I could hear her voice and feel her warmth in the words as she slowly penetrated the scar tissue that had formed around Jason's bruised and beaten 'psyche.'

Chapter Twenty-One

Next morning after breakfast I decided I had to talk to Victor S to find out what was happening. Was it, as Jason believed, a lost cause? Was Victor S doing all he could to find mitigating circumstances, even if he could not prove Jason's innocence?

I rang several times but kept on getting negative answers. 'He was in a meeting with a prospective client.' 'He was on the point of leaving the office.' 'Mr. Victor has been informed that you called and will get back to you as soon as he has a free moment.' I knew Victor S would never get back to me.

I had had no word from Asif, so I wrote off any possibility of meeting with the alleged rape victims. I now had to focus on convincing Victor S that a case could be made in Jason's favour by showing he had voluntarily opted to undergo therapy to put his life in order. The only way I was going to get Victor S to see me was to ambush him or camp outside the office building.

Victor S was the head partner in one of the country's top legal firms. They owned a six-storey building looking on to the old courthouse with its awe-inspiring Doric columns and heavy wooden doors. The security guard at the entrance made it as difficult as he could for me to enter. However, I was able to show him my vaccination certificate and the results of the Covid test I'd had the previous day, so at least that was one hurdle he could not stop me from crossing. However, when he was told - from upstairs - that I had not made an appointment, he shook his head with exulting satisfaction. He had fulfilled his role as fortress keeper.

"I'll just have to wait until Victor S leaves the building then," I said. "I need to see him today. It's urgent."

"I'm very sorry, Sir," he intoned in a patronising air that made it very clear he was not in the least bit sorry. "But I should warn you that Mr. Victor leaves the office very late."

"I'll put up a tent outside the front door, if I have to."

The security guard looked perturbed. He had taken me literally. "I'm afraid that's not allowed Sir. The passage must be kept clear."

"I suppose there's nothing wrong with just standing, is there?"

"It's rather nippy outside today, Sir. It could snow later."

"Let it snow. Let it snow. Let it snow," I chimed in a poor imitation of Dean Martin. The guard had either little knowledge of Christmas songs or had no sense of humour. He looked at me as if I'd totally lost it, reinforcing his decision to deny me entry. I was being frivolous, I know, but he was seriously getting on my nerves.

I paced in the warmth of the lobby, absorbing as much heat as I could from the radiators. I knew the guard was not going to let me loiter there for long.

"I'm afraid you can't wait here, Sir. This is a restricted area."

"Am I bothering anyone?" I asked.

"I'm afraid it's not allowed Sir."

"Who said?"

"The building regulations, Sir."

"I'd like to see the building regulations, please. As the security guard in a legal firm, you no doubt have a copy of the building regulations there behind your desk."

"No, Sir, I don't, but I know …"

"In that case, I'll stay here until you produce a copy of the building regulations."

"I can't do that, Sir."

"What a pity. It seems I'll be here forever then."

"I'd like you to leave the building, Sir," he said more aggressively this time, as he came out from behind his desk and headed resolutely in my direction.

He put his hand on my arm, indicating he was prepared to use force, if necessary.

"Going to use violence, are we? I can see the headline now 'Security guard in top legal firm injures prospective client.' Are you sure that's what you want?"

He immediately withdrew his hand and went to the phone. He

presumably dialled Victor S's private secretary. "The gentleman who wanted to see Mr. Victor refuses to leave the building. He says I can't stop him from waiting in the lobby until Mr. Victor appears. Yes. Yes. All right, Ms. F. I'll tell him." He put down the phone and gave me a disgruntled look. "They'll see what they can do."

"That's more like it," I said.

Sometimes making a bloody nuisance of oneself can produce results.

I had to wait another five minutes before another guard appeared from the upper regions to escort me to the sanctum sanctorum and hopefully to see Victor S. In the lift, the guard eyed me suspiciously, keeping his distance, as if at any moment I might produce a lethal weapon from somewhere on my person. He was extremely taciturn; no doubt having got the message from his superiors that I was a serious pain in the backside.

I got similar disaffected looks from other members of staff who came and went from the inner office. I was clearly someone to be wary of and, if not a serious threat, an item of curiosity. I was not offered a seat. I had to suffer a little for my sins.

Eventually the phone tinkled on the secretary's desk, and I could just make out Victor S's peeved voice on the other end telling her to send me in. "You may go in now, Mr. G."

Did I detect a slight twinkle in her eye and a faintly amused curl of her lower lip? Not many would have dared to defy the mighty Victor S. In retrospect, I wonder how I managed to get away with it.

Victor S looked up from behind his desk, making no attempt to hide his displeasure. "What is it, Patrick? I'm inundated here."

"Are you ever not? I want to know how things are going with Jason's case. Are you making any progress? Are we dealing with a lost cause here? Why haven't I been informed?"

"I was not aware you were my client, Patrick."

"You know perfectly well that I am the next best thing to Jason's guardian. I need to know."

"I believe Jason B is his own guardian. He's not a child, as far as I know."

"It seems to me you need all the help you can get. Why have you cut me out?"

"Look, Patrick, this is a pretty straightforward case. Whatever the circumstances, whether force, drugs or violence were used, he is guilty of statutory rape, because of the age of the victims."

"Why are you so certain he had intercourse with them? Has he told you so?"

"He doesn't need to."

"The boys were sixteen, right?"

"At the time, they were fifteen."

"But they're sixteen now."

"What difference does that make?"

"A few months off sixteen."

"The law states categorically…"

"What is the voting age in this country?"

"Sixteen, but…"

"Surely if you're old enough to decide who should run the country, you're old enough to decide who you should have sex with."

"Patrick, the law is intractable. They were fifteen at the time of the alleged rapes. Please let me do my job. It's far more complicated than you are trying to make out."

"Why?"

"It has to do with the difference in age between Jason and his victims and Jason's social position. Both would allow him to exert undue influence over the boys. Now if the accused were, let's say, only a year or two older than the victims then it would be a different story altogether. But in this case, the prosecution will argue that the boys were immature, that they were easy for the older man to manipulate."

"So, what you're saying is that Jason is being condemned because of his age and position? You're not even sure he had intercourse with them."

"It's not as simple as that, but in effect, yes."

"Would it make any difference if Jason was in therapy for nearly six months with my wife?"

"With Alice? If you can prove that he was genuinely endeavouring to seek help, then yes. I don't see how you can prove that."

"I have her notes in her own handwriting."

Victor S pondered the idea for a moment. "It might help, I suppose, but…"

"What if the boys were to retract their stories?"

Victor S laughed sardonically. "Now you are being ridiculous, Patrick." He looked at his watch. "Your time is up."

"I've contacted someone at the Refugee Centre who says he can introduce me to the boys. They are very keen to get together enough money to leave the country."

Victor S looked at me in horror. "Are you suggesting that we bribe these boys to lie?"

"How do we know they were telling the truth in the first place? What proof do we have that Jason even had intercourse with them, let alone, forced them to have sex with him, even if by law it boils down to the same thing?"

Victor S looked at me sternly. "Patrick, I am doing all I can for Jason. Unfortunately, the burden of proof lies on both sides. One of the reasons I got Jason to deny having sex with these boys is precisely because of what I said before. If it comes out that you have been tampering with the witnesses, then it could seriously damage our case."

"All I want to know from these boys is whether Jason raped them or not. Would it make any difference if they were paid to have sex with Jason?"

"It would certainly show that the boys were not entirely innocent but…"

"Look, Victor, Jason's career is finished, whether he's acquitted or not. Surely that is punishment enough. He may have to do time, but it is very important that time is minimal. Otherwise, he will not survive. I know him. He is extremely vulnerable. I believe I can get him to agree to continue therapy, if I can find the right therapist."

"You're meeting with this man from the Refugee Centre, can you be sure it was not filmed or recorded?"

"One hundred percent, no, but if it were, they would also see I gave him one hundred fifty for his services. It would also be very fuzzy as it was a dark night with no lights in that part of the square."

Victor S shook his head doubtfully. "This is a mistake, Patrick. You're getting in over your head. Is Jason aware of what you're doing?"

"No, nor do I have any intention of telling him."

"Good, keep it like that. And please do not come to my office again.

The less we see of each other the better. I do not want there to be any suspicion I have aided or abetted in your actions. You are doing this entirely off your own bat. If you need to talk to me, call me on this number, preferably after seven o'clock at night. I am interested in any information you get, but it must be entirely undercover, you understand?"

He wrote a phone number on a piece of paper and handed it to me.

"Absolutely."

"I am interested in looking into the possibility of pleading lenience on the grounds that he was in therapy with your wife, presumably until she died?"

"Yes, I am slowly reading the notes from her sessions with him."

"Keep them safe. We might be able to use them, with Jason's consent of course."

"Yes, absolutely."

"Right, Patrick," he said, getting to his feet and extending a hand. "I'm sorry for pulling up the drawbridge on you but I had a feeling you were here to break my balls."

"As I am wont to do," I said with a smile.

"You said it, not me."

"By the way, when are they likely to set a date for the trial?"

"They already have. Next Thursday."

"Next Thursday! Does Jason know?"

"I'm going to see him today."

"Will you be ready?"

"I'll be ready. The question is, will you?"

I understood what he meant. He was indirectly giving me the green light. "I'll have to be, won't I?"

I let myself out of his office but had to wait until a guard came to see me off the premises. As curious members of staff eyed me in passing, I couldn't help feeling I was some kind of urban terrorist in disguise. The young secretary, however, was very genial. "Did it go well, Mr. G?"

"Considering that the police didn't have to be called, I think it went remarkably well."

"I'm sure it did," she said, and added in a whisper, the flat of her hand shielding the side of her mouth, "I didn't hear any raised voices."

I laughed but couldn't help wondering how long she would keep her job.

~ * ~

I felt the meeting with Victor S went remarkably well. Though he hadn't accepted my ideas, he hadn't rejected them either. He simply didn't want to be compromised in any way. The onus was entirely on me if anything went wrong. If they went right, of course, he would get all the credit, but that was of little concern to me.

It was lunchtime. So, I decided to stop off at a small family restaurant on my way home, where they made a delicious chicken stew. I was halfway through their homemade profiterole when my phone pinged. It was a message from Asif. 'We meet tonight. Come alone.' So, it was going to happen after all.

~ * ~

After finding out that the trial was set for the following week, I began to feel under pressure. However, there was very little I could do to speed things up. So, I decided to read another of Alice's sessions with Jason.

'I felt we were making great progress, even though we were only ten weeks into therapy. I believe Jason feels the same. He appears far more optimistic about the future. Now in its seventh week he is able to dissociate Da from his personal life. It has become spontaneous, though he believes his personal experiences with his own father influenced his direction of the play and his portrayal of his character.

I asked him why he chose the theatre as a career. He said there were a number of reasons. Firstly, he believed that through the theatre he could get closer to his father, understand him better. Secondly, through theatre he could be someone other than himself. Make believe was not only permitted but encouraged. Through the characters he played he could live other lives, experience other worlds, feel emotions he could not feel in real life, in other words, "cast off my own skin and wear someone else's." Each play is a microcosm, and the actor and director can "shape that world into something consequential," which you can seldom do in real life. Thirdly, he felt that the theatre was his element, *"a kind of twilight zone between reality and fiction,"* in which he could become totally immersed and, in this way, forget who he is and where he comes from.

I wanted to explore his relationship with his father, as I believed this too was an issue that needed some closure. So, I read him a poem by Eleni Sikelianos entitled *In the Airport* and asked for his reactions:

A man called Dad walks by
then another one does. Dad, you say,
and he turns, forever turning, forever,
being called. Dad, he turns, and looks,
at you, bewildered, his face a moving,
wreck of skin, a gravity-bound question
mark, a fruit ripped in two, an animal,
that can't escape the field.

Jason expressed his reactions to the poem in more or less these words. *"I think I wrote off my mother at a very early age. At some point—I'm not sure when—I stopped looking for her. I never stopped looking for Dad, not just in my own Dad but in others too. I was so envious of other children whose dads actually played with them, showed them love and affection. Like the narrator in the poem, all I wanted was recognition, an indication he saw me, as someone he loved, as his son, but all I got was that pedestrian question mark that said, 'Do I know you?' Worse still, that look of bewilderment, 'What can I do with you?' Yes, he was like an animal that wished to escape, to escape his responsibilities as a father. Yes, although I saw him sometimes as a ripe fruit, not to be devoured, but admired, which fell apart in my hands when I tried to touch it. Thinking about it now, I wonder if he too had a similar upbringing to mine. Maybe self-destruction was a family trait—I once said I thought it was in my DNA—that it was hereditary, bequeathed from one generation to the next. Had I not been gay it would no doubt have been perpetuated in my offspring. Fortunately, I've never had the desire to have children. I often think some enlightened intelligence made sure the buck stopped with me.'*

I then asked him to write a poem about his dad. He produced the following, which he entitled *The Book*:

Within a glass casing
A book, open at the first page,
Thick with knowledge,
Meticulously bound in aged leather,
Sacred, mysterious, erudite.
I imagined it friable to the touch,
Smelling of whisky and stale tobacco,
Its title beguiling,
The Art of Magic.
Dad? I cried. It's me.
But the magic did not work.
Dad sat emotionless on the podium,
Forever encased, untouchable.
Unreadable beyond the first page.

I asked him to interpret his own poem. "I think I saw Dad not as a human being but as a source of knowledge, as a living book. Just to look at him aroused awe in me. Yet, there was something exciting about that too. I always believed if we could somehow connect, magic would take place, but it never did, or perhaps we just never connected. The book that was my father remained forever closed like a brittle old volume that has been carefully preserved. Only the restorers could touch it, certainly not a child. I wanted to get my hands on all that knowledge, all those experiences and emotions that I believed were contained within those yellowing pages, but I could never penetrate the austere leathery exterior. So, my relationship with him remained sterile, distant, impersonal, like a book open at the first page in a glass casing."

I believe another shutter has been erected. I wonder how many more windows there are to board up.'

Every session seemed to produce more pearls. Client and therapist were ideally suited, their sharp, insightful minds a perfect match. Alice knew the stimuli that would bring out the repressed memories and emotions. I couldn't wait to read on.

Chapter Twenty-Two

It was still light when I set off for my meeting with Asif and his protégés. I took just enough money to use as bait, if required.

It was warmer than it had been, but it started to rain as soon as I came out of the underground station. As agreed, I waited near the sign, trying to protect myself as best I could from the drizzle. seven thirty came and went but I remembered that Asif had been half an hour late the previous time, so I waited in hope. Fortunately, I was wearing an overcoat that kept out most of the rain. To keep warm, I paced up and down and did a bit of running on the spot, but I couldn't help feeling that I was on a fool's errand. The chances of getting them to change their testimony were very small indeed. There was too much at stake for them. On the other hand, why had they agreed to meet me?

Suddenly, four sombre figures appeared like commandos out of the shadows. I was surprised I hadn't noticed them. Perhaps I had been expecting to see them in the park opposite. Within seconds I was locked between two hefty lads, who swept me along the pavement, my feet hardly touching the ground. I didn't recognise Asif, but he could have been one of them under the ski hat and the surgical mask.

"Where are you taking me?" I said, but there was no answer.

All I could hear was the hurried patter of feet as we swished along the wet pavement.

We must have been walking for at least twenty minutes, without a word being spoken. We had taken such an erratic course I would have had difficulty retracing my steps. What I did know was that we were in a part of town most sensible people avoided, especially at night. It had a reputation for drugs, muggings, and brothels. Even the lights seemed dimmer and sparser than in other districts, making the red lights over the knocking shops even more conspicuous.

Many thoughts went through my head as we whooshed down murky alleys, none of them particularly heartening. Had they decided I was a threat and would summarily dispose of my body parts in bins around the city? Were they just being ultra-careful? Whatever their designs on me were, there was little I could do but accept my fate.

We stopped outside what looked like an abandoned building. The walls had long lost any paint that might have once clung to them. They were now covered in scrawled dyslexic graffiti, the angry outpourings of disgruntled citizens. Some of the shutters were hanging precariously off their hinges. There was no sign of life within. We went up some steps to the front door. One of the men rapped on it three times with no immediate response. Then, I could hear someone descending wooden stairs within, followed by bolts being shot back and a key turning in a lock. I was hustled inside, and the door was once again secured behind us.

I was taken to a room at the back of the house, which looked as if it had once been a functioning kitchen. The stench was horrific. The sewage must have been backing up. A camping gas stove was perched on a battered table, surrounded by the remains of takeaway food and greasy packaging. I was placed at the end of it to await interrogation or whatever it was they had in store for me.

I couldn't help feeling that they were not quite sure what to do, now that they had me in their power. They huddled around, whispering in a language I didn't understand. There appeared to be a dispute going on, but I couldn't tell what it was about.

Finally, one of them sat at the other end of the table. As soon as he spoke, I recognised Asif's brash, macho voice. "So, I bring them here. Now you pay me."

"The deal was I'd pay you if I got some results. How do I know these guys are the ones accusing Jason B?"

"I show you ID." Asif got them to produce their temporary residence permits, which he pushed across the table towards me. I recognised the names at once.

"Okay, let's talk. If I get the information I want, then you'll get your money. Tell them to sit down. Do they speak English?"

"Not good, but they understand."

He ordered them to sit down, indicating the chairs on either side of the table.

They could have been anything from fifteen to twenty-five, as no facial hair, or lack of it, was evident under the surgical masks. They looked at me silently, their dark eyes mistrustful and devious.

"I am not here to bribe you to make a false statement in court," I began. "Or to ask you to withdraw your accusations. I am here simply to find out the truth."

"How much you pay?" said one of them.

I could tell from his voice that he was no more than a teenager, young, greedy, and impatient.

"It all depends on what *you* give *me*. If I am fully satisfied that you are telling the truth then I will give you five hundred."

"How you know we tell truth?"

"I'm an actor. I can tell," I bluffed. "If what you tell me happens to be in Jason B's favour and you are prepared to testify to that in court then I'll give you an extra five hundred." I had no idea how much would satisfy them, but I imagined they would consider one thousand quite a large sum of money. "However, if Jason raped you, as you claim, I won't try to get you to change your testimony. He needs to pay for his crime. Do you understand?"

They both looked at Asif, who clarified what I said. "They understand," he said.

"So, I want to hear the whole story from the beginning. I want the truth, whatever the truth is. When did you meet Jason? Under what circumstances?"

They looked at each other, whispering in their incomprehensible tongue. Then, they fidgeted silently for some time, avoiding eye contact with me. Eventually, the taller one spoke. "We want no trouble," he said timidly.

"From the moment you testified against Jason, you're in it right up to your necks, whether you like it or not. Do you want to be known for the rest of your lives as the guys Jason B raped? I wouldn't. Wipe the slate and your character clean. You'll feel a lot better for it. Besides, do you want to see an innocent man rot in jail for something he didn't do? However, if you stick to your story, I can do little about it. On the other hand, if the story you told the judge is untrue, I would be delighted to know what the real one is. So, when did you meet Jason?"

After some time, the tall one spoke again. "Jason come to Centre about six months ago. He say he start theatre group and he look for actors."

"Young men? Or women as well?"

"He take girls and boys. He say he make us big stars."

I smiled. That sounded just like Jason. "I think he was exaggerating a little. So how many were in the group?"

"Eight. Five boys, three girls."

"Did you start rehearsing a play?"

"No. He say we make our own play."

"In English?"

"He say we can use our language but we all say we want English because English very important language."

"Did you like Jason?"

They looked at each other again. Then, the shorter one spoke this time. "Jason nice guy. He make theatre fun. He say we make comedy out of tragedy. We think of funny things that happen and make them into story with happy end."

"How did that go?"

"Good. We laugh a lot…and cry a bit too."

"Do you feel the theatre group benefitted you in any way?"

They looked at me blankly.

"I mean, do you feel it helped you to come to terms with your situation?"

They looked towards Asif for interpretation. He apparently explained what I said in their language. They looked puzzled that I should ask such a question, but the smaller one responded. "Jason, I think he help me. He make me see new life possible."

"I see," I said. It was clear to me by that simple statement that Jason's intention was to help these people, not to use them.

"When did Jason invite you to his home?"

"Two, three month after we begin theatre, I think. He say he have party with big actors."

"So, you went."

"Yeah, we go," he said, looking away sheepishly.

"What was the party like?"

"Crazy. Everybody drink."

"How did you feel about that?"

"Not good but everybody do it. We think this is party in West."

"Did you have sex?"

"We say no."

"And Jason?"

"He go into room with man. Then come out looking like he have sex."

"So, Jason didn't force or encourage you to have sex with him or anyone else on that occasion?"

"No."

"He invited you to other parties." They nodded. "Why did you go?"

They thought for a moment. "We go to meet big actors," said one.

"No, we go to have fun," said the other blushingly.

"So, the next time you drank. Did you have sex?" They said nothing, just looked edgily around the room. "I want the truth. No money if I don't get the truth."

"Yeah, we have sex," said the tall one.

"With Jason?"

"No. Everybody have sex, but not Jason."

"You did have sex with Jason on another occasion?"

"No. We have sex with other guys."

"Did they force you?"

"No."

"You took drugs and alcohol on previous occasions. What was different?"

He hesitated for a moment. "Nothing different. That's what big lawyer fella tell us to say."

"Which lawyer is that now?"

"The lawyer fella from Centre."

"Why did you need a lawyer?"

"Police raid party for drugs but not find. They see us and say we illegal, say we have drugs and put us in jail."

"What did Jason do?"

"Jason no there but he come later. He say we legal but they no listen."

"Why not?"

"I don't know. They not like person with dark skin, I guess."

"So, this lawyer from the Centre came and bartered a deal to get you off the drug charge. You agree to give them Jason and he'll get you off, right?"

They shrugged their shoulders and looked away. So, that was what happened. Someone was trying to pin something on Jason. Was it some sanctimonious do-gooder at the Centre who wanted to see Jason out of the picture? Or was it someone in high places who had a score to settle with him?

"We get our money now?" said the tall one unashamedly, undeterred by his inadvertent confession.

"Well, you've certainly earned some of it. Are you interested in the rest?"

"What we do for that?"

"Withdraw your testimony."

I could hear a sharp intake of breath.

"We can't do that. Lawyer man promise we won't go to prison if we say Jason rape us."

"Did they find drugs on you?"

"No. We have no drugs."

"So, they're just bluffing. They're after Jason not you."

"And nationality? They promise us that too."

"I thought you wanted to go to Germany?"

"We want. But this country okay. Better than nothing. So, where our money?"

I took the five hundred from my pocket and laid it on the table. "You know you can have double this is if you withdraw your testimony."

They grabbed the money and ogled it as if it were pure gold.

"So?" I repeated.

They were too busy counting the money to heed my question. When they finished, one of them looked up. "We think about it."

"Don't think about it for too long. Jason's trial is next week. Now, if you decide to withdraw your testimony, I cannot be seen giving you money because it will look like a bribe. So, I will have to give it to Asif on the quiet after the trial. Are you happy with that?"

They hesitated for a moment and then said, "Okay. We think about it."

I gave Asif his money and we left the building. I thought they were going to march me back to the underground station. Then, suddenly I realised I was alone. I looked around to see where they went but they had disappeared as furtively as they appeared.

I wondered whether the money I offered was sufficient to induce them to withdraw their statements. However, I had learnt enough for Victor S to work with. I was sure he could somehow use it to Jason's advantage. There was no question of their being unwilling participants in Jason's games. They knew exactly what it was all about, and no coercion was involved. They voluntarily attended the parties and took alcohol and drugs. Would this make any difference?

It was abundantly clear to me now that it was all a set-up to get Jason out of the picture, one that involved the Centre's lawyer and someone in the DA's office. How was Victor S going to prove it? Who was paying the lawyer and why did they have to resort to such underhand tactics?

When I got home. I checked to see what the age of consent was in countries around the world and was surprised to find out that in Austria, for example, it was only fourteen, while in most countries it was either fifteen or sixteen. Surely Victor S could get some mileage out of that.

I was so relieved with what the boys had told me that I wanted to share the information with someone. So, I rang Valerie. She picked up at once and sounded pleased to hear my voice. "Patrick, I was hoping you'd call."

"I met Jason's accusers today."

"You did?" she said apprehensively. "How did it go?"

"I was virtually abducted. I must admit I was pretty scared for a while. They took me to an abandoned house somewhere in the city. I have no idea where it was."

"You were taking an awful risk."

"It was worth it. They admitted that Jason didn't rape them. There was a lot of alcohol and drugs going around. Do you think it will make any difference, given that they were minors?"

"Hard to say but it should. What is the age of consent in this country?"

"Sixteen."

"Oh, I see. Did you hear that someone else has accused Jason of rape?"

"Damn it, really? He took his time about coming forward."

"Well, he's a she now. Apparently, it happened ten years ago before she had a sex change. You may have heard of her. She's a budding actress now, Suzy Queen."

"I can't say I have."

"She was in that TV series, *Goodbye Mama*. She played the part of the wayward elder daughter."

"Sorry. I didn't watch it."

"You didn't miss much. It was dire. Anyway, feel like going out for a drink?"

"Love to."

"Shall we go to Sully's place? I feel like slumming it."

"That really is slumming it, but why not? See you in about half an hour then?"

"Perfect."

Chapter Twenty-Three

Though I had been looking forward to an hour with Alice and her notes, the evening with Valerie was a pleasant interlude from self-imposed sequestration. We bumped into some friends of hers, a producer, and his wife I was vaguely acquainted with. As far as I knew, it was a chance meeting, though Valerie didn't appear surprised to see them. It did occur to me that she wanted to show me off, though God knows why. At seventy I was hardly a young stud a gal would be proud to flaunt in public. Anyway, it meant I had to be sociable. Surprisingly, I quite enjoyed it. They were an affable couple, who were supportive of my desire to help Jason.

While going to the bar for drinks, I caught a glimpse of Marcus V, the actor who gave me Asif's number. I felt I should thank him for his help. At first, he pretended not to know me and then did his best to ignore me. The others at the table also glared at me with obvious disdain. Clearly, anyone with sympathies for Jason was little better than vermin in their books.

I could have just walked away but I believed Marcus V might be able to help me with something else that had been bothering me. So, I insisted. "Can I have a word with you, Marcus?"

"What is it, Mr G? It's been a long day and I'm trying to chill with my friends here."

"I just wanted to ask you something. In private, if you don't mind."

Marcus V grudgingly got to his feet, and we went into an alcove outside of earshot.

"I want to thank you for introducing me to Asif. My meeting with him proved very fruitful."

"For God's sake, Patrick, I told you not to make contact with me in public," he said in an irate whisper.

"Yeah, I'm sorry. I just saw you here and…"

"What do you want?"

"Have you any idea who might want Jason put away?"

"I can think of any number of people, but you obviously have someone in mind?"

"The boys were told by the Refugee Centre's lawyer to claim Jason raped them, in exchange for their dropping a bogus drug charge. Naturally, they agreed. But someone must have put the Centre's lawyer up to it. Have you any idea who that could be?"

"All I know is that when it came out about Jason's wild parties the Board were not happy with him doing a theatre group at the Centre. They knew that sooner or later the shit would hit the fan and some of it would end up in their faces, which is exactly what happened. Of course, they have denied any knowledge of his private life, so the Centre has come through it unscathed. Fortunately, media attention has entirely focused on Jason."

"Why didn't they just scratch the theatre group? I'm sure they could have found some excuse."

"Give the Director of the National Theatre the boot? You must be joking. People would ask questions. Besides, I think some of the more puritanical members were very keen to see him put away for good."

"How do you know?"

"My mother is on the Board... Please, Patrick, do not involve her. She prides herself on being an upstanding member of the community."

"I know."

"She's devoted years to charity work. The whole business with Jason is bad enough but if it gets out that the Board conspired to bring charges against him it could turn into a massive scandal."

"If it's true, it can't remain under wraps. You must know that. We're talking about Jason's life here."

Marcus V looked at me imploringly. "Patrick, I've done my best to help you, the least you can do is keep me and my mother out of this."

"Don't worry, Marcus. I'll do my best not to involve you. I'm sorry for taking you away from your friends. I know I'm pretty much persona non grata at the moment. So, I promise that if I need to contact you again it'll be by phone."

"I'd be grateful, Patrick. Sorry about the charade earlier but, as you know, in the theatre business your career depends largely on who you know, or don't know. If public opinion goes against you, you've had it. If it got out that I'd been helping Jason, even indirectly, I'd be lucky to get a job delivering coffee."

"I understand. You've been incredibly helpful. Thanks to you I found out that Jason did not rape those boys."

Marcus V stared at me in surprise. "Really? You know, I'm very glad to hear that. I've never thought much of his private life, but I have nothing against him personally. He's always struck me as a pretty decent guy."

We parted company and I went back to Valerie and her friends. They seemed surprised that I should know Marcus V, a rising star in film and theatre. "Was he one of your students, Patrick?"

"No, long after my time. He did me a favour and I wanted to thank him, that's all." They must have wondered why I needed a full ten minutes to say thank him.

~ * ~

The following day, I needed to contact Victor S a.s.a.p. I wondered whether I should wait till seven o'clock in the evening, his preferred time. The clock was ticking, so I decided to call him a little after noon, possibly to catch him during his lunch break. It would also give me time to look at another of Alice's sessions with Jason.

'Professionally, no one could have been more successful than Jason. He received rave reviews as well as any number of awards both as an actor and director. However, I suspected his emotional life was in a mess. I asked him if he felt the love he felt for Rafi for anyone else.

He hesitated, looking at me with a slightly bowed head, gauging how I might react to what he was about to say. "Alice," he said, "I'm not sure I should tell you this, but you did take me on as your client - against your better judgement, I know - so I can't hide anything from you now."

"No, definitely not," I said, completely unsuspecting of what he was about to reveal. "I made it clear from the very beginning, there can be no secrets between a therapist and her client."

"In that case," he said at once. "I must tell you everything. I fell in love with Andrew the first day we met, and I realise now that he was the only *person I have ever truly loved."*

I tried not to show my astonishment. I had no inkling whatsoever of his feelings for Andrew. He hid it completely from me, and from Patrick too, I presume. I wondered if even Andrew knew. I had to ask. "Did Andrew know?"

His eyes began to brim with what I can only suppose were real tears. "I like to think he loved me, though it was completely Platonic."

I suddenly realised it had been a terrible mistake taking Jason on as a client. If I had known about his feelings for Andrew, I would never have agreed, but I suppose I should have anticipated such an eventuality. I was totally unprepared for this. I was at a loss how to proceed. I expected there was a lot more to be divulged about his relationship with Andrew that I did not want to hear. It meant revisiting our darling boy, those awful days before and after his death. I wasn't sure I could bear it. Like unrequited love, the death of a child is something you can never come to terms with. Patrick and I tried to rationalise Andrew's loss as best we could. We searched in vain for someone or something to blame other than ourselves. Yet, we could not escape the guilt, which made the loss that much harder to endure. When Andrew died, I know that part of me died too, and I believe parts of me will go on dying as the unremitting grief eats away at my vital organs. I was now suddenly terrified of what else might come to light. Yet, having initiated Jason's therapy (and made so much progress) I believed I had no choice but to carry on regardless.

I breathed in deeply and asked him to tell me about his relationship with Andrew. "Alice, this won't be easy for either of us. Andrew knew how I felt about him, which made our relationship very difficult, but also very special. On the one hand, he didn't want to give me false hope. On the other hand, he was unwilling to hurt me by rejecting me."

"In many ways, it might have been better if he had. I became obsessed with him. I realise now that it was a morbid, implacable obsession. In fact, I wonder how I managed to hold down my job. He was in my thoughts all the time. I was insanely jealous—which was totally unjustified because I knew that in his way, he would always remain loyal, both as friend and brother— for I did see him as my brother too. I was so afraid he was going to be snapped up by some Hollywood producer and I would never see him again. Or that he

might succumb to some female's advances and no longer want to spend time with me. In my attempt to keep him near me, I destroyed him, Alice, not consciously perhaps, but bit by bit, slowly but surely, I extinguished the shining star till it was nothing but a burnt-out shell, only visible to my tainted night vision. I know you will hate me for it and I will understand if you want to terminate our therapy."

I couldn't believe my ears. He was virtually telling me that he had killed our son. If it were true, then of course I would hate him. How could I not? Yet, what did he mean when he said he had destroyed Andrew? Was it merely a figure of speech? I was presented with the most testing dilemma of my life. I felt the instinctive urge to think like a mother, to stand up for my own, to reject the traitor who had insinuated himself into our home and destroyed our son. However, I knew I had to act like a therapist. Yet even that role was not totally clear-cut. Jason was like a son to me, whether he had a hand in destroying Andrew or not, he came to me, his surrogate mother and therapist, for help. Despite an almost overwhelming desire to banish him, both as a son and client, duty held me back. "Why do you say you destroyed Andrew, Jason?"

"I poisoned his life in every way, so that he would need me and always come back to me. I never gave up hope that we would one day be lovers. It was my sole aspiration in life. Even my work was of secondary importance. He had a brilliant career ahead of him. He had Patrick's name and his own considerable talent, but he was not pushy. He didn't know how to sell himself. As I advanced and gained more influence, I was able to hold back his career by insinuating to directors and producers he was unreliable, that he had a drinking problem or was into drugs. He would come to me in great despair after being rejected for a part and ask for an explanation, which of course I was unable to give.

"The irony is he always came to me because I would always make myself available to commiserate with him, console him and...put my arms around him. He knew I loved him. What he didn't know was that I was secretly and remorselessly maligning his character so that I was the only one in the whole world in whom he could find solace. In the end, when he almost gave up hope of ever doing anything significant in film or theatre, he did everything he could to further my career. He lived through me, vicariously

enjoying my successes, rejoicing in my awards. He came to my rehearsals, offering me invaluable advice, suggesting ways to improve my performance or my directing. If he could not succeed himself, he said, he would do everything in his power to help me reach the top, which of course I did, in the end."

At this point, he broke down, clasping his head in both hands and wailing like a bereaved mother, but I could feel no sympathy for him. My heart had turned to stone.

"He was the kindest, gentlest person I have ever known," he stammered between sobs. "And I killed him. After he was gone, life was not worth living. From there on, it was all downhill for me."

I was seeing a Jason I did not know, a Jason full of evil and self-interest, conspiratorial and ruthless in his endeavour to achieve his ends. I was no longer sure whether his emotional outbursts were genuine or mere charades to gain my sympathy. How could he have destroyed the only person he claims to have truly loved? I was so overwhelmed by what he told me that I felt faint. I could no longer continue and curtailed the session ten minutes before the end. As I made my excuses, he asked if he should come the following week at the usual time. I didn't answer at once. The mother, the surrogate mother and the therapist fought it out in my head. In the end, the therapist prevailed, and I agreed to meet him next week at the same time.'

I was utterly confounded by what I read. Was this the Jason we nurtured and showered with love all these years? Had we been harbouring a viper in our midst? Surely not? There must be an explanation. I wanted to read on, but I had to speak to Victor S first. Though, after what I had just read, I was tempted to let justice, or should I say injustice, take its course. Maybe that's what I should have done right from the start.

Yet, whatever he did to our son, I couldn't stand by and allow him to be condemned for something he hadn't done. In part at least, I believe he was already paying for the evil he had done to Andrew. All the drugs and rampant sex, were they not just a way of escaping from his nagging conscience? Of course, I could not be sure but the night he entered my house seeking my help I believe I saw a Jason weighed down by guilt and depression, not so much for what he had been accused of but for what he had done to Andrew. It all made so much sense now.

Darling Alice. What you must have been through. To relive Andrew's death and to find out that your 'adopted' son had a hand in his downfall. Keeping it all to yourself...but you were always a stickler for client confidentiality. Oh, my darling girl, why couldn't you have bent the rules just that once and shared your misery with me? I would willingly have borne some of the pain. I knew that Andrew's death was eating away at you, but Jason's confessions must surely have accelerated the disease. How could I ever forgive him for that?

I made a cup of coffee to give myself time to get over the shock. How was I going to face Jason? Would he not see the revulsion in my eyes? It would require a great deal of self-indoctrination to remain impartial. Was I capable of convincing him that my feelings for him had not changed? I must admit I was very close to abandoning Jason to his fate. All my enthusiasm was fast receding along with the euphoria I felt when I discovered he had not raped those boys.

Still, I had to hold out a glimmer of hope that his 'confession' to Alice was in some way an overstatement and that it was not exactly as he had put it. I had to believe that deep down he was not the monster he portrayed. Otherwise, there was no way I could continue to fight on his behalf. Call it self-deception, call it naivety, call it my inability to distinguish between fact and fiction - I still had many pages of Alice's notes to read—like the emotional need of someone reading a romantic novel I wanted to believe that a happy end was still possible.

With a heavy heart, I rang Victor S. I waited some time for him to pick up but he did eventually. "I've got some very important information, Victor, that could be a game changer in Jason's case."

"Haven't you heard? There's been another accusation of rape."

"Which happened ten years ago."

"It doesn't matter."

"Does this mean there's going to be a second trial?"

"Most likely, if the charge sticks."

"Surely, this Suzy person is just after a bit of cheap publicity?"

"Quite possibly, but it must be taken seriously until proved otherwise. Things don't look good, Patrick. So, I hope you have something very solid to give me."

The Return of the Dissolute Son

"I do. The boys admitted…"

"Not on the phone. An assistant will pick you up by taxi at around seven. She'll know where to find me."

"Is this cloak and dagger stuff really necessary?"

"Believe me, it is. If there's even a hint that you have interfered in any way whatsoever in Jason's case, it could ruin any chances we have of getting him off. So, seven, at the south end of your street. When you see the taxi arriving, hail it to make it look as if you aren't expecting it."

"If that's what you say, Victor."

"No harm in being cautious. We can't afford to make even the slightest mistake."

I looked at the date on my mobile. Only four days left before Jason's trial. Would Victor have time to prepare his case?

Then, I realised it was Friday and I had arranged to visit Jason that afternoon. Would it give me enough time to prepare myself psychologically? I had no choice. It was not something I could reschedule, and I had to see him at least once more before the trial and the sooner the better.

I had planned to read another of Alice's sessions but now I wasn't sure I could face more 'revelations.' I decided to put it off until after my visit to the prison.

Chapter Twenty-Four

I made myself a simple lunch and then lay down for an hour. I couldn't sleep. All the nervous energy in my body was making me jittery. Before a first night, I would walk through the play in my head a hundred times responding to the cues of the other actors. In this case, however, I could only imagine what my interlocutor would say. Yet, despite all that I learned about Jason from Alice's notes, I was unable to put evil words into his mouth or even heinous thoughts into his head. As much as I wanted to, I still had difficulty seeing Jason in an unfavourable light.

I read about sociopathic obsessions before, about successful professionals or quite ordinary people, whose colleagues or friends would never have suspected they could harm a fly, let alone carry out a malicious act. Yet, when the doctor's secretary, I. J., was arrested for throwing vitriol into an imagined rival's face, disfiguring her for life, they all said, 'Yes, I always thought there was something odd about her.' I've no doubt they would find something odd about all of us after the event. So, where did Jason's all-consuming obsession come from? Did it stem from some compelling need? Was it simply a way to get back at his early life, which had treated him so cruelly? His victim, the object of his passion, could have been anyone, I suppose. It just happened to be Andrew.

Could Alice and I have prevented it? Were we not close enough to either of our boys? I was aware that having a successful father was always a burden for Andrew. Sons in particular feel the need to emulate, or even outstrip, their fathers. Was he frightened by the idea of failure or was he more frightened of having to admit it to me? When he saw he was failing, instead of coming to me for help, he went to the person whose arms were forever open to receive him, the person he could always rely on to utter reassuring words. Perhaps it was better he never knew how he had been cheated out of a career and a life.

Of course, Andrew was not an ambitious man. He never had been. He tended to let circumstances determine the direction in which his life would go. I believe his need to succeed was more for our sake than his. I can only hope that he gained as much, if not more, satisfaction in having a hand in achieving Jason's ill-fated glory. At least he did not have to see its demise.

All these thoughts went through my head as I lay awake on my bed, but without Alice I could arrive at no conclusion. For today, at least, I said to myself, I would have to keep an open mind, whatever subversive thoughts were trying to undermine my endeavour to be positive about Jason.

I grudgingly got up and left for the prison.

~ * ~

I sat at the bare table in the visitors' room imagining Jason sitting opposite me. I went through the act of smiling and making impromptu hand and head movements, but they seemed wooden and forced.

The sharp click of the electrically operated door struck the side of my head like a blunt object, temporarily stunning me. I did not look up. I was unable to watch him approach. Instead, I tried to conjure up an image of the old Jason.

I could hear the chair scraping across the laminate floor and the shuffling of feet as he prepared to sit. I waited for him to speak before raising my head.

"Patrick, you look tired. I hope you haven't been moonlighting on my behalf."

I forced a smile. "I've been trying my best."

"I appreciate all that you're doing for me, but I'm afraid it's a foregone conclusion," he said with the nonchalance of someone who had not only accepted his fate but was almost looking forward to it.

"Not necessarily," I said. "I contacted Asif, who set up a meeting with me and the two boys."

"You mean Ali and Hassan? Christ. How the hell did you do that?"

"Through Marcus V."

"Ah, Marcus V. I always liked him. But how…?"

"Money. The great persuader. They haven't promised anything but they're thinking about altering their statements. There is of course this Suzy person. You are aware of who she is, I suppose?"

"She—or was she a he then?—was quite a handful. She was so keen to get a part in a play I was directing at my old school she virtually raped me. It wasn't easy to resist her but fortunately I did. Obviously, she still entertains wild dreams."

"Rape or no rape, it's going to be hard to prove after ten years, surely?"

"I should think so but as Victor S pointed out it's not an isolated case. God knows how many more supposed victims will jump onto the bandwagon."

"Are there more?" I asked tentatively.

"They're still hatching," he replied with a wry smile.

"I'm seeing Victor S this evening. I don't know if he'll be able to use the information I've gathered but... Oh, I also found out that the Refugee Centre had a hand in having you charged. The boys were forced into making a plea bargain. You or them. Did you know that?"

"No. I had no idea."

"Did you ever meet their lawyer?"

"Percy. T. What a swine. He's capable of anything."

"It will all depend on whether Ali and Hassan are prepared to retract."

"On what they've been promised. If Victor S can prove they were offered immunity and nationality, it shows they were not entirely disinterested in their readiness to accuse me."

"But can he? I'm afraid it could go either way."

"I'm not holding out much hope, Patrick. Not only the judicial system but the whole of society is against me, it seems. They want me to pay for the crimes of generations, in the hope that it will absolve them of their sins. I am the lamb being prepared for the sacrificial slaughter."

"We have to believe in the justice system," I said pathetically.

He smiled at my ingenuousness and laughed, as I would have done.

"But I haven't been wasting my time here. I've got palsy-walsy with this narcotics trader who's pretty high up in the cartel hierarchy. It appears he has some beef with a couple of guys near the top who blackmailed him into taking a fall to save their asses. He's been blabbing away to me as if I were his father confessor. It's strange how celebrity status seems to inspire confidence. Or perhaps it has to do with the intimacy of a prison cell. Anyway, he claims it was one of those guys who put out a contract on Andrew."

I sighed and turned away. "I'm not sure I really want to go there, Jason. It's too disturbing. Scratching old wounds."

"But you said…"

"I know what I said but it's not going to bring Andrew back."

"Right, but vindication can bring closure. I would willingly put out a contract on the guy who ordered Andrew's murder. Apparently, he's doing time in a prison up country. If I'm lucky enough to be incarcerated there, I might even do it myself."

I looked at him in dismay. I could see he was serious. Was it guilt speaking or were they the words of someone who had nothing to lose? "We're fighting to get you out of here, not so that you can go and kill someone."

"Patrick, I know you're a peace-loving man. If you knew the name of the guy who had Andrew killed, wouldn't you want to seek revenge? Especially when you know that is the only way that justice will be done?"

I thought about it for a moment. "I don't think so, Jason. There would be a strong temptation certainly, but what would I gain in the long run? Temporary gratification? Just to spend the rest of my life looking over my shoulder?"

"Yes, but think of the satisfaction it would give you!"

"It would soon wear thin, I think. No, there comes a time when you must let bygones be bygones."

"That's you, Patrick, and I admire your ability to put things behind you, but I can't. I loved Andrew."

"I know," I said, looking at him coldly.

"You know? Alice told you?"

I had to lie. "I could tell."

"Really? I knew you were a perceptive man, Patrick, but I clearly underestimated you."

We studied each other for a few moments trying to gauge each other's sincerity.

"There's one other thing I have to ask you before they kick me out,"

I said. "It would help your case considerably if Victor S could tell the court that you were in therapy with Alice. They might ask to see her notes, though. Would you be alright with that...if I can find them? I still haven't got round to clearing out her office."

Jason looked at me intently, defying me to look away. Was he trying to ascertain whether I had read her notes? "No, Patrick. I would not want those notes to become public knowledge. I told her everything there was to know about me, both good and bad, mostly bad. I put my life in her hands." His lower lip juddered uncontrollably for a moment or two. "Because I believed she was the only one who could save me, Patrick. Sadly, it was not to be. She kept going as long as she could, for my sake, I think, but in the end, it was too much for her. She was hardly able to walk from her chair to the lift unaided."

"You don't have to tell me, Jason. She insisted on going to the office, despite my entreaties. I drove her there, in fact, against my better judgement. She said, 'There is too much at stake.' She never told me what it was exactly, but I guessed it had to do with you."

"I went a bit crazy when she died. I had already lost Andrew. Then I lost Alice. I had put so much hope in both of them."

"You still had me, Jason. Why didn't you reach out?"

"I think I was ashamed. I bled them dry. I even felt that I may have been partly responsible for their deaths. I didn't want to do the same to you."

"I was always there for you. Surely you knew that?"

"I wasn't sure what Alice had told you...whether confidentiality applied between husband and wife."

"It did with Alice, I assure you."

A bell rang and a warden's authoritative voice ordered all the prisoners to leave the visiting room in an orderly fashion.

~ * ~

I left the prison with a heavy heart, not sure whether I would be able to see him again before the trial. I still found it hard to believe he callously destroyed Andrew. I needed to read more of Alice's notes to be sure.

It was a dark, chilly early spring evening as I trudged down my suburban street. I felt like a Cold War spy about to hand over vital information to the other side. I didn't want to get Marcus V and his mother into trouble but there was a strong likelihood they would have to be called as witnesses if Victor S was to establish Jason had been set up. I only hoped it wouldn't be necessary. I kept glancing around to make sure I was not being followed by paparazzi or spied on by long-range cameras hidden behind garden fences. I realised I was becoming paranoid.

I didn't have long to wait. A taxi appeared almost the second I reached the end of the street. I hailed it, as I was told to do. The back door was opened, and I got in. I was pleased to see that sitting next to me was the attractive young secretary I had shared pleasantries with during my incursion into Victor S's office a few days earlier.

"Mr. G, so nice to see you again," she said with a sparkling smile. She must have had a very good orthodontist, I thought. "I'm glad you didn't have to pitch your tent outside our building. Jan, our security guard, would have had a shit freak."

I smiled at her teenage phraseology.

"I think Victor S quite enjoys all this hugger-muggery," she added. "It gets him out of the office."

I laughed. I liked this girl. She was as sharp as a pin and a past master at lightening an oppressive atmosphere.

We took a meandering route through the city. At some point I had no idea where we were or where we were going. As we turned down one dark alley after another, the bright little secretary gave me an 'oh, here we go again' look, raising her meticulously groomed eyebrows in jocular frustration.

Victor S's Mercedes was parked under a bridge, as yet empty of the city's homeless, who gathered there soon after nightfall. I was instructed to get out of the taxi and join Victor S in the back seat.

As I slid in beside him over the shiny leather upholstery, I was hit by a blast of stiflingly warm air and expensive eau de Cologne.

"Patrick, what do you have for me?" he demanded.

No beating about the bush for Victor S.

"I visited Jason today."

"Good. Now give me what you've got."

I told him everything I gleaned from the boys and Marcus V. "Do you think this might help Jason's case?" I asked.

"Not if it gets out you met the boys and offered them money."

"They were offered a deal by the Refugee Centre's lawyer. I was merely trying to get at the truth."

"The trouble is no one knows what the truth is any more. Are you sure the boys were not just telling you what you wanted to hear to make sure they got the money?"

I hadn't considered that possibility but at the time their confessions seemed genuine. "I believe they were telling the truth. It was almost as if they were sorry for what they did. I think they were aware of how much working on the play with Jason helped them, psychologically, I mean. They didn't say that as such, but it sounded as if the theatre group gave them some support. From what I can gather, Jason was doing a form of psychodrama with them. I know he took an extended course on it in the past."

Victor S was busy taking notes, getting rather frustrated because of the poor light in the back of the car. "Damn it, Patrick. I've forgotten how to use a pen and my eyesight has gone to the dogs. What you've just told me could prove very useful. At least it shows that his motivation for helping these boys was ostensibly selfless. Why the hell did he invite them to his parties? He must have realised the risk he was taking…and the temptation, given his proclivities."

"I think he genuinely wanted to give them a good time. You know what Jason is like. He won't talk about it."

"He seems incapable of thinking like a prosecuting lawyer. If they get him on the stand, they'll tear him to pieces."

"He needs to be coached. If only I can get him to see the trial as a performance, in which he has to convince his audience of his innocence. In that way, it might make some sense to him. Today, when I saw him, he seemed indifferent to his fate. It was almost as if he wanted to atone for something. Maybe he realises that it was wrong to expose those boys to all the temptations available at his parties. Or maybe it was something else. I don't know." I didn't want to go into his relationship with Andrew. It had nothing to do with Victor S or Jason's case. "Oh, and he doesn't want Alice's notes produced in court. He says they're too personal."

"Obviously their content is confidential, but we may need to verify that the notes are in Alice's handwriting."

"That should be easy enough."

"Now, Patrick, I want you to keep a low profile. Don't go near this Asif person or the boys again. Not until this is all over. I may need you to see Jason again before the trial. How about Monday afternoon? I'll arrange it all. I think you are the only person who can convince him to take this whole thing seriously. Now he's lost the theatre, he seems to have created a whole new agenda, which could turn out to be very self-destructive."

I agreed but said nothing. I decided not to mention Jason's threat to kill the man who put a contract out on Andrew. It was too far-fetched for anyone to take seriously. Nobody in their right mind would believe that Jason wanted to be convicted so that he would have an opportunity to kill Andrew's killer, but was Jason in his right mind? When he got something into his head, he became like someone possessed. He wasn't able to let go until he achieved his aims.

Chapter Twenty-Five

The taxi driver waited and took me home after my meeting with Victor S. Sadly, the chirpy little secretary changed cars. I could have done with her spirited chatter. Instead, I was left alone with my uninspiring reflections on life. I thought of Alice and how I missed her native wisdom. Even though I was often loath to admit it, she was invariably right about most things. We had our differences, of course. What couple doesn't?

I liked to think I was the centre of her life, as she was the heart and hub of mine. I now know that I wasn't. Her work took precedence. As she said herself, her clients needed her more than I did and in a way she was right. All I needed was her reassurance, love, and intuitive wisdom, all of which she gave bountifully. The rest I could take care of myself, though my sullen presence was not always my best guide.

As I entered the unheated house, it didn't feel as if I was coming home. It ceased to be a home the day Alice died. It was now a mere habitation, a place to sleep, eat and rest. For some time after her death, memories would crawl out of the woodwork, flit around like stray ghosts unsure of their domestic status, sitting on the sofa beside me or looking askance at me from a vaporous mirror. As time passed, they timidly withdrew into their lairs. The truth is I did not welcome their unholy visitations and I invariably shooed them away. Their departure left a vacuum that I could not, or would not fill, for fear of losing her forever. As a result, I remained in an emotional limbo, a kind of sensory paralysis, unable to move forwards or backwards.

I collapsed on to the sofa in front of the cold hearth and tried to elicit the timorous ghosts from wherever they were holed up, but they were unmoved by my pleas. I drove them away once too often. I was tempted to turn on the TV. However, I had no desire for vapid news or mediocre entertainment. I was no longer moved by realism but yearned for the plasticity of fiction.

I realised I had to do something soon or I would sink into one of my nihilistic states and start questioning the whole of existence. At that moment my phone rang. It was Valerie. "Hi, stranger! I've been calling all afternoon."

"Sorry, I turned my phone off in the prison and I forgot to turn it back on. It lit up at a very opportune moment. I was sinking into a rather morbid state."

"Patrick. You do know how to use a phone, I suppose? Look, I know it's late and you're probably tired so I won't drag you out tonight, but tomorrow I have the day off and I thought we could go for a ride somewhere, to the sea or the mountains—your choice. What do you say?"

"I'd love that. I need to get away for a few hours, preferably from myself, but I know that's not possible."

"I think a change of environment is what you need. What time shall I pick you up?"

"Would ten be all right?"

"Perfect. You can tell me how things went with Jason."

"Or not. I want to forget about Jason for a few hours."

"Patrick don't shut me out. I have a right to know what's going on with him. Have you forgotten that he's partly my son too?"

"Yeah, I'm sorry, Valerie. You're not the first person to get angry with me for not sharing. Just blame my stiff-upper-lip upbringing."

"I don't want you to feel that you're alone in this. I honestly care about Jason, but above all I care about you."

I was taken aback by what I discerned in her words. I didn't know how to respond for fear of making a fool of myself. Yet, there was also a part of me that refused to believe she was professing her affection for me, possibly because it was too much for someone of my age to hope for. Furthermore, Alice was still very much present in my life, and I wasn't sure there was room for someone else. I was suddenly bombarded by a series of unanswerable questions. Was she falling in love with me? Was I capable of loving her back? Would Alice always come between us?

"Patrick? Are you still there?"

"Yes, sorry. It's fatigue kicking in."

"I must let you rest then. Sleep well and see you tomorrow."

"Yes, yes. I'll look forward to that," I said in a dazed voice.

After I hung up, I kicked myself for being so offhand. I hoped I didn't sound indifferent or ungrateful. I knew I should have felt lucky to have someone who cared about me, whatever her true feelings for me were.

I needed to fall into a deep slumber in the hope that a new and brighter day would dawn on my awakening. I poured myself a long whiskey and began to read Hardy's The Three Strangers for the umpteenth time. Fate (today they call it DNA), chance and circumstance, the three elements that determine our existence.

~ * ~

I woke up feeling reasonably refreshed, despite a rather disturbed night, not that there was anything unusual about that. I looked out of the window and saw a clear blue sky, ideal for a brisk walk before breakfast.

After clearing away the breakfast things I saw I had a good hour before Valerie's arrival. Though I had been dreading it, I knew I had to read Alice's notes to the end. Yet, it was like re-living the pain of those last days before she was admitted to hospital. I poured myself a cup of tea and settled down at my desk.

'The doctors tell me I don't have long to live. I've been trying to keep it from Patrick, though I think he suspects. Besides, my failing state constantly betrays my deterioration, but I will continue for as long as I can. What good would it do mourning my fate at home? Being concerned for others' pain allows me to temporarily forget my own. Jason has been constantly on my mind since our last session. I must do my best for him but to do that I have to vanquish all thoughts of animosity. Above all, I must remain objective, treat him as I would any other client, however difficult that will be.

He said he did not consciously destroy Andrew and I must take him at his word. Andrew, after all, was not a child. It was his choice to let his defences drop and submit to Jason's will. Yet, it is important that I know the full story. So, I asked Jason to tell me what led to Andrew's conviction, incarceration, and death. I was surprised at his eagerness to tell his story and it occurred to me that this was possibly the reason why he came to me in the first place. I got the impression he was riddled with guilt and regret, which weighed heavily upon him, like a monolith he could no longer carry around alone. The following is what he told me:

"For a time, we were inseparable. My love for him was returned to me in the form of hero worship. He saw me as a kind of idol. A theatrical Midas. Everything I touched in the theatre turned to gold. I even began to think that I was in some way invulnerable, that I could live a life of drugs and sex yet remain untouched by the world.

At first, Andrew watched, reluctant to participate. As you know, by nature he was shy and cautious. Then, slowly he began to join in with the rest of us. Our parties invariably turned into rampant orgies. It was not long before he began to lose control. The drugs allowed him to overcome his inhibitions and to commit acts he would not normally have contemplated. I must admit I was worried because I began to see a radical change in his personality and behaviour. He became reckless and irresponsible, less caring about himself and others. He was becoming another person. He was no longer the Andrew I loved.

For a time, I called a halt. No more wild parties. It wasn't long before he started protesting. I told him it was for his own good, but he rejected what he called 'my mollycoddling fretfulness,' saying I was not his keeper, and I had no right to treat him like a child. I tried to find other ways to entertain him. Yet, it was clear he was hooked on drugs and sex. They were the only things that made any sense to him now. After all, he had nothing else, no career, no permanent relationship, no prospects. I had seen to that. I told him if he didn't clear up his shit I would have nothing more to do with him. He laughed in my face and went looking for other parties. It wasn't long before friends started calling me in the middle of the night asking where I was, that I should come and pick up my 'friend,' who was totally out of it.

As he had no income, he was virtually dependent on me. So, one day we had a terrible row. I told him I would give him no more money unless he agreed to go into rehab - I was convinced his addiction was going to kill him. He told me to piss off and left in a huff. I was desperately worried, but I realised I could not force him to do something against his will. Then, one day he left and didn't come back the next morning. I had no idea where he was. He completely disappeared. I was frantic. Any free time I had, I spent searching for him. I went to every crack house and drug den in the city. Eventually I found him. He was in a terrible state. At first, he begged me to take him back, but my answer was the same, 'only if he agreed to go into rehab,' which I offered to pay for. Presenting him with this ultimatum was probably the worst mistake of my life.

I expected him to give in to blackmail, as I thought I saw in his eyes a yearning to be saved, but apparently, he was now supporting himself by selling drugs and he no longer needed me. He was living on a knife's edge, eating badly and ingesting substances that were rapidly destroying his mind and body. He was also mixing with desperate, unscrupulous people, who would kill at the least provocation. He seemed totally unaware of the danger he was in. Or perhaps he didn't care. All he cared about was making enough money for his next fix. I suppose I should have told you and Patrick, but I blamed myself for the state he was in and felt it was up to me to get him out of it.

By now, we were totally estranged, and I had lost all the influence I once had over him. So, I decided to arrange a party and asked him to supply the drugs. As it was a business arrangement, he agreed. At about ten o'clock that night, my place was raided by the police. Anyone found in possession of drugs was arrested, including Andrew. I did my best to plead with the officers. I even played the celebrity card, but it didn't work. They were determined to make an arrest and it appeared that their primary target was Andrew. I later found out why.

At the time I wasn't too worried. In fact, I kind of hoped that this would bring Andrew to his senses. In detention he would be forced to undergo cold turkey and possibly then be able to see things in a different light. I saw it as an opportunity for him to clean himself up. I would hire the best lawyer and devote any free time I had to getting him back on the straight and narrow. You see, I assumed by the time the police raided my flat he had got rid of most of the drugs and whatever they found on him he could claim was for personal use. However, it turned out that he still had large quantities in his pockets. Afterwards, I found out it was a set-up and that they had their eye on him for some time. They were just looking for a chance to catch him in delicto flagrante. It occurred to me later that they may even have planted the drugs on him to make their charges stick.

Of course, you were informed about his arrest and together we found Victor S to defend him. Even at this stage I was convinced he'd be let off with a warning. After all, it was a first offence and he was Patrick's son. Victor S was also confident that he'd get off with a light sentence. It appears the DA was under pressure from the police department to stop the spread of drug use in the richer areas of the city. They also believed that Andrew would give in to duress and hand over important names. I had always assumed Andrew was a small-time street dealer but it appears the bosses saw potential in him, as he was able to infiltrate the wealthier strata of society. So, he was in possession of facts, figures, and names that the ordinary peddler would not have been. The drug bosses were aware of this too. They knew that sooner or later he would buckle under interrogation. So, they arranged his 'suicide' before he got the chance to grass on them.

When I found out about his death I was devastated. Only the day before, I visited him jail. He told me he was finished with drugs, that he was going to start a new life and wanted me to help him get back on his feet. In fact, he was going to embark on an anti-drug campaign and write a book about his experiences. He had seen too many lives destroyed, not least his own. The police were prepared to make a deal and offered him witness protection. It would mean having to disappear for a while, but he didn't mind. He wanted to get as far away from his old life as possible. The next time I saw him he was lying bloodless in a coffin."

Jason bowed his head and covered his face with his hands to hide the tears streaming down his cheeks. Between sobs, he said, "The day he died was the day my life ended."

I wanted to say that my life ended on that day too, but I didn't. I know losing my darling boy triggered my illness, and my inability to come to terms with it is now slowly sucking the life out of me. I was so distraught I was unable to speak. I desperately wanted to let it all out, to explode in a flood of tears, but I had to be strong. I had to maintain my role as therapist. Had our son died in vain? Was Jason to blame? Would things have been different if Jason had told us earlier of Andrew's situation? There were so many questions I needed to answer as a mother before I could continue as a therapist. So, I simply got up, held him in my arms for a moment or two and told him we would meet next week as usual.'

Jason told me smatterings of these events so it did not come as a complete surprise to me, but I could only imagine the effect it had on Alice. I remember that day very clearly. It was when I picked her up early from the office because I was worried about her. It was about a month before her death. She hardly said a word in the car on the way home. I assumed she was tired but it was not unusual for her to remain tight-lipped as she ran over the day's sessions in her head. I remember making her a cup of tea when we got home, which she left undrunk. She pleaded fatigue and I helped her to get ready for bed. I offered to make her a light supper, but she said she was not hungry. At the time, I remember wondering whether that would be her last day at the office. As it turned out, it wasn't. She managed to make it twice more, which meant I still had two more sessions to read.

I looked at my watch. Valerie would arrive at any minute. I had to try to be cheerful, though I felt far from joyous. I was already on the pavement waiting when she pulled up. Her bright face immediately lifted my spirits. I was determined to make the most of the day.

She of course asked me about Jason, and I told her an abridged and slightly expurgated version of what he told Alice. Perhaps for fear of losing any remaining sympathy for him, I avoided telling her some of the more damning details.

"I'm sorry," she said, turning her head towards me. "I can't imagine how awful it is to lose two sons."

"I haven't given up on Jason," I said truthfully. "I just hope Victor S does a better job of defending him than he did with Andrew."

"Do you think he was to blame for his conviction?"

"Partly. He thought he had the judges in his pocket. None of us realised Andrew was a marked man, and I'm very much afraid Jason is destined to play the same role."

We decided to go to the mountains. Valerie said she read about some quaint villages a couple of hours north of the city. We could leave the car in the square and follow the mountain path to the next village for lunch. It would take us about two hours each way, which meant we would be back before nightfall. The idea sounded perfect, especially as it appeared that spring had finally sprung. The wind had turned to the south-east, bringing with it invigorating salt-saturated air and growth.

As we made our way along the rugged path through a mixed forest of oaks, birches, maples and limes with outcrops of spruce and birch, the city seemed very far away. We crossed streams coursing down the mountainside, which required leaping from boulder to boulder to avoid getting wet. We held hands like teenagers, screaming when we nearly lost our footing, pretending we were about to topple into the crashing white water below.

After a particularly energetic climb we came to a clearing with a view right down to the sea. In the distance, a yacht moved imperceptibly across the water like a toy boat on a pond attached by string to a little boy's finger. It brought back images of a carefree, happy childhood that belonged to another life, someone else's perhaps. I began to think this whole outing was unreal and felt guilty for allowing myself such unearned pleasure.

I gathered some dry leaves and made a comfortable spot for us to sit. The sun was surprisingly hot but we lapped it up like cold-blooded creatures emerging from hibernation, craving the life-giving warmth that would resuscitate us.

"Look," she said, pointing up into the sky. A large falcon was wheeling in the currents of air in search of prey. Suddenly, it swooped down into the undergrowth, and we heard a muffled screech as it grabbed its prey. On such a day, wildlife could easily be addled by the bustling activity of fellow nature and overlook lurking danger.

"How are you feeling?" she said, laying her hand on my arm.

I turned to look at her. She was resplendent. Her cheeks took on a pinkish hue and her dark green eyes were sparkling with contentment. "Good," I replied. "Thanks to you."

"Have I succeeded?"

"I have no doubt you have but what are you referring to exactly?"

"Getting you out of yourself."

"It was a resounding success. In fact, I'm dreading having to go back there."

"Don't then. Not yet at least. Let's enjoy the present. Moments like these are so few and far between."

"Do they have to be?"

"Yes, Patrick, I think they do. If we did this every day, it would quickly lose its charm. Besides, we both love our work." She took my hand

and kneaded it gently. "This day will always be important to me," she said coyly. "I hope it will for you too."

Again, I reacted like a gauche teenager. It was such a long time since I courted a girl, it felt strangely inappropriate. "I hope we can do this again," I said ineptly.

"You know I'm falling in love with you, Patrick? Does that seem unfitting to you?"

Again, she read my mind. "It's just I don't want you to be disappointed. You don't know me well enough yet."

"Patrick, I'm not asking you to marry me. I just want to spend time with you, to get to know you better. I love your company. You're intelligent, witty and kind. We don't have to think beyond the moment. We're both too old to make plans. Let's just allow things to find their own way."

"That's exactly what I would like too."

"I know."

Women and their intuition, I thought. *We men cannot compete. Logic and reason always get in the way of a man's heart.*

The rest of the day went swimmingly. We had a beautiful lunch in the next village. Most people were eating inside, afraid of the cold, but the waiter was kind enough to put a table outside for us. So, it was as if we had hired a team of cooks and waiters to serve a three-course meal in the middle of the forest just for us. I felt very privileged.

Chapter Twenty-Six

Valerie dropped me off just after nine that evening. I think she would like to have been invited in, but I didn't want to spoil the magic of the day. There would, I hoped, be other opportunities for quiet intimacy in front of a warm fire.

I was about to get ready for an early night when Billy rang. I imagined it was a courtesy call. Before the business with Jason flared up, we had been in the habit of speaking regularly on the phone or meeting for coffee in the Bohemian part of town where he had his pad. Billy is one of those rare people who never ages, mentally at least. One always feels young in his company. He still thinks like a twenty-year-old; anti-establishment, anti-authority, anti-anything that smacks of restricted civil liberties. For Billy the world has remained an oyster, available to all, but which sometimes needs to be prised open, even if it means taking on the riot squad.

"How are you, mate? I felt guilty for not ringing you."

"No need to. I understand. Rightly or wrongly, I couldn't abandon Jason. Everyone else has."

"I should have been more understanding. I was trying to look out for my mate, that's all."

"I know you were."

"Have you made any progress?"

"Some. I'm getting to know Jason better."

"Yeah? Good or bad?"

"Some good, some bad."

"I see," he said dubiously. "Do you still want to defend him?"

"It's never been a question of defending him. All I've tried to do is understand him…and find out the truth. Like most things the truth is never absolute."

"Do you understand him better?"

"It's not easy. We're talking about a highly complex individual, who had a very solitary and emotionally deprived childhood. It's almost as if he has two personalities. I don't mean he's schizophrenic or bipolar. Although, he is very much a Dr Jekyll and Mr Hyde. I find it almost impossible to get inside his head."

"Jekyll had to be punished for what he did, however sympathetic Hyde was?"

"Yes, I don't deny that. But I'm sure what's left of his soul can be saved. With a little persuasion, I'm certain he'll go back into therapy."

"He was doing therapy?"

"Yes, with Alice. Didn't I tell you?"

"No, mate, you didn't."

"I've been reading Alice's notes and it's pretty horrific stuff, but I believe there's hope."

"Are you sure it's not just wishful thinking?"

"I haven't totally ruled out that possibility, but I don't think so."

"Look. I rang to ask if you feel like coming into town tomorrow for coffee and a natter. If it's too much of a hassle, I can come up your way."

"No, I'd like to get out of the house."

"Okay then. The usual place at around eleven?"

I was tired after all the fresh air and exercise and slept soundly for a change. I woke with a more positive outlook on life and was keen to read Alice's second-last session with Jason. I anticipated it would be painful. Her voice had been getting progressively weaker, an indication of the decline in her physical condition. There was also an awareness that her time was limited, which added to her concern that she might not be able to complete therapy with Jason. She knew he was teetering on the brink and, unless she succeeded, he could easily fall back into a life of rampant dissoluteness. I settled down on the settee with a fresh pot of tea.

'I fear that my time is up. The doctor says I should already be receiving treatment in hospital but as long as I can still bear the pain and put one foot in front of the other, I will continue. I must continue, for Jason's sake. I feel we are so close to a breakthrough, but I am worried about the effect my death may have on him. I have always been aware of his attachment to me and have played the role of surrogate mother to the best of my ability,

however uncomfortable I have felt about it. I believe I must tell him of my imminent death, though I know it may have an adverse effect on his therapy.

I need to focus now on the future, not on the past, on how he is going to cope with his remorse and Andrew's...and my...absence. I know that he has not fully rejected drugs and his wanton life. So, I asked him to imagine that if Andrew were to write a letter from the other world, what would he say?

He spent some time writing the letter, pausing to bite the end of his pen, closing his eyes, tilting his head back in deep thought. When he finished, I asked him to read it out to me. "Jason, my old friend, and dear brother, I made a mess of things, didn't I? I let my life go to hell. You were always much stronger than me. I allowed myself to be led, manipulated, and ultimately annihilated. You, on the other hand, were always untouchable. You are a survivor. I realised too late what I had done to myself and to others. I didn't appreciate your love and didn't give you credit for your efforts to help me. The truth is I reached a point where I felt life had no meaning for me. Already in my forties, I had achieved nothing. I didn't deserve to go on living.

Jason, you have a brilliant future ahead of you. Please, for my sake, turn over a new leaf. Start over. Give up drugs and young men. You must know the harm you are doing them and yourself. As you know, I am not religious but, if I were, I would say there is still time to repent. I know that you have a kind, generous soul. You proved it to me many times. However, the life we led slowly, no, quickly poisoned the soul, so that we ended up feeling nothing, trying to lose ourselves in the excesses of drugs and sexual paroxysm. I beg you Jason, now, before it's too late, give it all up. Devote yourself to the theatre, your big love. Forget about all the rest. You can do without it. You said once that you wished to do psychodrama. Do it. You have the qualifications. Find a cause and go for it. For God's sake, don't let your past life drag you back into the mire.

I am sorry I was not always your loving brother. From heaven I can see I was wrong to doubt you. Be strong, brother. You have so much to live for.

Always yours, Andrew."

I was stunned by how well Jason had captured Andrew's tone and turn of phrase. I had no doubt his love for Andrew was deep and true. I was also surprised by how well he could see his own situation and what he needed to do to emerge from the darkness into light. Would he be able to take his own advice? I asked him what the letter meant for him. I thought he'd be able to answer immediately but he seemed unable at first to interpret what he had written. It was as if Andrew had written the letter and not he.

His comments were more or less the following: "Andrew was never able to see me as I am. He saw me as strong and self-disciplined but I'm not. I'm weak, much weaker than he was. I give in to my passions knowingly. He did not. He tried to resist them and, in the end, he would have got his life back together if he survived prison. I would have helped him, I think, because I was aware of how I had destroyed his life. I'm not sure I could have parted with him. I would have tried to find ways of tethering him to me. You see, Alice, I am incurable. I could not envisage a life without Andrew. And now that he has gone, I cannot move forward, at least emotionally. I wish I could see hope. Things would be so different if he were here."

I tried to point out to him the importance of the advice that 'Andrew' gave him in his letter but all he said was that the advice was good, but he wasn't sure he could act on it. He would try. He knew an actor friend called Marcus V. He volunteered at a camp for young refugees, who in many cases were severely traumatised, suffering from PTSD. Many were lost or separated from their parents and family. He had always been interested in therapy and did an extended course in psychodrama. He believed that this might give him a chance to right some of the wrong he had done and in so doing find a more fulfilling purpose in life. His job at the National, though challenging artistically, had lost a lot of its charm. He sometimes found it a drudge, as it involved far more administrative work than he anticipated.

I am ambivalent about how the session went. I was uplifted by the letter he wrote in Andrew's name but was disheartened by his reaction to it. I have seen this so often in therapy, the ability to see what is right but the inability to act on it.

I wasn't sure how long I would be able to continue and felt it my duty to warn him. It was not easy, but I told him as gently as I could that my condition was terminal. A look of total desolation appeared on his face. It slowly dawned on him what the implications were for him. He said that he had been aware that I was not well but had no idea how ill I was. The effect on him was as I feared. He visibly shrunk into his chair and started to weep uncontrollably, stammering almost unintelligibly, 'Why, Alice? Why? Not now. Not now. I don't think I can go on without you. I feel I am at last becoming the person I have always wanted to be and now you are going to desert me. Please, Alice, tell me it isn't true."

All I could do was tell him he had to be strong, and I would recommend another therapist in whom I had complete faith. At this he laughed dryly and said, "I can't go through it all again. I don't want another therapist. You are the only person I can truly be myself with." I pointed out to him that it would merely be a continuation of the work we had done together, which of course was not entirely true.

I said it was very important we meet at least one more time and he agreed. I was not happy with the way things turned out, though there was very little I could do about it. I only hoped he would be willing to see my colleague.'

I always knew what a difficult profession Alice was in, but I had no idea how dependent a client becomes on their therapist. Alice was on the end of a lifeline she had thrown out to him. He had grabbed it, believing that she could save him. Suddenly, the lifeline snapped, just as he was about to be pulled ashore. Now, he could feel the current slowly dragging him back out to a merciless sea and he was once again confronted with the prospect of drowning.

I took the underground into town. The Coffee Pot was only a ten-minute walk from the station. It was Sunday and university students, and aging 'eternal' students were overflowing out of the coffee shops and restaurants onto the pavements. They all seemed engrossed in animated conversations. About what, I wondered? I always marvel at our ability to take life so seriously and to find meaning in our ephemeral existence. I thought of Andrew and Jason. I realised how thin the line is between passion and despair. Do we not daily walk this line, like tight-rope walkers constantly at risk of hurtling into the abyss?

Billy was sitting at a small table under the green awning of the Coffee Pot. He was smoking his favourite cigarillos. I once told him they would kill him. His answer was predictable, "I've got to die of something," and the truth is he is still very much alive. Looking deceptively young, sporting a salt-and-pepper beard, and thinning greyish hair tied back in a ponytail, he could have been a university professor fraternising with his alumni. He rose when he saw me and clapped his arms around me. We were in student territory, on neutral ground, so to speak, where everything goes, even trying to understand the mentality of an alleged paedophile and why I still loved him.

We ordered coffee and he told me about a play he was in, which had been deferred because of the Covid epidemic. He was hopeful that now with more than half the population vaccinated they would have a normal season.

"I have some good news," he said with his inscrutable smile, the smile which has largely defined his career in cinema.

"Yeah?" I said dubiously.

"They haven't found anyone for the role yet."

"But?"

"Yeah, there is a but. Before they can contact your agent, they want to be sure."

"I'm not going to turn on Jason, Billy. I've told you. You know me, I'm almost as stubborn as you are."

"Don't I know it? They aren't asking you to do anything. It will all depend on the outcome of the trial. If Jason is convicted, then they will consider you for the part. They're convinced that once Jason is inside, the general public will forget all about him, along with your involvement in his defence or whatever you like to call it. It appears that the interview you did with Valerie what's-her-name gained you a lot of sympathy. Whose idea was it, anyway?"

"Valerie's."

Billy leaned back in his chair and gave me a sassy grin. "Just a moment," he said. "Are you...? No, surely not? I thought you said that after Alice there could be no one?"

"Life goes on. The truth is I sometimes get hellishly lonely in that house of ours. I want to move on. I just don't know whether I can."

"So, you're actually.... You know...with this Valerie person."

"Oh, for God's sake, Billy. I'm seventy years old. I'm not going to jump straight into bed with a woman. We hardly know each other."

"I would."

"I know you would. You're still twenty, but some of us actually age."

"Paff. Grab the opportunity, old man, or the bird may fly."

"I don't think so."

"Oh, so it's serious... I have to say I'm happy for you. I haven't had a proper relationship for years. You've given me hope. Ask her if she's got a friend, not too haggard, and preferably doesn't walk with a Zimmer frame, you know, someone who would like to meet a handsome young bachelor of sixty-nine."

"I'll think about it. If I do, it'll be done extremely subtly and I'll pray to God, I won't regret it."

"Of course you won't. You know me. I'll go very gentle on her."

"Oh, yeah. Sorry if I'm a little sceptical, but after three marriages...and how many relationships?"

"Are you serious? Do you think I've notched them off on my belt?"

We chatted about old times. I said very little about Jason. I knew he would not be very sympathetic. He had not lived with a psychotherapist all his life like I had and experienced second-hand the infinite range of psychological conditions that can torture our fellow beings. Alice shared them all with me, admittedly anonymously and in layman's terms, but I felt that I could at least call myself an honorary therapist.

I left Billy around one o'clock and walked across town to a small restaurant where Valerie and I arranged to have lunch. It would probably be the last time I would see her until after the trial. She had booked a table next to a window that looked out on to a shady pedestrian alley, a catwalk of interesting people of all ages and backgrounds. She was in a reminiscent mood and talked about Ares. "I never stopped loving him, despite his remoteness. The thing about Ares was that he was never totally present and never totally absent. One minute he'd be saying how beautiful and intelligent I was. The next he'd be immersed in his latest play or article, hardly aware that I was sitting in the same room. It's strange how someone can be so sensitive with words and so insensitive with people. Are all geniuses like that? Is Jason like that, I wonder?"

"In a way I suppose he is."

"Before I met Ares, I hero-worshipped actors and writers because I had this false belief that to be able to express such depth of sentiment and emotion, they must be unbelievably sensitive and empathetic people. I now realise it's all a bit of an act. I knew an actress once who could cry at will, and very convincingly too. Just like turning on a tap."

"I'm afraid you're probably right. You've got yourself involved with both a writer and an actor. God help you."

"Oh, sorry, Patrick. I certainly wasn't referring to you."

"But you're right. To be an actor or a writer, you must be perceptive and able to get inside people's heads but that doesn't mean you're more sensitive than others. We're just more observant, that's all. The big problem is that actors and writers tend to have very large egos, which can upset the apple cart somewhat."

"Patrick, would you like to meet Dory?" She looked at me warily.

"Yes, of course I would. Do you think he'd approve?"

"He already does."

"Oh, so you've told him about us."

"Well, hinted at it."

"And?"

"He's happy for me. He hasn't always liked my male friends."

"I'd better be on my best behaviour then."

"Don't be silly. He'll love you."

"Has he never asked about his father?"

"Once, but I told him his father wasn't prepared to commit and left it at that. That seemed to satisfy him. We've always been pretty content with each other."

"I'd like to meet him and his family, of course, but I think I'd better wait till after the trial. I have no idea how it's going to go. Either way it won't be easy for Jason. Once you've been condemned by society, an acquittal is not going to change his life much. Somehow, he's going to have to start over, but the stigma will follow him forever."

As we walked back to her home through the city, I felt rather like a tourist enjoying the sites, as if seeing them for the first time. She told me stories of her childhood and how she used to walk these streets on her way to school. Nothing much had changed, she said. I told her about a very different childhood in a primitive Dublin, where horses and carts still delivered coal and milk to people's doors, before the Celtic Tiger reared its majestic head.

Again, something prevented me from accepting her invitation to go in for tea. I don't think it had anything to do with being old-fashioned. I just wanted to relish the anticipation of better times to come.

Chapter Twenty-Seven

I arranged to see Jason one more time before the trial. In fact, it was Victor himself who put me on the 'list.' He was convinced I was the only person who could make Jason see that a trial is about winning over your audience and he should avail of his thespian skills. In Victor S's view, appearing innocent was more important than being so.

I didn't have to leave for the prison for an hour or two, so I decided to read Alice's last session with Jason. I was dreading it, for several reasons, but primarily I didn't want to say goodbye to her voice. Ever since I started reading her notes, it was as if she were with me again. I could imagine her leaning over her desk and hearing that sigh of satisfaction when the last phrase was put down on paper.

I remembered the morning of her last session. She had been in agonising pain most of the night until I persuaded her to take a double dose of painkillers. She was very weak and could hardly stand. I offered to call Jason and cancel the appointment, but she said it was crucial that she see him one last time. It was clear to both of us, though, that she could not go on working. Nor would we be able to deal with her condition at home. Sooner or later, she would have to go into the hospital.

"I feel Jason and I are so close to making a life-changing breakthrough," she said dolefully. "One more session could make all the difference."

"My love, you've hardly slept. You're in excruciating pain. How can you possibly go to work like this?"

"Patrick, please don't make a fuss. I promised Jason we'd have one more session and so we will. I can't let him down. It may do no good, but I must try."

I didn't argue. Alice was strong-willed, to put it mildly. When she set her mind on something, even a police barricade wouldn't stop her having her way. I helped her into the car and then had to virtually carry her into the building and up to her office. She had lost a lot of weight and was as light as an oversized bird. Jason was already there. He looked pale and drawn. He also had a somewhat neglected appearance. He was wearing a pair of shabby, rather creased pants. No one would have guessed that he was the Artistic Director of the National Theatre. Neither of us spoke. We were too concerned about Alice. We knew how seriously ill she was, though I think we were both inclined towards self-deception.

I opened her notes at the last session and then closed them again. "What's the point?" I thought. There's nothing more to find out, surely? Yet, a morbid curiosity egged me on. Initially, I couldn't focus on the page. It was just a blur, as if someone had poured drops of olive oil into my eyes. Slowly, however, I managed to pick out the words.

'I made an effort to put on a reassuring face, though I could see Jason was distraught. I tried to smile but the painkillers had ceased to have much effect and I know that the stabbing pain made my face twitch. Nevertheless, I had to make the most of our last session. I suppose in a way I was hoping and praying for a miracle, that a magic ray of light would burst through the window and erase his childhood traumas and turn his profound sorrow into hope. I had to focus on hope, hope for positive change. I chose a short poem by Thomas Hardy, one of Patrick's favourites. In my faltering voice, I read it too him.

Song of Hope

O sweet To-morrow!—After to-day There will be This sense of sorrow. Then let us borrow Hope, for a gleaming Soon will be streaming, Dimmed by no grey—No grey.

As soon as I finished it, I realised I had made a mistake. It never occurred to me that he would associate the poem with me rather than himself. He glared at me, eyes brimming, a look of near contempt on his face. 'How could you read that poem to me today of all days, our last session? How can there be any hope?' I told him that we were there for him, not me. My life was nearly over. His was just beginning. He said nothing for some time. Then, I asked him to comment on the poem.

'For people like me there is no hope. So, what's the point in pretending that there is? When everything is grey, when the sun has lost its

brightness, when the day never dawns, when a leaden shroud covers everything, when death is constantly staring you in the face, how can there be hope?'

For the first time in my life, I realised I had failed totally as a therapist. I decided to try one last time. 'At this moment you feel there is no hope, but I want you—my last request, if you like—to write a poem about hope. Try to envisage a state where you can contemplate the possibility of hope.' I knew he would do it for my sake, if not for his own. He would make that leap into the unknown, into the unfamiliar world of hope, which he had only ever glimpsed fleetingly. He sat without writing a word for so long I thought I had set him an impossible task but eventually he started writing. After some time, he read the following poem to me in a solemn voice, through which a ray of hope shone dimly through. At least, so I thought.

> *Hope in a Lunar Landscape*
> *The blackened stumps of charred trees*
> *Stand inert on the hillside,*
> *Lined up in marching order,*
> *Like regiments of carbonized warriors*
> *Prepared for a battle already lost.*
> *Where once the owl hooted and the nightingale sang,*
> *Deathly silence prevails.*
> *The bodies of fleeing creatures lie,*
> *Stiff, frozen in their tracks*
> *Like Pompeian figures*
> *Forever running from the ravaging flames.*
> *Yet, through the grey brushless soil*
> *A green shoot peeps through.*
> *Scarcely visible,*
> *But there, nonetheless,*
> *Pushing, pushing towards the life-giving light.*
> *Cutting through the greyness*
> *Releasing the sap,*
> *Allowing it to flow anew.*
> *All it needs is time.*
> *Time to revive,*

To spread its branches
To take to the wind once more.
There is hope,
Even in greyness.

I was taken aback by his ability to produce a poem that was so positive
after what he had said earlier. I told him sometimes we need to pretend to
keep going, in the hope the greyness will eventually fade into light. I asked
him what inspired the poem, and he told me the following. "Last summer
there was a terrible fire that ravaged thousands of acres of primaeval forest
near a friend's country home. I think it was the most depressing thing I have
ever seen. It made me realise how brittle we are, how fragile life is. Yet, after
the rains, I was amazed by the plants that only weeks earlier had been burnt
to nothing were showing signs of growth. It made me realise how resilient
nature is."

I told him that we are part of nature, that we too can be resilient. All
we need is to let ourselves revitalize - no need to force it, just let it happen
and in time it will.

I was not sure how the session went. All I could do now was pray that
in Jason's charred landscape hope would eventually push its way to the
surface.

I told him that I had been in touch with a trusted colleague who was
prepared to take him on in therapy. His reaction was almost violent.

"Alice, can't you understand? I agreed to do therapy only because of
you. I want no one else to know about my life." I gave him the name and
number of my colleague anyway, which he took grudgingly. If he did decide
to contact her, Patrick knew where I kept my notes. He could find them and
give them to her. I had done all I could. I just hoped he would change his
mind.

On his way out, Jason approached me and held me for a few seconds
and without saying a word hurried down the stairs. It was almost six months
before I saw him again, when he turned up on my doorstep, a fugitive from
the world.

I sat waiting while Alice wrote up her notes. It took longer than usual.
I could see by her bent back that it required great effort. I often wondered
whether she wrote those notes knowing one day I would find them and read

them, though now it seems unlikely. No. Alice liked to finish things. It would have been impossible for her not to write up a session, even if it meant expending her last ounce of energy. I remember too that she was very insistent that her office be left neat and tidy. Was she hoping for a miracle for herself too? Could she not let go of the idea that she would never be coming back?

I took one last look at the file. I felt a lump in my throat but knew I had to say goodbye. Had all her work been in vain? I closed the file and put it in a bottom drawer. Would I be able to hand it over to Victor S, if he requested it? It would be hard, but I had to think of what Alice would want, and I liked to think she would want what was best for Jason.

Though each session had been read with a mixture of dread and perverse pleasure, I now had nothing to look forward to. There was nothing to follow, no sequel, no second series. I left for the prison with a heavy heart, still ambivalent about my feelings for Jason. Yet, I kept on thinking about what transpired during therapy. Had she failed as she believed? Subsequent events would seem to indicate that she had. If she had had more time, would she have succeeded? It is difficult to say. Alice was the first one to admit that therapy didn't always work. Was Jason 'incurable,' as he said himself in one of the sessions?

In the visiting room, Jason did not seem unduly nervous about the trial. In fact, he seemed positively blasé, as if he had resigned himself to an inevitable outcome.

"I don't want to get your hopes up, Jason, but I believe you have a good chance of being acquitted."

"I admire your optimism, Patrick, but I don't share it."

"Is it because you don't dare hope?"

"Hope, yes," he said musingly. "In my last session with Alice, she insisted I write a poem about hope. She said I had to pretend. You know, it kind of worked...for a while. I even started a psychodrama group with some refugees and look where that got me. There was a time when I considered giving up the National and devoting myself to helping others in the way Alice did. But slowly hope faded and greyness covered my life again like a thick layer of ash, smothering everything. I could see no other outlet but through oblivion. I honestly believed she would live, and I would overcome my crushing depressions, but neither happened. Alice died and I reverted to drugs in a futile endeavour to overcome my melancholia, which led to where I am now. So, whether I win or lose tomorrow, it's all the same to me. I am incurable."

"Do you think Alice could have 'cured' you? If you had more time?"

He thought for a moment, looking vaguely around the stark, uninspiring room, as if trying to catch an elusive thought. "I honestly don't know, Patrick. You see, I don't think I was in therapy because I believed I could ever be well again. I was there for Alice. It was the only way I could justify spending time with her. I saw in her what you must have seen in her, wisdom, gentleness, perspicacity, understanding, but she was much more than that for me. She was the mother I never had. I wanted to monopolise her, to have total exclusivity, to have her for me alone. I was jealous of you and Andrew. It was wrong of me I know. I just couldn't help myself. I even felt that you couldn't possibly appreciate her like I did. When she died, I died for a second time. Honestly, as things stand, I wouldn't mind dying for a third time, for good this time."

"Jason, you must revisit that poem you wrote for Alice. There is hope even in greyness."

He looked at me quizzically. "Did she read that poem to you?"

I realised I had put my foot in it. "No, no," I lied. "You talked about hope and greyness, so that's why I said there is hope even in greyness."

He looked at me suspiciously for a few moments, then seemed to accept my stuttered excuse. "Yes, I wish I had kept a copy of that poem. I used to know it by heart, but I've forgotten it now. It's probably still in Alice's notes. I know she was very meticulous when it came to writing up her sessions."

"Would you like me to look for it?"

"No, it's all right. I remember the gist of it. She read a poem by Thomas Hardy, which she said was one of your favourites."

"Really? She had an amazing memory. I read that poem to her decades ago when we were going through a difficult time with Andrew. He was very ill with rheumatic fever. We thought we were going to lose him. We clung desperately to hope then."

"I can imagine."

"Jason, about tomorrow. Victor wants me to impress upon you the importance of appearing innocent, you know, take on that 'butter wouldn't melt in my mouth' look, which I know you can do very well. I believe he will present a very good case in your favour."

"You've all worked very hard for me. I thank you for it but I'm not sure I deserve it. I am weak, Patrick. The truth is I am not without remorse."

"I know you aren't, but this is not the time to be thinking about remorse. That can wait till after you are acquitted. When it's all over, I do believe that you should start therapy again."

"I probably should," he said apathetically.

"We are doing the best for you, but you must also play your part. You have a very good chance of getting off."

"Maybe I do," he said with a listless smile.

"If Alice were here, she would be giving you all the support that you need. I am afraid I am a poor substitute."

"Would she, Patrick? I let her down. I wanted to get well for her sake. I failed her. I know she was not used to failure."

"Jason, you must do your best tomorrow, for Alice's sake. Try to imagine what she would tell you. You know how much she loved you."

"Did she tell you that?" he asked urgently.

"Yes, many times. After Andrew's death, you were more of a son to us than ever."

"Ironic, isn't it?" he said wryly.

I knew what he meant but said nothing.

A harsh distorted voice blared out through the speakers ordering us to leave.

"I've got to go but I'll be there tomorrow rooting for you."

He must have found my feeble encouragement amusing. It was the kind of thing a father would say to his young son before a school football match. "When it's all over, I'll be waiting to take you home. I think you should stay with me until we sort out your life."

"Always the optimist, Patrick. There is hope in greyness. I will try and remember that."

He smiled and turned towards the exit where guards were waiting to take him back to his cell.

"Chin up," I said faintly, but I don't think he heard me.

Chapter Twenty -Eight

The night before the trial I slept badly. I kept thinking about Andrew and how badly his trial went. However, I felt that this time we were more prepared. Thanks to Marcus V, I had managed to unearth many facts that might otherwise have remained buried. I hoped Victor S would make full use of them. I hadn't made contact with him since our cloak and dagger meeting under the bridge, but I assumed that if he wanted elaboration on the information I had given him he would have communicated with me.

Though I felt the urge to talk to someone, I resisted calling either Valerie or Billy. I had to face this alone. Well, not entirely alone. Alice would be holding my hand throughout the trial. I would be drawing strength from her memory, imagining her reassuring words. It's surprising how comforting a memory can be.

It was going to be a high-profile trial. It is not every day a celebrity, and not just any celebrity, the Art Director of the National Theatre, goes on trial for a hideous crime. Reporters and paparazzi would have a field day, making their tenuous claims and shaky speculations. Rightly or wrongly, Jason had already been found guilty. All that remained was to find out whether the sentence would be jail or eternal damnation. One way or the other, his life was in pieces and it was very difficult to contemplate a new beginning for him.

As expected, the crowd outside the courthouse was overflowing across the street, causing a massive traffic jam, resulting in a cacophony of car horns, drivers venting their frustrations. The chaos was compounded by TV transmission vehicles parked on the pavement opposite, thus narrowing the street even further. Apparently, traffic rules don't apply to the media.

The one good thing was that, aided by my surgical mask and tatty yellow baseball cap - the one Alice detested - I was able to slip unnoticed through the madding crowd. On this occasion, my threadbare baseball hat came in handy as it gave me the appearance of a down-and-out enjoying the free entertainment. However, some observant individual did notice me as I was presenting my credentials to the security guard. I heard them call my name, but it was too late. I didn't even look back. I just continued up the steps to the courthouse.

I found a seat near the back. I didn't want to be intrusive. Victor was already there with an assistant, but I decided not to make contact. Not long after me, the jury trooped in. They were a motley crew, mostly young people in their thirties or forties - from all walks of life, I guessed. I wondered how many of them had already made up their mind about Jason. Then, the defendant himself was brought in by two guards and left in Victor S's care. Finally, we were told to stand while the judge entered. I was pleased to see he was young, in his early fifties.

I do not intend to transcribe everything that transpired during the proceedings. It would require a book. I will merely give a brief outline of what was said, omitting what I believe is irrelevant.

The public prosecutor was a woman in her late thirties. She gave the impression of being assertive and self-confident, but I suppose that goes with the territory. Her contempt for Jason manifested itself with every word she uttered. "I intend to show that Jason B is a predator, who has used his exalted position as Artistic Director of the National Theatre to prey on minors. I will also show that he callously offered his services, free of charge, to the Refugee Centre for unaccompanied minors with the sole intention of gaining the trust of his prospective victims, waiting for the right moment to pounce. Reliable witnesses, former friends of the accused, will testify that Jason B is a serial paedophile. I will also present sworn statements by two of Jason B's rape victims, who at the time of their abuse were only fifteen years old. These defenceless refugees were taken in by the apparent 'altruism' of the accused which, as it turns out, was a mere ploy to further his odious ends. I will show that Jason B is a danger to society and should be given the severest possible sentence permissible by law."

She returned to her seat, looking very smug. She was obviously a good lawyer who knew her job, but she lacked the ability to connect with the jury, which I knew was Victor S's forte.

During her diatribe, Jason remained passive, occasionally closing his eyes, apparently indifferent to her accusations.

Victor S looked starched, ironed, and pressed in his tailored-made dark grey suit. You could almost smell the newness of his attire, as if it arrived that morning from the chicest haberdashery in town. His black hair was neatly groomed, with a discreet parting, securely gelled in place. He was wearing a purple tie that looked sharp enough to cut through flesh. He reminded me of someone out of the Godfather. I had to admit he was impressive. How could one fault such flawlessness?

He strode out into the arena with the confidence of a veteran gladiator who had taken on far worthier opponents. He oozed poise, avoiding blustering histrionics. Instead, he spoke in a gentle, rather condescending voice, as if the jury were slightly deluded friends who needed enlightening. "Jason B is a household name in our country. He has entertained and delighted theatre and cinema goers alike with his wit, sensitivity and perception, both as a writer and actor. I intend to show you, esteemed members of the jury, Jason B is innocent of the accusations that have been thrust upon him. Someone, like Jason B, who has reached the pinnacle of his career, is constantly at the mercy of vindictive and envious people, who will do anything to topple him from his ivory tower. I intend to call two witnesses who will testify to the impeccability of his character and his social conscience. The heinous crime in this trial is not the one my client is accused of but the elaborate plot woven by certain people in high places who, for reasons unbeknownst to him, wished to sully his reputation, destroy his career, and ruin his life.

"Thank you, friends, I can see from your faces that you wish for justice to be done here today. So, I beg you to consider all the facts carefully. Society has already condemned Jason B. You, however, must try to remain objective, however difficult that may be. You must erase from your minds everything you have read or heard in the media. You must see things afresh, as they are presented to you during the trial. When you are in possession of all the facts, I want you to ask yourselves two questions. Firstly, have the facts been sufficiently substantiated by the prosecution to ensure their absolute truth? Can the prosecution prove beyond the shadow of a doubt that Jason B is guilty of the crimes he has been accused of? If not, despite any suggestions of guilt that may have been sown in your mind by hearsay, you are bound to find him not guilty."

Victor S paused for a moment and scanned the jury with an avuncular smile, looking at each juror in turn.

It wasn't easy to determine the jury's reaction to Victor S's inaugural address. However, I did notice some nodding heads. He was getting through to them.

The prosecution began by calling two witnesses to affirm that Jason was in the habit of holding sex parties, where drugs and alcohol were consumed, and teenagers were present.

Victor S toyed with the witnesses. "You claim to have been present at these so-called 'sex parties' held at Jason B's penthouse apartment. Presumably you were guests and not undercover detectives. Did you yourselves partake of the sex, drugs and alcohol you claim were readily available there?"

"Objection, irrelevant," exclaimed the PP.

"I merely wish to establish if the witnesses are as guilty as the accused and, if so, to show they may have had an ulterior motive for agreeing to testify against him."

"Please answer the question."

"As you said, they were readily available," said the witness sheepishly.

"So, I'll take that as a yes. Is it not therefore very hypocritical of you to accuse a fellow actor—you are an actor too, I believe—of something you yourself indulged in?"

The witness said nothing.

"So, were you present at many of Jason B's parties?"

"Yes."

"Did you see Jason B indulge in intercourse with a minor?"

"He sometimes went into his bedroom with a guest."

"And you followed him and watched him have intercourse with this guest?"

"Of course not."

"So, you have never actually seen Jason B having intercourse with anyone, whether they were a minor or not?"

"No, but it was…"

"Thank you. No further questions."

Victor S had got off to a good start and was clearly up on points.

Then, came the turn of Ali and Hassan. The Public Prosecutor said she would not be putting them on the stand. Instead, she would read out their statements, which she did. However, it was obvious they had not been written by two teenage boys with little or no knowledge of legal terminology, especially as it was all in English.

Victor S insisted that they take the stand. The PP objected, saying they were minors, and their English was very poor. "I insist, your lordship, the alleged victims take the stand. Otherwise, no cross-examination can take place. How else can I establish whether these statements were indeed written by the plaintiffs or if they even knew what they were signing their names to? Besides, I do believe the plaintiffs are no longer minors, as they are now sixteen."

"These are sworn statements," said the PP, flapping a bunch of papers in the air.

"As you well know, anyone can swear to anything. It doesn't necessarily mean it's true. So, your Honour, if these young men are unable to express themselves in English, I suggest that an interpreter be found post haste. However, I have it on good authority that they can communicate adequately in English, certainly well enough to answer my simple questions."

The judge pondered Victor S's request and said, "I will allow it. Please call the first plaintiff."

Ali shuffled to the stand and swore on the Coran to tell the truth, the whole truth and nothing but the truth, so help him Allah. I suspected that both boys were devout Muslims and would not dare lie.

"So, Ali, I am going to ask you some very simple questions," Victor S said in his best kind-auntie voice. "If you do not understand what I am asking, I will rephrase it to make it simpler. If you still do not understand, then an interpreter will be brought. Is that clear?"

Ali nodded his head.

"Good. Is it true that Jason B did theatre with you at the Refugee Centre?"

"Yes."

"Did you enjoy doing theatre with Jason?"

"Yes."

"What did you think of Jason as a person?"

"We like him."

"Were you aware of why Jason volunteered to do psychodrama with you?"

"He say he want to help us."

"And did he?"

"I think, yes."

"All right. Is it true that you were arrested during one of Jason's parties and taken to the police station?"

"Yes."

"Is it also true that they found you in possession of drugs?"

"No. We no have drugs."

"I see. In that case why did they accuse you of having drugs?"

"I don't know."

"Do you know why the Refugee Centre's lawyer came to the police station?"

"To get us out."

"Right. So, he was able to tell the police you had no drugs on you when you were arrested?"

"No."

"No? So, what did he advise you to do? Given that being in possession of illegal drugs is a criminal offence."

"He say sign statement."

"What statement?"

"Statement saying Jason B do bad things to us."

"So, are you saying that the statement is not true?"

"I don't know. I not read it."

"So, you were asked to sign a statement you could not or at least did not read?"

"Yes."

"No further questions."

The Public Prosecutor became progressively more agitated as Victor S's questioning continued. "Your Lordship, I request a recess to talk to my clients."

"Yes, I think you should. We will reconvene in exactly thirty minutes."

After Victor S's skilful questioning of Ali, I assumed it was all over. It was clear to the jury that Ali at least had been hoodwinked into signing the statement. However, the PP was not going to give up without a fight. After the recess, she returned with renewed vigour. "Your Honour, I wish to recall the plaintiff, Ali, to the stand."

"I object, your Honour," said Victor jumping to his feet. "The Public Prosecutor has had ample time during the recess to brief her client and put words into his mouth. Ali stated quite clearly that he did not know what he was signing."

"I will allow it."

Victor was clearly displeased.

"Ali, you said you did not read the statement you signed," the PP began, "but is it not true that your lawyer read it out to you and explained its contents?"

"Yes."

"So, you were aware of the contents of what you were signing?"

"Yes."

"Thank you, Ali."

Victor S rose to his feet with a look of fierce determination on his face. "Ali, were you given a translated version of the statement to read?"

"No."

"So, your lawyer could theoretically have read you his own version of the statement you later signed?"

"I suppose so."

"Let me ask you straight out, Ali—and I would like to remind you that you have sworn an oath on the Coran to tell the whole truth—were you offered anything in exchange for signing the statement given to you by your lawyer?"

The boy hesitated, looking nervously around the room. His gaze alighted for a moment on a squat, frog-like man sitting behind the PP. "Yes."

"What exactly were you offered?"

"He say I get nationality."

"Let me clarify this. You were told that a deal had been manufactured with the Ministry of the Interior whereby you would receive nationality or citizenship if you were prepared to sign a statement claiming that Jason B had raped you?"

"I think so." Ali looked very flustered, unsure whether he had said the right thing.

"Did you understand what I just asked you or would you like me to have an interpreter brought in?"

"I understand."

"Why did you agree to sign this statement when you knew it was clearly false, after all Jason had done for you?"

"Nationality very important. I want to join family in Germany."

"So, you believed that by signing the statement you would obtain nationality, which would permit you to travel to Germany, where you would join your family. It was certainly a very generous offer on the part of your lawyer. However, I'm not sure that he was in a position to make such an offer. One last question, Ali, did Jason B rape you? Remember you are still on oath."

Ali again looked nervously around the room. For a second, he made eye contact with the frog-like lawyer but quickly withdrew it. He bowed his head as if in prayer and then raised it with a look of humiliation on his face. "No."

"Thank you, Ali. No further questions."

It was clearly a total debacle for the prosecution. Their whole case had fallen to pieces before Victor even called his character witnesses or cross-examined Hassan.

The PP, however, was not going to give up easily, though I couldn't imagine what else she might have up her sleeve, unless she was planning to write a completely new scenario for Hassan, who had still not been called to the stand. "Your Honour, I would like to call for an adjournment until tomorrow as I wish to confer with my clients who are clearly unnerved and confused by the proceedings."

"It is highly irregular, but I will adjourn until tomorrow on condition that an interpreter be found for the plaintiff Hassan, which is something that should have been arranged for the cross-examination of Ali too."

"Thank you, your Honour."

The trial lasted a little over one and a half hours. It seemed clear to me Jason had won. After what Ali said, how could Hassan's testimony be taken seriously, even if he were to stick by his statement, which must have been identical to the one signed by Ali?

Before exiting I watched Jason being taken away. He didn't search for me in the courtroom, as I thought he would. I raised my hand to get his attention, but he left with his head down. I was worried about his psychological state. Might he do something foolish? I couldn't be sure. I had learnt over the previous few weeks to expect anything from him. His soul remained a mystery to me.

I considered congratulating Victor S on his handling of the case but decided against it. I had promised to keep my distance until after the trial and that is what I would do. I had done all I could do. It was up to him now.

I felt elated as I made my way out of the courthouse. Thanks to my investigations it looked as if I had saved Jason from prison at least. I was still not sure whether I could save him from himself.

With my tattered hat pulled down over my eyes and the collar of my jacket turned up, I slipped quietly through the stunned crowd. It seemed Ali's testimony had already been leaked. Would it change public opinion in Jason's favour? I doubted it. They had created a monster, a monster worse than themselves, and they would not willingly give up their creation.

Chapter Twenty-Nine

On my return, I felt as if I were floating on air. I ran into my office, opened the bottom drawer of my desk, and took out Alice's notes. I wanted to tell her how well the trial had gone, but as I sat staring at the folder, I realised the utter futility of talking to a pile of papers. I put the file back in the drawer and pushed it shut.

I had a light lunch, then decided to have a short siesta to make up for all the sleep I had lost in previous nights. However, just as I lay my head on the pillow, my phone rang. It was Victor, who sounded uncharacteristically agitated. "Patrick, I need your help."

That's a first, I thought.

"I'm very worried about Jason. He insists on taking the stand tomorrow. It would have been a last resort, if I saw the trial was going badly for him, but now that we are winning its utter foolishness. It'd be like stepping into a lion's den, but he won't listen to me. He wants his voice to be heard, he says. He doesn't understand that in a court of law it's better your voice isn't heard. When he's been acquitted, he can speak as much as he likes. But he won't budge. I think you're the only person who can make him change his mind."

"I'm not sure he'll listen to me either. He didn't even look at me in court today."

"You've got to try, Patrick. You're a writer. Compose an email in your most eloquent prose, pointing out the foolishness of taking the stand. If he insists, I can't stop him, of course. It's his prerogative but it could be a disaster. The absurd thing is we're just a stone's throw from winning the case. Whatever stunt the PP is planning to pull tomorrow, it can't override the fact that Ali denied being raped by Jason."

"I will do my best, Victor, but I don't believe I have much sway over him anymore."

"It was you he went to for help and I know for a fact that he has great respect for you."

"I believe he does but I'm afraid he suspects I've read Alice's notes, which contain certain details about his life he would not want anyone, not even me, to know. I think he's ashamed to face me."

"It's all in your imagination, Patrick. How could he know or even suspect you read her notes? No. The man is clearly deeply troubled. When this is all over, I will recommend he see a psychiatrist friend of mine, who'll prescribe a few antidepressants. That should set him right."

"I'm afraid his problem is not something that a few pills can solve, Victor. He needs therapy. He was making great progress with Alice."

"You know better than I do. All I know is that you've got to stop him from taking the stand tomorrow."

"I'll do my best."

"You need to do more than your best."

Victor S had successfully passed on his anxiety to me. It would indeed be a disaster if Jason took the stand. I know how crafty lawyers can be. They can twist you into knots until you don't whether you're coming or going. Then, they get you to say exactly the opposite of what you mean.

I thought it best I speak to him directly. So, I called the prison but either they could not locate him, or he refused to come to the phone. So, I had no choice but to write him an email and hope he'd read it. I made it very simple, explaining the dangers of taking the stand and pointing out that once acquitted he'd have plenty of time to say whatever he liked to the world; give interviews, write a book, whatever. TV presenters would only be too pleased to have him on their show and I suspected that a publisher might even see the opportunity to make a buck or two out of his autobiography.

I waited all afternoon for a reply, with one eye on my phone and the other on my computer, but nothing arrived. Why was he so insistent on taking the stand? Had he totally gone off the rails? I had no idea what his motivation might be unless he thought the court was the best place to clear his name. It would certainly be reported widely, but would the PP trick him into saying something that might be misinterpreted, which would no doubt overshadow anything positive that might come out of it?

In the end, I gave up waiting for a reply. I had planned to invite

Valerie for a drink to celebrate but all my enthusiasm had melted away. I just felt like having an early night.

I was about to turn in when Valerie herself rang. "So how did the trial go? I heard it went well."

"Yeah, it did, and I was planning to call you. I thought we might go out for a drink to celebrate but it seems Jason has decided to take the stand tomorrow - against everyone's recommendation."

"You can't stop him."

"Yes, I know, but both Victor and I are afraid he's going to end up saying something that might incriminate him."

"I don't think he'd be so foolish, Patrick. Stop worrying. Would you like to come over?"

"Do you mind if we take a rain check on that? I don't think I'd be good company tonight."

"I understand. It won't be long before it's all over and we can celebrate in style."

"I sincerely hope so. I'll call you as soon as I have news."

~ * ~

The next day the crowd outside the courthouse was considerably reduced. It seemed even the press were not expecting the PP to overturn Ali's retraction.

The second day of the trial began punctually. The jury looked a great deal less enthusiastic than they had the previous day. I could tell from the weary looks on their faces that they were hoping for a quick resolution.

I was not so sure, however, that was going to happen. The PP would certainly have something up her sleeve and there was now the variable, Jason himself. Although I only saw them briefly, I got the impression that Ali was the timid one, while Hassan was cocky, even a bit arrogant. With some incentive, she could probably get him to stick by his statement, in which case the jury would have to decide which of the boys was telling the truth.

The PP surprised us all by calling the Refugee Centre's lawyer to the stand. He was not a prepossessing man. He looked like an oversized frog and talked with a throaty voice that resonated in his barrel chest like churning buttermilk.

"Mr. F, what exactly is your function at the Refugee Centre?" the PP began.

"To help any young person who finds themselves in trouble."

"So, on the night of the twenty-third of February, why were you called to the police station?"

"I was told that two of our boys had been arrested for possession of illegal drugs."

"I see, and what did you do to help these boys?"

"I had planned to plead with the police and the magistrate to let them off, as they were minors and refugees. However, during our discussion the boys confessed to me that they had been raped by Jason B."

"So, what did you do?"

"I explained to the magistrate that the boys were extremely vulnerable and if charged with possession of illegal drugs they would be sent to prison. To cut a long story short, we all agreed that it was in the boys' interests that the police drop the charges."

"So, why did you get the boys to sign a statement that claimed that Jason B raped them?"

"A serious crime had been committed. I wanted to make sure it was not repeated."

"Did you offer the boys nationality if they signed the statements?"

The frog chuckled. "I do not have the authority to do so."

"So, how did they get the impression that you offered them nationality?"

"I believe I may have said that I would try and get them nationality."

"Thank you, Mr. F. No further questions."

As Victor got to his feet, he looked pensive. "Mr. F. I understand your concern for Ali and Hassan but Jason B was an illustrious volunteer at the Centre, did you have no concern for him?"

"No. Rumours had already reached us that he was indulging in sex with underage boys."

"Rumours, I see. So, you wanted to get rid of him. And for good, it seems. Why did you not just ask him to leave instead of instigating a police raid on his apartment?"

"We had nothing to do with the raid."

"According to police records—and I have the transcript here—someone from the Centre called the police at exactly ten-o-six on the night of the twenty-third of February and told them illegal drugs were being used at Jason B's apartment. Now, was that you, Mr. F? Please do not lie because you have a very distinctive voice and I believe the officer on duty that night could recognise it, if called to do so."

"I believe the secretary at the Centre may have called the police."

"Why would she have done that?"

"We were worried about Ali and Hassan, who had come under Jason B's influence. We had also heard people took drugs at his parties and indulged in orgiastic sex."

"So, your intention was to have Jason B arrested. However, your plan backfired. Ali and Hassan were arrested instead. Do you know why Jason B was not arrested?"

"No."

"I think you do, Mr. F. Jason B was not there, was he? He was on tour with a play called Da, which he directed and was playing in. Jason B gave permission to a close friend of his to hold a party at his flat, to which Ali and Hassan were invited. Is it not true that the police did not find drugs in Jason's apartment? However, the police arrested Ali and Hassan anyway, according to your instructions. Is that right?"

"Objection. Badgering the witness," exclaimed the PP.

"I merely wish to show, your Honour, that this was a plot to have Jason put away, a plot which failed, initially at least. As a result, they devised another plan, to blackmail Ali and Hassan into accusing Jason B of rape."

"I will allow it."

"Please answer the question, Mr. F."

"The boys said they had been raped."

"So, are you saying Ali lied?"

"No. I believe he is still under Jason B's influence and is afraid to admit the truth."

"This is what you believe. Do you have any proof this is true?"

The lawyer had lost his croak.

"Please answer the question."

"No," he said faintly.

"In his statement Ali claims that Jason raped him on the eighteenth of November last year. Are you aware, Mr. F, that at the time Jason B was supposedly raping Ali he was giving a speech to a select group of film critics and directors at a film festival in the north of the country?"

"No."

"You should have checked your facts, Mr. F."

"He may have got his dates wrong."

"I think you got your dates wrong, Mr. F. No further questions."

The PP then called Hassan to the stand. He had none of the timidity of Ali. He strode confidently to the stand and stood defiantly waiting to be questioned.

"Hassan, I have read out your statement to the court in which you claim that Jason B raped you. Is it true?" began the PP. "If you wish to answer in your language an interpreter is on hand. Do you understand?"

"I speak English good."

"So, please answer the question."

"Yes, it's true. I not lie."

"So, you are saying that Jason B raped you. I know that this may be painful for you but for the court I'd like you to tell us exactly how he raped you."

"He take me into bedroom and he say, 'I take you to heaven.' I say, 'No. I not want' but he very strong man."

"I see so he forced himself on you. Is that right?"

"Yes."

"No further questions."

Victor got to his feet and paced for a few seconds before fixing his eyes on Hassan. "Hassan, on the night of the eighth of October last year when you claim Jason B raped you, had you taken drugs or alcohol?"

"No. I am good Muslim."

"I have no doubt. And Muslims do not lie either, right?"

"No, they not lie."

"So, tell me, first of all, why did you agree to go into Jason B's bedroom? Had you no idea what his intentions were?"

"He say he wanted to show me something."

"I see. Didn't you ask what he wanted to show you?"

"No, I trust Jason."

"Oh, you trusted him. But he betrayed your trust by forcing himself upon you?"

"Yes."

"Hassan, what height are you?"

"I don't know."

"Irrelevant, your honour."

"Please get to the point, Mr. S."

"At once, your Honour. I would say that you are at least one metre eighty-five. I would also say that you are around seventy-five kilos. You also look quite powerful. I suspect you are very athletic. The defendant, on the other hand, is around one seventy-five and can't weigh much more than sixty kilos. Nor is he particularly athletic. So, why, Hassan, were you not able to resist his overtures?"

"He stronger than he look."

"He certainly doesn't look very strong. You, on the other hand, look very strong indeed. Hassan, you said earlier that Muslims don't lie. Isn't that correct? Especially if they have taken an oath on the Coran. So, are you lying?"

"No, I no lie."

"Was your friend Ali lying when he said that Jason had not raped him?"

"I not know."

"Are you aware that Jason B could be sentenced to many years in prison if the jury accepts your testimony?"

For the first time, he looked a bit sheepish. "Yes, I know."

"Yet, you persist in lying."

"Your Honour, he is clearly badgering the plaintiff."

"Yes, Mr. S, Hassan has said he is not lying."

"Very well, your Honour. Hassan, in your statement you claim that Jason B raped you on the eighth of October last year. Is that correct?"

"I think so."

"You think so. Might you have got your dates muddled up like your friend Ali seems to have done?"

"No, I know."

"That is very good because on the eighth of October last year Jason B was on holiday with friends. I have written confirmation from the hotel where he stayed from the seventh to the tenth of October. How do you explain that, Hassan?"

"I must have made mistake."

"It seems both you and Ali are prone to making mistakes or is it your incompetent lawyer who keeps making mistakes? Therefore, let me suggest to you that you were not raped by Jason B at all but your lawyer convinced you to state that you were. No further questions."

Again, Victor had pulled a couple of rabbits out of the hat. Once again, it seemed a foregone conclusion Jason would win the case. Certainly, if I had been on the jury, I would have serious doubts about both Mr. Frog's and Hassan's testimonies.

"Do you wish to call any further witnesses? If not, then we can call a recess before the summing-up."

Victor and Jason were engaged in a heated discussion. I could only hear snippets, but I gathered Victor was trying to prevent Jason from taking the stand.

"Is there something wrong, Mr. S?" asked the judge. "If not, may we proceed please?"

"Your Honour, my client wishes to take the stand, against my recommendation, I may add."

The PP perked up but could not hide her surprise.

"Then, let's get on with it, shall we?"

Victor raised his hands in a gesture of despair and flopped back into his chair.

Jason came to the stand. His face was blank, expressionless, like someone who has made up their mind to end their life, to exit a world that has nothing more to offer them.

"Jason B," began the PP. "You have come to the stand for a purpose. Do you wish to confess?"

"I wish to set the record straight. I did not rape these boys. During rehearsals we became very close. I had nothing but love and respect for them."

"So, why did you invite them to your parties, where alcohol and it appears drugs and sex were available?"

"It was wrong. I corrupted them. When I first met them, they were pure, unadulterated, and innocent, but they acquired a taste for bad things. That was my fault and I wish to be punished for it."

"You say you did not rape these boys, but did you have sex with either or both of them?"

"I had sex with Ali."

A subdued sigh rippled through the audience, followed by a charged silence. Jason had done the unthinkable. He had deliberately incriminated himself.

"Are you aware, Jason B, that having sex with a minor is considered statutory rape and therefore you are liable for the same sentence as you would if it had been ordinary rape?"

"Yes, I am, and I wish to be punished."

"Then it seems your wish will come true. No further questions."

Victor looked troubled but had not lost all his fight.

"Jason B, I wish you had admitted this in the first place and spared us the trouble of a court case."

"I have had time to think. Yes, I am guilty of having sex with a minor, but I did not rape these boys or any others."

"I'm afraid consensual sex with a minor is an oxymoron. You have committed a crime, and you will be punished accordingly. However, if your honour will permit, I would like to mention certain mitigating circumstances."

"I will permit it."

"Jason B has been through several traumatic events that have disturbed his mind. His best friend was brutally murdered in prison. This was followed by the death of a woman whom he dearly loved. In fact, he was having therapy with her when she was diagnosed with a terminal illness. However, my client has assured me he will continue therapy and hopefully come to terms with the issues that are having such a disturbing effect on him."

It was a foregone conclusion now. He chose to be punished. Why in an open court? Surely, he could have found other ways to punish himself.

The PP and Victor S said nothing new in their summing-up. Victor merely stressed Jason took the stand because he wished to atone for what he did and turn over a new leaf.

The PP doubted a serial paedophile could ever change and again asked for the maximum penalty allowed by law.

The judge then made it clear the jury had no option but to find Jason B guilty of statutory rape. After a very short deliberation, the decision was returned. All that remained was for the judge to pronounce the sentence.

"By his own admission, Jason B has been found guilty of statutory rape. However, his willingness to come forward and admit his guilt indicates a desire to reform. The fact he also underwent therapy for a period of six months also shows a disposition to overcome any psychological problems he may have. However, it is quite clear he has broken the law and taken advantage of a minor. I therefore am obliged to sentence him to four years in prison without remission. I would also recommend that he begin therapy as soon as possible."

Jason left the courtroom accompanied by two guards, this time, however, with his head high. He had, in his eyes at least, left the court with dignity. He did not turn his head in my direction. He had written me off. I wondered when, or if, I would ever see him again.

Chapter Thirty

I know Jason got what he deserved. According to his confession, legally and morally he had done wrong. Yet, I could not help wondering whether his admission of guilt was genuine. Why did Ali state categorically that he had not had sex with Jason? Did he want to protect the man he 'loved?' Or was Jason lying? Why did he insist on taking the stand? Did he have something else in mind? I had been aware of Jason's death wish for a long time and I was afraid that this was his way of fulfilling it.

I made every effort in the weeks that followed the trial to visit him in prison, but he refused to see me. I was deeply hurt as I had always had nothing but his best interests at heart. I know I committed the grave sin—in Alice's eyes at least—of invading the confidentiality of her notes, but how else was I to find out the truth?

Valerie was a great comfort to me. We spend a lot of time together. We share a love of walking, and she took me to places near the city I had never been to before. Alice was seldom free to take day trips. Her work always took precedence, even at weekends. Valerie and I also shared a common interest, theatre and the performance arts. We were both performers in a way, she as a presenter of herself and others, me as a presenter of others through me. In so doing, we became very self-critical, while indulgent towards others. While Alice talked about clients and their psychoses from the point of view of an expert, Valerie and I were able to discuss life and people on equal terms.

Despite her busy schedule, Valerie found time to devote to our deepening friendship. There was seldom an evening when she felt too tired to meet me, albeit for an hour or so, at her place or mine. We became steadily closer until the inevitable happened. We became lovers. The idea of becoming part of a new family was appealing but also frightening. I didn't want my curse to spill over onto others. However, Dory was slowly beginning to see me as the father he never had, and his children were delighted to have a second grandfather. I was also looking forward to meeting her second son, who, it appeared, was also keen to get to know me.

Starting a relationship at my age has its advantages. Neither partner expects a great deal of the other. We know our time is limited, and we simply want to make the most of it. Nor was there any of the jealousy or possessiveness of youth to interfere with our undemanding love. Yes, I think we were in love, but in a calm, staid way, without the destructive passion that can accompany first love.

Still, the thought of Jason languishing in jail made me feel guilty and inadequate. I wanted desperately to be able to lighten his pain, but I saw no way of doing so. He had a rotten deal, at least in early life. That he later turned things around and reached the peak of his profession was all his doing. He got little or no help from his father, or from anyone else for that matter. I suppose my recommendations did help in a way, but he could not have achieved what he had if it hadn't been for his talent and profound intelligence.

Yet, it all collapsed overnight like a house of cards. There was no doubt he was ultimately to blame but I still could not get over the fickleness of the public who once adored him and the media that clambered for his attention at the height of his career. Perhaps it was for that very reason they turned on him with such vehemence. They believed he had betrayed them. He had deceived them into believing he was someone else.

I suppose I should have hated him for what he did to Andrew, but I couldn't. I did not believe he alone destroyed Andrew. Andrew himself was equally to blame. It was Valerie who helped me to see things in a clearer light. "I know you love Jason, Patrick. There is obviously a lot to love about him, but you must remember he willingly confessed to having abused a minor. There comes a time in life when you can't go on blaming your upbringing for everything. You must take responsibility for what you are. He's an intelligent man. He knew what he was doing was not right but he gave in to his desires, however much he may have loved this boy. The fact he wished to atone for what he did is certainly in his favour. However, he was guilty and needs to be punished. In the same way, Andrew allowed himself to come under Jason's influence. His gullibility was his, no one else's. He allowed himself to be manipulated. Admittedly, it was wrong of Jason to do so but in the end,

I think he knew it and was racked with guilt, which was why he chose to admit his crime. He realised he needed to be punished to make sure he would become a better person."

I didn't entirely agree with everything she said but summing it up like that helped me to clarify things in my head.

For me at least, things started to look up after the trial. My agent rang me the day after it was over. He sounded unusually ebullient. "Patrick, you've got the part."

"Really?" I said, unsure whether I still wanted it.

"You don't sound overjoyed."

"It's just been a trying time with the trial and everything."

"Don't tell me you're going to turn it down? The money is fantastic, considering you're a bit over the hill."

"Thanks a lot."

"Only joking, Paddy. There's plenty of sap in you yet. So, shall I send you the contract?"

"Sure, why not? I'll look it over."

"Good. I think you'll find it very satisfactory. If you want to change any details, let me know. They are negotiable. It's just they're in a bit of a hurry. They were waiting around for you, believe it or not. When shall I tell them you'll sign?"

"Can I think about it?"

"Paddy. How many opportunities like this are you going to get?"

"I just want to discuss it with a friend."

"Oh, I see, do I take it the friend is female?"

"None of your business, Max. A man is entitled to a private life, I think."

"Em, not all men. You won't be able to keep it quiet for long."

"Not now that you know, you old tattler. Can you please do me a favour? Just keep it under your hat for a bit."

"I'll do my best, though there is talk of you having a fling with a certain Valerie F."

"Oh, for Christ's sake, Max, you're worse than a scullery maid."

"Scullery maid? Don't flatter me, darling. So, are you going to confirm it? I need to get my facts straight."

"Max, have I ever told you to f. off."

"Many times, but not recently. I can see you're getting your old spirit back. So, I expect a yes, no later than tonight. Don't let me down, Paddy. I could do with the cash. Things have been a bit slack lately, what with Covid and everything."

"I'll bear that in mind, Max. Though, the truth is I couldn't give a shit about your financial situation, you old skinflint."

"Paddy don't be like that. You know how much I love you."

"Yeah, yeah. I love you too, Max, most of the time. I'll call you tonight."

About an hour later, Billy called me. "Max rang. He says you're having second thoughts about whether to take the part. Please don't do this to me, Patrick. I've stuck my neck out for you."

"Yeah, Billy, I appreciate all you've done for me, but it'd mean being on location for a month or two and I'm not sure I really want that at this time."

"You mean you don't want to be away from Valerie."

"Well, that's part of it."

"You always let women control your life, Patrick. I think a little bit of independence would do you good. Apart from anything else, mate, it'd be great working together again. It's a lead role, or almost. No one turns that sort of thing down."

"I'm very tempted, I have to admit."

"Great. See you on set. Oh, sorry the trial didn't turn out as you would have wished. However, it's nice to know Jason has a conscience at least. If he keeps his nose clean, he should be out in a year or two."

"His life is over, Billy. He has nothing else to live for."

"I disagree. I think he is more resilient than you give him credit for. I don't see why some sort of comeback is not possible."

"No, Billy. He's a marked man. No one will employ him now. He might as well join a monastery."

"Well, maybe that wouldn't be a bad thing."

That evening, I told Valerie about the film but pretended that it was not all that important to me. I wanted to give her the chance to show her real feelings about my being away for so long. "It'll mean my being on location for a good month or so."

"Patrick, I'm delighted for you. I know it's what you want. You must take it."

"The idea of not seeing you for a few weeks doesn't appeal to me in the least."

"We'll have plenty of time to be together when it's over. Unless of course you fall madly in love with some young thing on set, in which case I will be very upset," she said with a half-smile.

"I think I'm a bit beyond that. There aren't all that many young ladies around with hang-ups about their grandfathers. Besides, I don't think I have the stamina any more to keep a young woman happy. It'd be too much like hard work."

"I'm very glad to hear it."

That evening, I made Max's day, and told him I'd sign the contract.

"Oh, you darling boy, I knew you'd see sense in the end. It'll be a smash hit. Maybe your chance to get an Oscar."

I let out an ironic laugh. I was not in the Oscar league, however well the film did. Nevertheless, I was looking forward to the challenge and the total immersion that making a film requires. While it's happening, nothing else matters, though I had the feeling this time I would have Valerie constantly in the back of mind.

I was spending a lot more time at her place now. I'd usually have a meal ready for her when she got home from work. We were becoming very much like a married couple but without the bickering that comes with over-familiarity. We'd usually have a glass of wine, then settle down in front of the telly, watch the news and then an episode from a series.

It was about three weeks after the trial ended that we heard the shocking news. We were watching the Nine O'Clock Roundup when I saw the headline at the bottom of the screen. I was totally gobsmacked. At first, I couldn't believe it or didn't want to. I had to read it a dozen times before I could fully assimilate it - 'Jason B dies in prison brawl.'

In stunned silence we listened to the correspondent give his report. "It's not yet absolutely clear how Jason B died. One version, which seems unlikely now, is that he was set upon by a group of homophobic prisoners. However, there are clear indications that he may have planned an attack on Tony Q, the notorious drug lord. It appears they had a score to settle concerning the death of Andrew G, the son of Patrick G, who died in prison two years ago. His death was believed to have been suicide, but it appears that Jason B told friends he believed Tony Q had him killed. CCTV cameras show Jason B clearly attacking Tony Q and attempting to thrust a homemade stiletto into the side of his neck. Those around Tony Q managed to drag Jason B off him before he could stab him a second time. In the scuffle that followed, Jason B was fatally wounded with his own knife. He was immediately rushed to the City Central Hospital but lost a lot of blood on the way. Doctors tried to stop the bleeding, but he died shortly after admission. Tony Q is now in intensive care fighting for his life. It remains to be seen whether he will pull through or not."

I was horrified. I couldn't speak. Valerie took my hand and squeezed it. "I'm sorry, Patrick."

Slowly, I emerged from my daze. I had lost my second and last 'son.' Why did he do it? In revenge for Andrew's death? Was it an act of suicide? Or both? Had he deliberately incriminated himself in the hope he would be incarcerated in the same prison as Tony Q? It was so utterly implausible but now it seemed the only likely explanation. He planned it all along. The reason why he didn't want to see me was not because he resented my reading Alice's notes but because he didn't want me to try to dissuade him from going ahead with his act of folly. He was aware of the risks. He knew it was tantamount to suicide. Tony Q would have been constantly surrounded by his goons. In fact, I was surprised Jason managed to get close enough to stab him even once.

"I've got to go to the hospital," I said getting to my feet.

Valerie pulled me back. "You can't go tonight. It's far too late. I'll see if I can get the morning off and come with you."

"What have they done with him?" I stuttered.

"We don't know, Patrick. He's most likely still at the hospital."

"Who's going to claim the body? He has no one. It must be me."

"You never actually adopted him, did you?"

"If no one else claims him, I'm sure they'll let me have him. The state doesn't want the expense of a burial."

"For your peace of mind, I'll call the news team at the Channel. I'm sure they'll know."

Valerie called the head of news who gave her the number of the reporter covering the case. It appeared Jason was in the hospital morgue. However, the police were still investigating the circumstances of the incident. Until they established exactly what happened they would not release the body.

"I feel I ought to do something, go there, make my presence felt."

"There's nothing you can do, Patrick. If no one claims the body, then we will offer to arrange for the funeral. I know you want to give him a good farewell."

I think it was the word farewell that struck a chord with me. I broke down in a flood of tears. I was beset with feelings of guilt and sorrow, just as I had been when Andrew died. Had I done enough? Could I have saved him?

Valerie seemed to know what was going on in my head. She said, "Patrick, you know you couldn't have done anything more than you did. He took it upon himself. He didn't want that on your conscience too."

Between my childish sobs, I think I said, "How much he must have loved Andrew."

I realised how much we all loved Andrew - and Jason too.

Fortunately, a lot of preparations had to be made before filming could begin. Max wasn't exactly telling the truth when he said they had been 'waiting around' for me. I just hoped that I wouldn't have to take a day off filming to attend Jason's funeral.

I waited a day or two before going to the hospital to see if anyone had claimed his body. It appeared the police had finished their investigation. Their conclusions were that Jason had indeed attacked Tony Q in the yard. Apparently, he had been planning it for some time as the knife he used in the assault went missing from the refectory a week before the event. He had obviously been slowly sharpening it to a lethal point, waiting for the right moment to stick it into Tony Q's neck, intending it to be a fatal blow. The police were unable to establish his motivation other than what a cellmate claimed, Jason had a score to settle with Tony Q.

The news was that Tony Q was pulling through and would soon be returned to prison, which didn't give me any joy, I have to admit.

At the hospital I told them who I was and asked if anyone had claimed the body, expecting a negative reply. To my surprise, they told me that a certain Mr. Harry B had come in that morning, who claimed to be a close relative of Jason's. He was going to arrange for an undertaker to pick up the body the following day. I had no idea who Harry B was and was surprised Jason had not told me about him. All they could tell me was that he was an old man in his late seventies or early eighties. I assumed it must be a very distant relative hoping to claim Jason's inheritance. There was probably very little I could do to prevent him from claiming the body or Jason's estate, but I was going to do my damnedest to stop this unknown person, who had had no contact with Jason for as long as I knew him, from arranging the funeral.

I spent the rest of the day calling all the Harry Bs I could find in the telephone directory but in vain. None of them claimed any kinship with Jason. My only hope was Victor. Jason may have mentioned this distant relative to him or he might be able to help me locate him. However, I wasn't sure Victor would spare one of his staff to work on such a trivial matter. I could only try.

Victor was surprisingly friendly on the phone. It appears he had got over the embarrassment of Jason's trial. "Harry B, you say. No, Jason never mentioned him. He sounds like someone trying to make a fast buck. Do you want me to look into it?"

"I'd be most grateful, Victor."

"It's the least I can do. Did you know that Jason left quite a sizeable fortune?"

"I knew he must have made quite a bit of money over the years. I kind of assumed he spent most of it on fast living."

"No. Surprisingly, he was very careful with money. His solicitor called me and wants us to meet. He didn't say much on the phone, but it may have to do with his inheritance. In the meantime, I'll try and locate this Harry B person."

"If you could Victor, I would be very grateful. He may be genuine; in which case I'd like to share the expenses of the funeral. If not, he may be glad if I took it off his hands."

"I'll get back to you as soon as I can."

For the rest of the day, I kept racking my brain trying to come up with who this mysterious Harry B was and why Jason never mentioned him. Was he a distant relative who went abroad and recently returned to spend his retirement in the homeland? I hoped that Victor's man would track him down quickly so I could pay him a visit. My only other option was to wait outside the hospital and ambush the undertaker when he came for Jason's body.

Chapter Thirty-One

Victor got back to me surprisingly quickly. "We found your Harry B. When he separated from his wife some thirty years ago, he went abroad and only returned recently, two weeks ago, so I'm told. It appears he was had up for child abuse. That's how we found him—because of his criminal record. As a convicted child abuser, he has to inform the local police of his current address and report in on a regular basis. It wasn't hard to find a tame officer to help us out. We scratch their backs, and they scratch ours."

"I was thinking of going to see him. Do you think that's wise?"

"I see no harm in it. You don't have to say how you got his address. It would be interesting to see what his intentions are. Let me know what happens."

Harry B had rented a small apartment through Airbnb near the centre of the city. I decided to waste no time. I thought it better to sort things out directly with him rather than confront the undertaker at the hospital.

When I rang the bell to the apartment, he buzzed me in, which meant that he didn't mind receiving unknown visitors. I think he was quite relieved to see that I was someone not much younger than himself. "I'm sorry," he said, looking me up and down. "Do I know you?"

"No," I said. "We've never met. I'm Jason B's guardian."

"*Legal* guardian?" he said uneasily.

"No. Unofficial guardian. I believe you've arranged to pick up Jason's body tomorrow. I was wondering if we could talk."

"You can't stop me," he said defensively. "I'm a relative. As far as I know his only close relative. His father had no siblings. My sister and brother have both passed. My brother and I had no children. Jason was the only offspring."

I suddenly realised who he was. I should have put two and two together long before, but in my eagerness to take charge of the funeral it didn't cross my mind. Well, the truth is Jason implied that he was most likely dead. I immediately felt repulsion for this man who had abused Jason repeatedly over a period of nearly three years.

"Come in," he said in a pleasant voice. "They provide basic facilities. I think I can make us a cup of tea."

My instinct was to decline. I had no desire to drink tea with a man who had damaged Jason, but my curiosity got the better of me. For some reason, I needed to know more about this man. Was he as evil as I imagined?

"I'm sorry," he said apologetically. "I didn't recognise you at first but you're Patrick G, aren't you? I'm so glad you came to see me, though I don't know how you found my address."

He gave me a quizzical look, but I was not about to enlighten him.

Harry B must have been in his mid to late seventies, but he was not well preserved. He was thin and wizened, with a deeply furrowed, weathered face. He walked with a marked limp.

I decided not to confront him. What was the point? It was unlikely that he was going to tell his life story to a stranger. It was evident he was not a rich man. In fact, he looked rather shabby. Was his intention to get his hands on Jason's money? I could think of no other reason why he would be prepared to spend a small fortune on his funeral.

"I've been working abroad. Menial jobs, you know. Anything I could find. I'll be leaving as soon as Jason is safely in the ground."

"Was that your reason for coming back?" I ventured.

"No. I was very upset about the outcome of the trial and intended visiting him—being his only living relative. We had once been very close."

"I don't think he'd have wanted to see you," I said, contravening my decision not to confront him.

"I beg your pardon," he said, stopping in his tracks and fixing me with an indignant glare.

"He has nothing but utter loathing for you, Uncle Harry. You are his uncle, aren't you?"

The man seemed to wither when he heard the anger in my voice. I saw him reach for his chest and wondered if he was about to have a heart attack.

"How do you know that?" he said. "I was the only one to show him any love. My sister and brother-in-law were unable to give him the love he yearned. They were too engrossed in themselves and their own lives. Their behaviour was nigh on criminal. They treated him as an encumbrance. I, on the other hand, had genuine love for Jason."

"Love? Do you call abusing a young boy love? Have you any idea what you did to him? How you irreparably damaged him?"

"How can you say that? I loved him. My marriage was ruined because of him."

"Not because of him, Harry. Because of you."

"You don't understand. I loved Jason," he repeated mournfully.

I almost felt sorry for this pitiable creature, but my anger got the better of me. "Weren't you aware of what you were doing to him?"

"No, you're wrong. Our love was reciprocal. He loved me a much as I loved him."

I honestly think he believed what he was saying. I could only imagine he deceived himself into thinking Jason loved him to justify his heinous acts. "He was just a child, Harry. He had no idea what love was. You never gave him the chance to feel real love. What you taught him was that love has to do with sex, sex of a violent, clandestine nature. You burdened him with an unbearable load of shame. There is a reason why sex with a minor is considered statutory rape."

As I spoke, I was aware of him sinking into a semi-catatonic state. His eyes became inert, staring motionless into the void. I waited for a response but got none. I wasn't sure what to do, get up and leave, shake him until he emerged from his hypnotic state...

Eventually he spoke. "I should have broken the vicious circle, I know, but I was too weak. The urge was too strong. You cannot imagine how I loathed myself. I still do, for I am not an insensitive man. I knew what I was doing was wrong."

"You could have sought help."

"I suppose at the time I couldn't admit to myself I was sick, that I needed to be shut away. But I have paid the price. I have had to live in exile half my life, alone and friendless. I am a pariah, a reject. You cannot imagine what that feels like."

"I can, but you're talking as if you had no choice. You did."

I wasn't sure why I was bothering to talk to this vile individual, who had preyed on Jason, and on others too no doubt. "Anyway, the reason I'm here is to ask you to let me handle the funeral."

He looked up at me with a glint of defiance in his watery eyes. "So, you have a guilty conscience too."

"We all have," I said. "We all could have done more than we have."

I think perhaps he hoped that I would admit to abusing young boys too, but I disappointed him. His hopeful stare faded, and his sagging jowls dropped again. "Can I at least attend the funeral?" he asked pleadingly. "I would like to pay my respects. Maybe he can forgive me from the other side."

"I can't stop you but don't be surprised if I ignore you."

"I won't intrude. I know you were good to him, Patrick G."

I wondered how he knew that, but I said nothing.

"You loved him like I did."

I wanted to say I loved him but not like he did. "As the next of kin, I suppose you will inherit his estate," I said.

"I could have done with it a few years ago but it's too late now. I've been given six months to live. I have terminal cancer, fourth stage."

I was taken aback but was unable to say I was sorry.

"I will go back into exile and die a pauper. You will probably say I deserve no better and you may be right."

Who was I to condemn a man who had been abused himself? He was no worse and no better than Jason had been. Neither had been able to break the vicious circle.

"Where were you planning to bury him?" I asked.

"In the family vault, in the First Cemetery. I'll give you the details. Here is the undertaker's card. I won't need it now. I've kept the number. I'll call him to find out the time and day."

Though indiscreet of me, I couldn't help asking. "Do you intend to be buried there too?"

He laughed. "No. I couldn't afford it. Anyway, who's going to come to my funeral?"

I wanted to say I would, but I didn't. I might not have been able to keep my promise. "So, you will remain in exile."

"They're very good at disposing of bodies there. The state will pay and the funeral will be attended by one man."

I was curious to know who that one man was but decided not to ask. It was none of my business. I got up to leave. The feeling of revulsion I initially felt for him had turned to disdain and pity.

"That man is my psychiatrist. I can't afford him now but he sees me every so often pro bono. I have tried, Patrick G."

So, he had tried to overcome his vice. That at least was in his favour.

"Won't you have a cup of tea?" he said piteously.

I could tell he was in need of someone to talk to, a father confessor perhaps, but I was not prepared to do him that favour.

"No, thank you. I have things to do."

"Can I shake your hand at least?" he said, extending a shrivelled, limp hand.

I tried to hide my distaste but, despite myself, took the hand, which felt weak and brittle, the hand of my dying mother.

"I'm glad we were able to talk," he said

I wished I could have said the same.

"I have always been a great admirer. I am also very grateful for what you have done for Jason all these years. I would like to have done the same."

For the first time, I wondered whether his feelings for Jason had been more than just pure lust. I would never know. Perhaps I didn't want to find out. "Goodbye," I said.

"I will see you at the funeral, but I promise to keep my distance. I will not embarrass you. There will almost certainly be someone there who will recognise me, though I have aged greatly since my conviction."

I couldn't wait to get out of the apartment, which was stifling and claustrophobic. I no longer wanted to breathe the same air as this pitiful wreck of a man. Yet, I could not help muttering to myself, 'There but for the grace of God go I.'

~ * ~

I rang Victor that evening as promised.

"So, who is this Harry B then?"

"I'm surprised you didn't know. He was convicted of child abuse about thirty years ago."

"I knew that."

"What you didn't know is that he also abused Jason."

There was a stunned silence at the end of the line. "Oh, my God."

"I looked into the case and found that it was his wife who took him to court. He was sentenced to five years and served four. After that, he left the country, only returning when he heard about Jason's incarceration. However, Jason died before he got the chance to see him."

"So, he was taken to court because he abused Jason?"

"No, Jason had already left by then. It was another boy he'd picked up somewhere."

"Which is why Jason was never mentioned at the trial."

"Exactly."

"So, is he going to attend the funeral?"

"He said he'd keep a discreet distance. I can't imagine there'll be much of a turnout."

"You never know, Patrick. The public is very unpredictable, as you know. Now that Jason's dead, his old fans are beginning to see him in a new light. I wouldn't be surprised if there are two factions, the lovers and the haters, those who want to pay their respects and those who want to pillory his memory. Let's hope they don't clash."

"I've talked to the undertaker. I want it to be a quiet funeral. He's promised not to send an obituary to the newspapers. So, with any luck, no one will find out until it's all over."

"You'll be lucky."

"It's at ten o'clock on Wednesday. Will you be able to make it?"

"I'll do my best, Patrick. I don't promise anything."

I knew he wouldn't come. Any association with Jason might be damaging for his firm's image, after the embarrassment of the trial. Victor hadn't changed, nor would he, despite our temporary reconciliation.

"Anyway, thank you, Victor, and I have to say I hope I won't be in need of your services again."

"So do I, Patrick. You've been a right pain in the arse."

I think I detected a half-smile in his voice.

~ * ~

That evening Valerie called and said she'd be late home. She didn't tell me why, but I assumed it had to do with work. I prepared dinner, salmon linguini with cream and a demi-sec white wine. I set the table. Everything was ready. As we always ate at more or less the same time, I was surprised.

When she finally arrived, she looked tired and taciturn. She was not her usual smiley self. Had we reached that point in our relationship when we no longer needed to make an effort?

"Are you going to have a shower before dinner?" I asked. "Or shall I pour you a glass of wine?"

"A glass of wine, please, Patrick."

I poured us each a glass of wine and we went and sat in front of the fire. Neither of us was in a particularly chatty mood, though I wanted to tell her about my meeting with Harry B.

Valerie sat looking at the fire. The flickering flames in the dim light brought out the fire in her face. I was worried and wondered if it had anything to do with us.

"Are you all right, love?" I said, cautiously reaching for her hand.

There was no reaction, as if she wasn't even aware of my hand on hers.

"I think I may have made a terrible mistake," she said at last.

"Why?" I said anxiously.

"I told Dory who his father was."

"Oh," I said, taken aback.

We usually discussed such things, but presumably she felt it was a personal matter between her and Dory.

"He was angry with me, which is very rare for him. We have always been so close."

"So, what did he say?"

"He couldn't understand why I wanted to tell him now. He would have preferred to remain in ignorance. He says he now must live with the knowledge his half-brother was a paedophile and his father a heartless philanderer."

"Why did you tell him?" I said gently.

"I felt he ought to know. I should have told him long ago. I thought if he was going to be with us at the funeral, he ought to know that Jason was his brother."

"So, you left on bad terms."

"Yes, and I hate it when we fight."

"I'm sure he'll come round. Sometimes ignorance is bliss, but knowledge, however upsetting, is better in the long run. Are you hungry?"

"Not really, but I suppose I should eat something."

"I can always heat it up tomorrow."

"No. You've gone to so much trouble. It's a pity."

She smiled and laid her head on my shoulder.

Over dinner I told her about Harry B and the feeling of nausea I had in his presence. "Yet, in the end I felt almost sorry for him. He seemed genuinely contrite. He said he felt utter self-loathing."

"No doubt his intention was to gain your sympathy. He sounds like a very sad, lonely old man."

"He said there would be only one person at his funeral, his psychiatrist."

"You can't feel sorry for him, Patrick. He brought it on himself."

"Did he? Or was he just a victim like Jason was? Harry B said something that made so much sense. He loathes himself because he could not break the 'vicious circle' of child abuse. Jason said something similar."

"The truth is, Patrick, that life is full of vicious circles, beaten children become child beaters, children who have seen their mothers maltreated end up maltreating their wives, children who have bullies as fathers become bullies themselves, etc., etc. And the only way to break the cycle is by punishing those who perpetuate it. There needs to be a very strong deterrent. I see no other way."

Of course, Valerie was right.

Chapter Thirty-Two

I had forgotten what a business organising a funeral can be; deciding on what casket you want, plain, deluxe or super deluxe, what flowers to have, whether there should be a choir and so on. I told the undertaker that this would be a close family funeral and so there was no need to make a show of it. A simple casket and one or two bouquets of white flowers would suffice. He asked me if I would arrange for the pallbearers, but apart from Dory and Marcus V I couldn't think of enough men who would be willing to carry out such a task. So, we agreed that he'd pay some professionals to do it instead.

I picked Valerie up from her place and was pleased to find Dory there. I suspected that the contretemps he had with his mother wouldn't last long. His initial reaction to finding out who his father and brother were, was one of shock rather than anger. I'm still not sure whether Valerie should have sprung it on him like that, but I suppose it was only right that he should know he was attending the funeral of his half-brother.

As there were only three of us, we all went in my car to the First Cemetery. Fortunately, it was not a busy day for burials, and I found somewhere to park close to the front gate. It wasn't until I got out that I saw the crowd. Someone had leaked the day and time the funeral was to take place. Why were they there? To gloat, I wondered, or to pay their respects. There were also a couple of reporters standing outside the gate. I considered going around to the back entrance, but it would mean walking about half a kilometre and risking being late for the service. So, we had no option but to face them.

Valerie held my arm as we approached the gate. They saw us almost at once and charged at us brandishing their microphones. "Patrick G, would you say a few words?"

"I have nothing to say. This is a private funeral. Jason was like a son to me. I think we should be allowed to mourn in peace. So, I would be grateful if we could be left alone."

"Valerie, are you here to give moral support to Patrick or to mourn Jason?"

"I'm here primarily to be with Patrick but I wish to be able to say farewell to Jason too."

"Were you close to Jason?"

"No, but I was close to his father. Now, can we pass? The service is about to begin."

I looked around to find Harry B but I couldn't see him. He was probably there somewhere, but he was not someone who would stand out in a crowd.

When we reached the church, I saw Marcus V standing alone at the bottom of the steps. I left Valerie for a moment and went up to him.

"Thank you for coming," I said.

"I came for you, Patrick, but I see you are not alone."

"It would have been a very sad funeral if I had been the only one to say goodbye to Jason. Thank you. I appreciate it."

"Patrick, one of the reasons I came today is because I wanted to tell you something I should have told you a long time ago. Please forgive me."

"I'm sure there's nothing to forgive."

"You see, I wasn't sure. After following the trial, I now know what he once told me was true."

"Yes?" I said wondering what this could be all about.

"He said he loved young men but he would never seduce a minor."

"He admitted to having sex with Ali in an open court."

"It was not true. It was simply a ploy. For some reason he wanted to go to jail. You probably know better than I do why."

"Are you sure, Marcus?"

"Yes, I made a point of asking others what they knew about Jason. They told me he would never touch a boy. It was a matter of principle. I think he may have been abused as a child. He hinted at it one evening after we'd had a few drinks. I'm sorry for telling you this on the day of his funeral, but I thought it important that you should know."

"Thank you, Marcus. Yes, it is important. All I ever wanted was to find out the truth about Jason. I was prepared for the worst, but I always clung to the hope that he was innocent. There were times when I thought it was just wishful thinking or self-deception, but I could never give up on him."

"It was a good thing you didn't."

"If you hadn't come today, I would never have known the truth. I thank you from the bottom of my heart. I hope you will come for coffee afterwards."

"Of course I will, Patrick. It's the least I can do. I am with some friends of Jason's. Would you mind if they came too?"

"Of course, not. I am so glad that others feel the need to mourn him."

There was an air of profound sadness about him. I suspected that he too had lost a good friend.

As I entered the darkness of the church, I saw Victor standing half hidden in the wings. "I thought you said you weren't coming," I said wryly.

"What we say is not always what we do, Patrick. You should know that."

"I appreciate it anyway. You won't be rushing off afterwards, I hope."

"No, of course not. Besides, I have something important to tell you, which you will find very interesting, I think."

I was curious to find out what this 'very interesting' thing could be but the priest was approaching the altar. So, I returned to Valerie and Dory who were standing next to the coffin.

At some point in the service the priest asked if I would like to say a few words. I thought there was little point in making a speech to such a small assembly of mourners but what I had planned to say was not so much for them as for me. I had not managed to see Jason after his conviction and there were so many things I wanted to tell him. I considered reading the poem he had written for Alice, Hope in Greyness, but after what Marcus told me there were other things I needed to say. Besides, what hope was there left, only a vilified image of an innocent man?

"Now is the time to remember the bright moments in your life, Jason, and I like to think there were many. We met in Drama School, or should I say we clashed in Drama School. You were one of those students a teacher hates because I knew you were going to teach me more than I could ever teach you. You knew it all. At least, you thought you did. Nevertheless, I believe I was able to teach you some things, like humility, self-knowledge and self-discipline. From your first performance I knew you would reach the top of your profession. You were a natural. So, I simply encouraged you to let your instincts guide you. After class, when I was dying to get home after a long day's work, you would engage me in endless discussions on the deeper meaning of Beckett's or Shakespeare's plays. What a pain you were, but I loved every minute of it.

"Then you became part of our family. Alice, Andrew, and I welcomed you with open arms. You were the son Alice had lost in childbirth and the brother Andrew had been cheated out of. I like to think you loved us as much as we loved you. You did fulfil our expectations. You gave us all so much joy on those numerous weekends when you came to stay. You would keep us entertained with your subtle wit and juvenile antics."

"You didn't disappoint your teacher either. You won numerous awards, including Actor of the Year, and then you became Artistic Director of the National Theatre. That in itself is proof of your talent and brilliance."

"But, Jason, you had some shortcomings that were not of your own making. They were inflicted upon you by others, shortcomings that you fought valiantly to overcome. And in the end your love for my son Andrew made you commit an act of folly—or was it courage—that resulted in your death. Yet, if you stayed alive, would you have been able to get your life back together? Would the merciless public have given you that chance? I think you knew they would not and so you felt there was only one course of action open to you. So, you exited this world in a final act of daring that you hoped would make up for all the wrong you believed you had done. I am in no position to say whether you did the right thing or not. You and only you know that. I only hope that you will find peace in the next life."

I'm not sure what I said made much sense to those present but it was the only way I knew how to say goodbye.

A large crowd had gathered outside the church, waiting to follow the pall bearers to the vault. I was glad to see they were mainly people who wished to pay their last respects. By the side of the vault, people I was only vaguely acquainted with came up to me and shook my hand and expressed their condolences. It gave me joy and comfort to know I was somehow recognised as his spiritual father. I wondered what they would have thought if they knew Dory was his brother.

We walked slowly back to the coffee shop where mourners traditionally meet after a funeral. As we were entering, I caught a glimpse of Harry B. standing near the entrance peering in my direction, hoping to catch my eye. He looked more bedraggled than ever and even at that distance I could see he was unshaven. Was he hoping to be invited in? I felt sorry for him and gave it some thought but I couldn't bring myself to ask him to join us. I think he realised my dilemma but kept his promise not to embarrass me. He raised his hand in salute, and I raised mine but that was it. I wanted no more to do with him. I watched him turn and shuffle out under the arched gates of the cemetery.

Normally, a whole room of the coffee shop would be filled with mourners, but we were so few they put us in a corner around one table so that another party could take up the rest of the space. Victor came and sat between Valerie and me. He seemed unusually empathetic and even put an arm over my shoulder in an unprecedented expression of sympathy.

We ordered coffee and brandy and exchanged pleasantries, but I could tell Victor was eager to tell us something.

"Yesterday," he began, "I met Jason's solicitor. As I mentioned to Patrick the other day, Jason left a sizeable fortune. Two days after being incarcerated, he called his solicitor to draw up a will. It was almost as if he knew he was going to die and wanted to leave everything in order. In short, his last wish was that the majority of his estate should be used to set up an Arts and Cultural Centre for young refugees. He wanted it to be called the Andrew G Cultural Foundation."

"The Andrew G Foundation!" I exclaimed.

"The purpose of the Foundation will be to provide a meeting place for unaccompanied teenage refugees and immigrants where they can meet and practise the arts. It will also provide a place where recent arrivals can learn the language and familiarise themselves with our culture to facilitate their integration into our society."

I was so flabbergasted I could hardly speak.

"The only proviso, Patrick, is that you become the Foundation's first Director."

I didn't know what to say. The task seemed monumental. "I will certainly help but I'm not sure I'm up to being its director. It's a great responsibility. A full-time job."

"No, Patrick, you'll have to attend some meetings, but the running of the Foundation will be entrusted to a professional with experience in the field. It's a prestigious position and I have no doubt we will find someone suitable."

"It's certainly a great honour but..."

"You can't turn this down, Patrick. Jason is relying on you."

"I'll certainly do my best," I said, still in a fluster.

"Please raise your glasses in a toast to Jason B," said Victor, raising his glass of brandy. "And to the success of the Andrew G Cultural Foundation."

We all raised our glasses. No doubt we would have cheered if it had not been such a solemn occasion.

"I do have one more thing to say regarding the will," said Victor. "It's of no real concern to most of you but I thought you ought to know. Jason wanted a sum of money set aside for Harry B, his uncle. Apparently, the man doesn't have long to live. He wanted the money to be used to ease his passing and allow him to die with some dignity."

My ebullience was temporarily dampened by this news but, as Victor said, it was no concern of ours. In a way, I was quite glad the sad old man would not die a pauper's death.

~ * ~

That evening as we sat in front of the fire at Valerie's place, I kept thinking about Jason's decision to help his uncle in his last hour. Why would he want to ease the pain of a man he loathed? Did he have feelings for his uncle after all? It was evident they corresponded or else how would Jason have known about his illness and imminent death? So, what kind of relationship did they have? I suppose we will never know. I asked Valerie what she thought.

"Either he didn't loathe Uncle Harry as he claimed, or he wanted to show forgiveness."

"It's possible his feelings for Uncle Harry were ambivalent. He didn't know whether to love him or hate him. From what Harry told me, their relationship was not without some affection."

"How could Jason feel any love for a man who abused him over and over?"

"As we said once before, the human psyche is an abyss."

"I suspect that he saw in Uncle Harry a kindred spirit, someone like himself who could not break the vicious circle of abuse."

"But he did," I said emphatically.

With all the excitement following the news of the Foundation, I had forgotten to pass on to her what Marcus told me.

"What?" she asked, looking at me as if I had lost my mind.

"He did break the vicious circle. Marcus V told me outside the church. Apparently, he told others too that he would never lay a hand on a minor. It was a matter of principle for him."

"Do you think it's true?"

"Yes, I do. I don't believe Jason would deliberately harm anyone, particularly a young boy. He knew first-hand the devastating effects of abuse."

"That is good news!" she said elatedly. "So, he was innocent after all. Your efforts to help him were not in vain. In the end, you found out the truth you were seeking."

~ * ~

That evening, I decided to put my house up for rent and move in with Valerie. It would only be for a couple of days as I had received my filming schedule and would soon be off on location for a couple of months. I promised to visit whenever I had a day or a weekend off, but we both felt what we had together would stand the test of time and the two-month separation. And it appears it has.

As for the film, well, it was not a great success. Reviews were mixed. It didn't remain for more than a couple of weeks in the cinemas but that is the way with the arts. It often depends on what the public want at any given time or whether the media have decided it is worth hyping up. It is up to future generations to decide whether a creation is a work of art or not. The good thing is it didn't damage my reputation, and, despite my age, I am still being offered roles in films, which keep me off the streets, as my father would say.

The Foundation too keeps me busy even though my position is purely honorary, at least according to Victor.

I wish to make a go of it for Jason's sake because I now know for sure that he volunteered at the Refugee Centre not to molest young boys but to help them, because he saw in them youngsters like himself who had been abandoned, neglected and unloved. He believed as a trained psychotherapist he could help them in a way that no one else could. However, he made the fatal mistake of inviting two of them to his parties and exposing them to the dangers of drugs, alcohol, and sex. That was what led to his downfall and which he ultimately paid for with his life.

On the evening before my departure, Valerie said to me, "You know you're going to have to restore Jason's image somehow."

"How do you propose I do that?"

"Well, we could do another interview but I'm not sure people would watch it. No. I think you should write a book about the events of the last few weeks. You're the only one who can set the record straight."

"I know Alice would want me to but I'm not sure it would do any good."

"Even if it doesn't help to clear Jason's name, I think it will do you a lot of good."

I had to agree with her. I believe in setting things down on paper so that past events become history rather than remain part of a legend that becomes distorted over time and is never fully put to rest.

I have the feeling that Jason will never be too far from my thoughts. I realise how close I was to giving up on him. Like everyone else, I had been swayed by the public outcry and the media condemnation, both of which were based on circumstantial evidence. There was no real proof, except the statements of two highly impressionable, frightened boys.

I often wonder how many other celebrities like Jason have been destroyed unjustly in a similar fashion. Unlike Jason, though, they did not have someone who loved them enough to go in search of the truth, whatever that truth was, good or bad. When all is said and done, I had no real reason to believe Jason was innocent. All I had to go on was my gut instinct, which could very well have been misguided. In fact, if it hadn't been for Marcus V, I, and the rest of the world, might have gone on believing that Jason had been unable to break the vicious circle.

Well, the book is written, admittedly with altered names and circumstances. It is a great relief; I must admit. So, it will be up to the reading public, if they are interested, to see the real people and events behind the story I have endeavoured to narrate in a truthful and unbiased way so that through the disguise of poetic licence they will recognise the man who was falsely accused and condemned.

However, I have the feeling that few will bother. What happened to Jason B is no longer of any interest to the fickle public, always hungry for breaking news, which they will forget once it has been devoured. Jason B is dead and gone. For the world at large, he will soon be ancient history. Only those few who genuinely loved him will remember him for what he was, a cast-off, scarred and damaged by life, struggling to overcome crushing shame and depression. For me, his greatest achievement, beyond the awards and titles, was his success in breaking the vicious circle of abuse.

About the Author

Ian Douglas Robertson is a graduate of Trinity College Dublin. He lives and works in Athens, Greece, as a teacher, actor and translator. He has had a number of poems and short stories published in online and print magazines as well as three books of non-fiction in collaboration with his wife Katerina. He has also published several novels: *Fo's Baby, Turtle Hawks, Break, Break, Break, Under the Olive Tree, The Frankenstein Legacy, On the Side of the Angels, The Reluctant Messiah* and *The Adventures of Jackie and Jovie.* He was chosen Poet of the month of May 2023 by *The Poet.* Contact Ian Douglas Robertson at eireian@yahoo.co.uk or through his website www.iandouglasrobertson.com

Made in the USA
Columbia, SC
02 October 2024

42859004R00137